DEATH IN PIECES

DI DREW HASKELL & PROFILER HARRIET QUINN DETECTIVE SERIES BOOK 2

BILINDA P. SHEEHAN

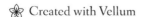

ALSO BY BILINDA P. SHEEHAN

Watch out for the next book coming soon from Bilinda P. Sheehan by joining her mailing list.

A Wicked Mercy - DI Drew Haskell & Profiler Harriet Quinn Detective Series Book 1

Death in Pieces - DI Drew Haskell & Profiler Harriet Quinn Detective Series Book 2

Splinter the Bone - DI Drew Haskell & Profiler Harriet Quinn Detective Series Book 3

Hunting the Silence - DI Drew Haskell & Profiler Harriet Quinn Detective Series Book 4

All the Lost Girls-A Gripping Psychological Thriller

Wednesday's Child - A Gripping Psychological Thriller

DEATH IN PIECES

CHAPTER ONE

RAISING THE KNIFE, he twirled it between his fingers and studied the image. Perfection was not easy to achieve, but perhaps this time he'd come close. Or at least as close as any human being could.

Pressing the craft knife down against the picture, he felt the satisfying pop as it slipped through the card like a hot knife through butter. Excitement thrummed in his veins. Soon, everything would change.

And then it would begin again.

This was his favourite part, the building anticipation creating an insatiable appetite that could only be satisfied by the spilling of blood.

Glancing over at the wall, he eyed the newspaper clipping he'd so carefully cut out from the paper.

Would she be worthy?

They never were but it was nice to dream.

Chuckling, he returned his attention to the image he'd begun to carve up and studied his progress. It had to be just right, or the game would fail before it had even started.

CHAPTER TWO

"THE DEBATE SURROUNDING INHERITED disposition is frequently discussed in terms of good versus evil." Harriet steadied herself against the podium and stared out at the hall. Before the Robert Burton case, it would have been unusual for the hall to be even a quarter full. Now, however, it was standing room only.

The microphone screeched--the noise tearing at her ears--and she cringed and took a step back. The lights glared down at her, blurring the faces of those who had come to hear her speak. Tightening her fingers into a fist, she struggled to control the panic that welled inside.

Perhaps it had been a mistake to return to work so soon.

The manuals she'd studied during her years of

training hadn't provided her with an exact timeline for the resolution of trauma. Everybody had warned her to take as much time as she needed. But staying at home, staring at the same four walls every day, hadn't helped. So here she was.

The note Dr Jonathan Connor had sent burned a hole in her pocket and it took every ounce of willpower she possessed not to pull it out and read the contents for the hundredth time.

"Many people refer to this debate as: Nature versus Nurture, and I'm sure many of you are familiar with the concept," she said, continuing the lecture.

A collective murmur of assent spread throughout the room. It was the one question to which everybody wanted an answer, yet nobody had a definite conclusion. Were you born a killer, or were you created?

"There are far too many variables involved in the topic to specifically pin the answer down. However, many experts agree that for the majority of studied cases, the answer is found in a complicated combination of societal influences and genetic predisposition."

"So, Dr Quinn, tell us are killers born or are they made?" The question came out of the audience and she smiled in spite of herself. She tried to pinpoint the man's voice but found it impossible.

"Well, that's what we're going to explore here today and in future lectures."

"Have you been to see Robert Burton since his incarceration, Dr Quinn?" The second question came from somewhere near the back of the room and splintered her concentration. Raising her hand to shield her eyes from the harsh lights, Harriet tried to focus on the owner of the disembodied voice but nobody in particular stood out.

"We're here to discuss inherited dispositions, not the ongoing case involving Robert Burton," she said. Had there been too much emotion in her voice when she'd spoken his name? It seemed impossible for there not to be, yet Harriet knew, better than most, that allowing her emotions to well up would lead to nothing but chaos.

She'd allowed her emotions to cloud her judgement regarding DI Haskell and his fiancée's case and look how *that* had turned out.

She'd tried calling him once since their last meeting in the hospital, but the call had gone unanswered. And even if she'd wanted to leave a voicemail, the message minder had sounded almost gleeful when it had informed her that Drew's voicemail was full.

"But surely you've got an opinion on his most recent claim that you had agreed to let him end your life in exchange for a cessation of his actions."

Harriet drew in a deep breath and closed her eyes. It was a mistake; the moment her eyes were closed she was right back there in the basement, desperately scrabbling for purchase as her feet left the floor and the noose tightened.

The number of nights she'd lain awake, afraid to close her eyes in case the memories returned and sucked her under, had left her exhausted.

"I can't..." she said, her voice a low murmur as she stumbled toward the edge of the stage.

The room seemed to close in around her. The neckline of her cream blouse pressed against her throat just as the noose had done and Harriet's fingers ripped at the delicate material.

The lecture hall tilted violently around her as she raced down the steps. The vague murmur of the crowd followed her, dogging her every step as she sought to escape the onslaught of panic that enveloped her.

She reached the exit door at the side of the stage and rammed it open, escaping into the back hall.

It was there that she remained, crouched low to the floor, her head between her knees, as she struggled to get her heartbeat to return to a normal tempo.

A gentle touch against her back made her jump, and she jerked her head up.

Dr Katerina Perez stared down at her, concern dancing in her rich brown eyes. "Are you all right?"

There was only a slight trace of an accent; it had

been mostly worn away by Katerina's years spent travelling between the UK and America, teaching and lecturing on psychology.

Sucking down a mouthful air, Harriet nodded. "I don't know what happened to me. One minute I was fine and then the next..."

Katerina nodded, a sympathetic smile curving her lips. "You had a panic attack."

Harriet started to shake her head and then changed her mind. Was that what it had been? Was the answer truly so simple? From where she sat on the floor, still recovering in the aftermath of the incident, it felt much too intense to be something so simple.

"I feel so stupid," she said finally. "I'm supposed to be a psychologist and I can't even figure out a simple panic attack?"

"They are not so simple," Katerina said, crouching next to Harriet.

Harriet recognised the move as one designed to put the other woman on a level with her, so as to ensure Harriet didn't feel intimidated or threatened by her presence. Such a simple act, but it had the power to set her teeth on edge. She wasn't some fragile little thing who needed looking after.

Then why are you the one on the floor with your head between your knees? The voice in her head taunted. Heat spread up her neck and into her face.

She was only too familiar with the emotion of shame these days.

"I've seen plenty down through the years," Katerina said. "Granted, none quite as spectacularly public as yours."

Harriet groaned and buried her face in her hands. "They're going to think I'm losing my marbles."

Katerina shrugged. "Doubtful. I'd expect an interesting write up in the morning paper though."

"Why?" Harriet tilted her head to the side to meet the other woman's gaze head on.

"The last question--the one that triggered your attack--was asked by a reporter."

Harriet sighed and shoved her hand back through her curly hair. "How did they get in?"

Katerina shrugged. "You know it's not difficult. Just about anybody could walk in off the street and attend a lecture if they really wanted to."

"Isn't that why we hand out student ID cards? You know, to ensure only those who are fully paid up are getting the benefit of our collective wisdom?" Harriet didn't bother to hide the bitterness in her voice.

The university had opted to decrease the student fee subsidy funds and she'd been one of the few dissenting voices on the matter. Not that anybody had cared what she thought at the time. Now, however, it was a different matter. It seemed that everything she thought and felt was newsworthy.

Katerina's grin broadened. "You and I both know the ID cards are merely an opportunity to keep tabs on them. Nothing more and nothing less." She reached over and patted Harriet's arm gently. "How are you feeling now?"

"Better," Harriet said. "Foolish."

Katerina nodded and returned her serious gaze to her hands. "You should talk to someone about it all."

Harriet sighed. "I've had enough people poking around in my head to last me a lifetime."

"You can't keep going on like this. It isn't healthy. And you don't need to suffer alone."

Harriet pushed up onto her feet and dusted down her navy wide-legged slacks. "Honestly, I'm fine."

"You're far from fine," Katerina said, and before Harriet could interrupt, she raised her hands in mock surrender. "But I know when to retreat. I'm not trying to make this more difficult for you. I just think you could do with a friendly ear to listen to everything going on in that head of yours. Especially after everything you've been through. There's a reason we suggest people go to counselling after traumatic incidents."

Harriet nodded. "I know that. But I'm used to being the person they come to see, not the patient."

Katerina's expression shifted and a broad grin

erupted on her face. "The age-old question, who shrinks the shrink?"

"Something like that."

Katerina's expression was compassionate. "Well, just think about it. Nobody is saying you need to make up your mind straight away."

"What brought you to my lecture?" Harriet asked. "This isn't normally your area of interest."

Katerina's gaze slid away to the floor. "I was passing and decided to drop in, that's all."

"Are you sure?" She wasn't able to keep the suspicion from her voice.

Katerina's head jerked up. "Yes, I'm sure."

"I'm sorry, it's just that everyone has been behaving differently since everything that happened."

"I can understand that." Katerina sighed and glanced down at her watch. "I'm late."

"Going somewhere nice?" Harriet asked, noting for the first time that the other woman was dressed particularly smart. The blue dress she wore clung to her body as though it had been poured on. It ended just below her knees and her toned legs were emphasised by the towering heels she wore.

Katerina glanced down and smiled. "Dinner with an old friend."

Harriet swallowed past the lump in her throat and nodded. Katerina's use of the word old friend had instantly brought Bianca to the forefront of her mind. Not that Bianca was ever very far from her thoughts these days.

When Bianca had been alive, had Harriet thought about her so much? Harriet was almost certain the answer was no, but it was as though her life before the incident and her life since had been split into two completely separate compartments. Almost as though the memories from that time before belonged to someone else. A different Harriet.

"Well, you enjoy your dinner," she said, as she tugged on the door to the lecture hall only to find it wouldn't budge. "Shit."

Katerina smiled. "It's locked from this side," she said. "To stop anyone re-entering the building during a fire."

Harriet drew in a breath and tried to let the tension in her shoulders go.

"Anyway, they'll all have left by now," Katerina said. "Nobody expects you to finish your lecture after that."

Starting down the corridor, Harriet gave Katerina a quick smile. "I know, but I didn't bring any of my things with me. I have to go back in there and pick them up."

Katerina glanced down at her watch again.

Harriet could sense her impatience. "You go to dinner," she said. "I'm fine now."

Hesitating, Katerina looked her over with an appraising eye. "Are you sure?"

BILINDA P. SHEEHAN

"Of course, I'm as fit as a fiddle." The words left her mouth before she could stop them and caused her heart to constrict in her chest. It was Kyle's favourite saying; a phrase he'd took great pleasure in overusing, much to her and her mother's chagrin.

Katerina gave her a crooked smile. "You are a strange one sometimes, Harriet Quinn."

Harriet shrugged. "So they say. Now go."

Katerina nodded, relief sweeping across her features. "Just think about the counselling," she said. "Promise me."

"I'll think about it."

"Good." Katerina started in the opposite direction down the corridor. "Goodnight."

"Have fun," Harriet called after her. "Don't do anything I wouldn't do."

Katerina's rich laughter drifted back toward her and Harriet waited until the other woman had rounded the corner before pressing her hand against the brick wall and drawing in a deep breath.

Perhaps Katerina was right and talking to someone else would be a good idea. The thought of it pained her but surely it couldn't be worse than what she was currently going through.

Pushing the thought aside, she straightened up and brushed her unruly hair back from her face, tucking it behind her ear. She just needed to take a better hold on her emotions. And she, better than anyone, knew how dangerous too much empathy could be.

She was sure she just needed time. Everything was just a little raw right now. Given time, the wounds would heal, and she would return to normal; whatever that was.

CHAPTER THREE

"ARE you sure you don't want to meet up tonight?"
Michael waggled his eyebrows in Gabriel's direction.

"I'm sure. I've got far too much study to catch up
on. And so do you--" Gabriel cut him off with a kiss
and his words dissolved into laughter. Pressing his
hand against the other man's chest, he pushed him
away playfully. "Go, or you're going to be late."

"It's just a coffee shop, they won't care if I'm a few
minutes late for my shift," Michael said. His blue
eyes had darkened as he snaked his hands around
Gabriel's neck and closed the distance between them.

Struggling to control his desire, Gabriel planted
both hands against the other man's chest. The feel of
his solid muscle beneath the T-shirt he wore brought
his skin out in goose bumps. How had he been so
lucky? It would be so easy just to fall back into bed
and run the risk of being late for the third time this

month. The image of Martha's shrewish face as she tutted about him missing his appointment, again flashed in his mind.

"No," he said, wriggling out from underneath Michael's wandering hands. "I've got to go and so do you."

"I'm sure she wouldn't mind you running late, especially when it's for such a good cause..." Michael batted his baby blues up at him and Gabriel felt his resolve wobbling.

"Dr Quinn has very graciously offered me extra time to work on my thesis with her. I cannot afford to screw that up now." Gripping Michael's shoulders firmly, he spun the other man around and frog-marched him toward the door of his bedsit. "And anyway, seeing Martha look at me like that again if I turn up too late is just going to ruin my day completely."

He felt Michael's shoulders slump as they reached the door. "But wouldn't it be worth it? I mean--"

"Go, already. My god, you're insatiable!" Gabriel laughed as he tugged open the door and gently pushed Michael out. "I'll see you tomorrow after lunch and we can--"

"I could always swing by tonight. You know, what they say, Gabe, all work and no play makes Gabe a very dull boy."

Laughing, Gabriel shut the door in the other

man's face and grinned as he crossed the apartment. The sound of Michael's insistent knocking brought a wide smile to his lips as he headed for the shower.

Thirty minutes later, showered and dressed, he left the apartment building behind and wheeled his bike down to the side of the road. Settling his rucksack on his shoulders, he swung his long leg over the bar and perched on the uncomfortably slim seat. One of these days he would find the time to bring it into the shop and have the seat changed.

Of course, the upside of keeping this particular seat meant he rode the bike standing on the peddles and even Michael had remarked on how muscular his thighs had become. Pausing at the traffic lights, he pulled the hood on his jumper up over his hair. It wasn't much but at least it kept the worst of the rain at bay.

Arriving at the university with only minutes to spare, he parked the bike and quickly locked it before he sprinted into the psychology building. Skidding across the tiled floors, he almost collided with the guy mopping the floor.

"Sorry!" He held his hands up as the cleaner stumbled backwards and pulled the right headphone out of his ear. "I'm really sorry," Gabriel repeated.

"You need to watch you're going," the bloke said, his face twisted into an unpleasant grimace as he slopped his mop back into the wheelie bucket.

"I said I was sorry," Gabriel repeated, this time

not bothering to keep his irritation under wraps. Just what more was this guy looking for? "Shouldn't you have a sign up or something to say the floor is wet?"

The cleaner repeated the words under his breath as he pulled a face, reminding Gabriel of his twelve-year-old brother at home. Side stepping around him, Gabriel gave the guy a wide berth and made for the stairs.

He made it to Dr Quinn's office only a couple of minutes late and grinned triumphantly at the dour faced bag that greeted him.

"Gabriel Hopkins reporting for duty," he said, making a mock salute at the woman on the other side of the desk.

"Didn't you get my message?"

He stared blankly at her. "What message?"

"The one I sent you telling you that your meeting with Dr Quinn has been cancelled for today."

Gabriel shook his head. "No." He fished around in his rucksack and pulled the phone from the bottom of the book bag. Clicking through to the home screen he stared down at the message Martha had mentioned.

"Where's she gone to now?" he asked, struggling to keep the irritation from his voice.

"What Dr Quinn does is her own business," Martha said imperiously. She glared at him over the top of her glasses. "Don't you have somewhere else you could be?"

"Well, are we still on for our meeting on Friday?"

Martha glanced over at the computer screen. "Unless I hear otherwise from Dr Quinn then I would assume so, yes."

"Do you think next time you could give me a little bit more notice?"

Martha gave him a withering look and he raised his hands in mock surrender. "Right, sorry for asking."

"You see, you wouldn't have this problem if you'd turned up to your appointments on time."

Rolling his eyes, he turned and headed out of the office.

Down on the ground floor, he was pleased to find the cleaner had cleared out. Sauntering across the floor he pushed out into the drizzly morning and made his way toward the coffee station.

If he'd known Quinn wasn't going to show up at all he'd have stayed in bed with Michael. As he pushed open the door to his favourite coffee shop and the familiar scent washed over him, he put all thoughts of Dr Quinn and her flaky behaviour out of his mind. There was no point in allowing her to ruin a perfectly good day.

CHAPTER FOUR

THE SOUND of the ringing phone caused Drew to pull the duvet up over his head, but it followed him there, penetrating the warm cocoon he'd created for himself. Groaning, he turned over in the bed and pulled what had been Freya's pillow toward his face. It had long since lost her scent but if he closed his eyes tight and concentrated really hard, he could almost swear a couple of faint, stray notes still lingered.

It was in his head, though; of that much he was certain. Freya was long gone and so was her scent.

That was the problem with death; every part of the person eventually disappeared, erased from existence as if the person had never truly been here at all.

The phone continued to ring.

"Fuck off already," he growled. What was so hard

to understand about a day off? Not that the day off had happened through choice. If he'd had his way, he'd be sitting behind his desk right now, catching up on the paperwork he'd allowed to mount up.

He sighed. Who was he kidding? He might be able to lie to the Monk, but he definitely couldn't lie to himself. There was no way he'd be filling out reports. Anyway, Maz lived for reports; not to mention the fact that he was so much better at it than Drew.

The phone fell silent and he flopped onto his back, staring up at the ceiling. Raising his hand, he traced the outline of what had been a patch of damp on the plaster. In the early days of their relationship, Freya had let the bath overflow and it had soaked through the floorboards above and into the ceiling plaster. He'd come home from work to find her frantically mopping it all up with every towel he'd ever owned, to absolutely no avail.

Even now, he could remember the look of panic on her face.

He'd tried to be angry; they hardly knew each other and here she was, a veritable stranger, trashing his place when he was out. But she'd been so miserable that anger had been impossible.

Had her carelessness been a sign of her illness, even then? He'd thought her absent-mindedness was cute, if not sometimes a little irritating, but had it been covering a darker truth, one which he'd missed?

Or was it simply that he'd known the truth, even then, and hadn't wanted to face it?

The possibilities were endless.

Covering his face with his hand, he tried to block out the memories. Before he'd met Harriet, blocking out memories had been easier. Since Freya's death, he'd considered himself the walking dead. Nothing touched him; well, not deeply enough for it to matter, anyway.

Harriet had awakened something in him; a side of him that craved true human connection. But ever since he'd uncovered her deceit, the memories of Freya and the emotions that came with them had returned with a vengeance. How was he supposed to concentrate when he was constantly haunted by a ghost?

He squeezed his eyes shut and balled his hand into a fist on his forehead. "Stop. Please, just stop."

The phone started to ring again.

Rolling over, he grabbed it from the nightstand and contemplated hurling it across the room. His gaze snagged on the caller ID and he faltered.

The Monk wouldn't call unless it was serious. His fingers were suddenly too big and clumsy for the screen and he found himself fumbling to answer the call.

"Yeah, DI Haskell," he said.

"You sound like shit," the Monk said. "Did I catch you at a bad time?"

"No, sir, not a bad time," Drew said, struggling to regulate his breathing. "What's up? Do you need me to come in or...?"

"You're on mandatory annual leave, Haskell, just accept it; even if this place was on fire and you were the only man alive with the ability to put it out, I still wouldn't let you back into this office."

Drew sighed and sat up in the bed. "Then why are you calling?"

"Arya said you'd taken some paperwork home with you."

Drew stared guiltily over at the box of files he'd snuck out of the office. Case files that still hadn't been closed. He'd reasoned that his enforced leave would be the perfect time to get a jumpstart on them.

"No, sir, I wouldn't."

"Cut the shit," Monk said. "Do you know where I am right now?"

"No, sir." Drew had a bad feeling about whatever his DCI was about to say next.

"I thought I'd pop over to the security booth and take a look at the CCTV footage from last Friday and guess what I'm looking at right now?"

Before Drew could get a word out, the Monk answered. "I'm watching you carry the box out on CCTV, Haskell."

"Sir, I need something to focus on. Something to keep—"

"I don't care what you get up to during your time

off," Gregson said. "So long as it's actual time off. I want those files back in the office before three o'clock today."

Drew sighed. There was no point in arguing with his boss, at least not while he was in this kind of mood. Not that DCI Gregson was ever in any other temperament.

"Fine."

"I mean it, Drew. And when I say I want the box back, I mean the box and *everything* inside it. Not just the few files you think will satisfy me."

"Got it, sir."

"Right, now go back to whatever it was you were doing." The line went dead, and Drew let the phone drop onto the mattress next to him.

When he got his hands on Maz he was going to kill the little snitch.

———

A COUPLE OF HOURS LATER, Drew carried the box of files back in through the doors of North Yorkshire's CID squad room. The place was a beehive of activity and he found himself wishing he was among the officers hurrying back and forth.

Hell, he'd even settle for a bit of phone action if it meant getting away from the silence that had taken over his own house.

He dumped the box of files onto the edge of

Maz's desk, crushing the other man's lunch beneath the cardboard weight. Maz jerked upright, away from his intense scrutiny of a paper file in front of him.

"What did you do that for?" He asked, picking up the box. "Oh, come on! It's ruined now!"

Drew stared down at the white and yellow flecked pale mush that looked like it had once been a tuna sandwich. The cling film wrapped around it prevented the mush from escaping over the desk but did nothing to keep the smell contained.

Drew wrinkled his nose in disgust. "Why do you keep bringing fish to work? You know I hate that shit."

Maz shrugged. "I figured that since you weren't here, I was safe to bring it in."

"Well, you thought wrong," Drew said gruffly, dropping into his swivel chair. Leaning back against the well-worn back, the chair creaked ominously.

"What are you doing in here anyway? Aren't you supposed to be off working on your tan, or catching up on some telly?"

Drew inclined his head in the direction of the box Maz had set on the floor. "I would have been doing a little light reading if somebody hadn't decided to rat me out to the Monk."

Maz's eyebrows shot up toward his dark hairline, his brown eyes wide and sincere. "I didn't rat anybody out."

"Pull the other one, mate, it's got bells on it," Drew said harshly.

"I swear, I haven't spoken more than two words to the Monk since you left on Friday."

Drew searched the other man's face, but he couldn't see any indication that he might be lying. "Well, shit," he said with some admiration.

"What?"

"Gregson pulled one over on me."

"What does that mean?" Maz asked, screwing his face up in concentration as he tried to scoop the remains of his sandwich together. "Do you think this is salvageable?"

Drew shook his head. "Seriously, just chuck it already." He pushed up onto his feet and started for the Monk's office.

"Where are you off to?" Maz asked.

"Got to have a chat with the boss man."

He crossed the office and rapped on Gregson's door.

"Come in."

Pushing the door open and stepping inside, Drew said, "I thought you might like to know I've brought the files back."

Gregson's attention was fixed to the screen of his computer. He nodded. "Great."

"Sir, was there something else you wanted me in here for?"

Gregson glanced over at Drew and waved him away. "No, I told you, you're on leave."

"Yeah but..."

"No buts, Haskell. Get out of here."

Disappointment welled in Drew's chest and he turned to leave.

"There's one thing I wanted to run past you," the Monk said, and Drew paused, anticipation swirling in his guts.

Don't sound too eager, Drew, keep it nice and causal.

"Yes, sir?" He'd aimed for only mildly intrigued and instead had managed to sound like a strangled cat.

"There's a fundraiser in city hall tonight—"

"No." Drew's voice was firm. The Monk had been wheedling at him to attend for what felt like forever and at every turn, Drew had found a reason to say no. Not that he really needed a reason.

As far as he was concerned, dressing up in a monkey suit and parading around in front of the top brass and the upwardly mobile turned his stomach.

And anyway, he wasn't cut out for the kind of schmoozing required for an occasion like the one Gregson was talking about.

"You seem to think I'm asking you a question," Gregson said, his voice icy.

"Sir, we both know that sending me to something

like this is a screw-up waiting to happen. I'm not a fundraiser type of guy."

"Yet, we both also know that you've got aspirations beyond DI."

"Even so, I don't think I'd do the squad any favours by turning up to something like that."

"And I happen to disagree with you," Gregson said. "Seems I'm not the only one, either."

"What does that mean?"

"Superintendent Burroughs seems to believe it would be to your benefit to attend tonight's function."

Drew started to shake his head, but Gregson cut across him.

"You might not like this, Drew, but what you did with Dr Quinn has brought nothing but good press our way. Burroughs wants to utilise some of that favourable coverage in the papers, to further our cause here."

"Sir, what does that even mean?" The simple mention of Harriet's name had caused his hackles to rise. The beginning of a headache was starting to rear its ugly head behind his eyes. He fought the urge to scrub at a point in the middle of his forehead.

"There's talk from higher up of setting up a specific force."

Drew felt the tension in his shoulders melt away at the DCI's words.

"What kind of force, sir?"

"Nothing is set in stone," Gregson said. "It's all

just pie in the sky right now but if we're ever going to stand a chance at getting something like it off the ground, we need all the good press we can get. Funding doesn't grow on trees you know."

Drew knew when he'd been beat. Gregson was a master at wielding both the carrot and the stick at the same time and he knew just how to work Drew into a corner he couldn't wriggle free of.

"And where do I come into all of this, sir?"

"Superintendent Burroughs believes you'd be an asset to the team. Alongside Dr Quinn of course."

Drew shook his head. "No."

"No?" DCI Gregson cocked an eyebrow in Drew's direction. "You don't think getting in on the ground floor of something like that would look good on your file?"

Drew swallowed hard. The DCI had him pinned down and knew it. Of course it would look good on his file. But he'd sworn he was done with Harriet and he meant to keep to his word.

"Sir, there was a complication in working with Dr. Quinn and I'd much rather not—"

"Don't tell me you crawled into her knickers, Haskell." The DCI's voice rose, and, from the corner of his eye, Drew spotted a couple of the other officer's in the room beyond the window casting a speculative glance in their direction.

"No, sir, nothing like that."

"What is it then? Spit it out."

"She lied to me, sir."

"Is that all?"

Drew bit back the sharp response that lingered on the tip of his tongue. "With all due respect, sir, you and I both know that a true partnership can only thrive on trust. If I can't trust Dr Quinn to tell me the truth with regards to the cases we work on, then how can I possibly enjoy a successful working cooperation with her?"

"You've put a lot of thought into this haven't you?" the Monk asked, as his gaze wandered back to the screen. "Look, nobody has said you have to work with Quinn. Forensic Psychologists are a dime a dozen these days. I'm sure there are plenty of others who'd be only too happy to jump at something like this."

The tension Drew had felt gathering between his shoulder blades released and he sighed. "That's true, sir."

"Good, so it's settled then."

"What is?"

"It starts at 8pm, I expect to see you there promptly. And for God's sake, man, make sure you scrub up properly."

Drew stared at his boss. He'd been outmanoeuvred, and he'd been so busy thinking about Harriet that he hadn't even bothered to put up a fight.

"Sir—"

"Dismissed, Haskell."

Drew knew when he'd been beat and so he

turned on his heel and strode out of the office. As he passed Maz, he caught the unmistakable whiff of fish and very nearly gagged.

"What did he want, then?" Maz asked, speaking around a mouthful of grey mush.

"I told you to dump that sandwich, Maz," Drew said.

Maz shrugged. "Seemed a pity to waste it and, anyway, it's only going to end up a mushy heap when I'm done chewing it. This way I figure I'm saving my teeth and jaws a job."

Drew shook his head and kept going for the door. If he had to spend another minute in the office with that smell lingering in the air, he was going to vomit. And anyway, he had to figure out just where he was going to get a suit from.

As much as he hated the idea of getting dressed up and parading around, he was intrigued by the potential the evening held.

Just what had Gregson meant by a new team? Only time would tell.

CHAPTER FIVE

PUSHING OPEN THE FRONT DOOR, Harriet stepped into the silent house and scooped the mail up off the carpet. Without bothering to glance down at it, she dumped it onto the small table in the hall. It was beginning to overflow. She'd have to pick her way through the correspondence soon enough, especially if she didn't want it to all end up back on the floor.

Setting her bag and papers down on the kitchen counter, she glanced over at the phone. The red light didn't blink back at her and her heart sank into her shoes.

Everything had been so quiet. Too quiet and it was beginning to mess with her head.

She should have just stayed behind at the office and caught up on the paperwork there. It wasn't as though there was anything waiting here for her except the ghosts of her failure, which seemed to lurk in every corner.

Flopping onto a stool next to the breakfast bar, she buried her face in her hands. Exhaustion overwhelmed her and the thought of heading upstairs for a shower and a change of clothes filled her with dread. The last thing she wanted to do now was put her best clothes on for the event at city hall. Not that she really had a choice. Dr Baig had been only too clear about his expectations.

It never ceased to amaze her that someone who considered themselves a psychologist could have so little understanding for their fellow humans.

The phone shrilled and Harriet raised her face from her hands and stared over at it suspiciously. She contemplated letting the call go to voicemail before she changed her mind and reached over and scooped the handset up.

"Dr Quinn," she said automatically and felt suddenly foolish for her air of professionalism on her own home phone.

"Harriet?" The woman's voice rang a bell deep in the recesses of Harriet's mind and she struggled to place exactly where she knew it from.

"Yes..."

"It's Urma," the woman said, as though her first name alone should have been enough of an explanation. As the seconds dragged between them, Harriet registered the frustrated sigh from the woman on the other end of the line. "Urma Skegsby. Bianca's mother."

The name was like a punch to the gut and Harriet found herself unable to form words past the lump that had formed in the back of her throat.

"Bianca Sommerland—"

"Yes, of course," she said, her voice broken and hoarse. She straightened up on the stool, as though Urma would somehow be able to see her through the miles of phone line that lay between them.

"I just wanted to give you a quick buzz to see how you're getting on, love." Urma's warmth was overlaid by her obvious grief over the tragic loss of her daughter.

"I'm fine," Harriet said, struggling to find the right words. Just what was she supposed to say? Everything seemed woefully inadequate in the face of everything that had happened.

Despite her years of training, Harriet found herself suddenly at sea. There was no amount of education or practice that could prepare you for the kinds of emotions grief could bring to your door, especially when the cause of said grief was so terribly personal.

Bianca had been a bright light in Harriet's world. Her only true friend, or at least the only friend who ever bothered to dig beneath the layers of professional veneer that Harriet preferred to keep between herself and the world.

Bianca had got under her skin. A hollow ache in the centre of her chest every time she was reminded of her was the price she had to pay.

"I know you and Bianca were close," Urma said. "Bianca spoke of you often. She always worried about you; you know?"

Harriet hadn't known but the admission from Bianca's mother still brought a smile to her lips because it was so quintessentially Bianca.

"I didn't know that," Harriet said. "But thank you for telling me. Bianca was..." Harriet trailed off, unsure how to finish the sentence. How could you encapsulate somebody like Bianca who was so much to so many? Words failed to do her justice.

"Yes, she was," Urma said, filling in the gap as though Harriet had managed to convey her feelings through the silence alone.

"The police have released her body," Urma said. "So we can finally lay her to rest—" Her voice broke up and Harriet's heart ached for the mother's loss.

"Is there anything I can do?" she asked. "Anything at all?"

"We'd love it if you'd come and say a few words about her," Urma said, using the momentary break in the conversation to compose herself. "I'll understand if you can't do it. But we'd still love to see you here. Tilly would too."

Harriet swallowed around the lump in her throat. "How is she?"

"The counsellor we've brought her to see has said children are surprisingly resilient and even though she keeps trying to put a brave smile on it all, something in her has changed. I can see that."

Harriet nodded and then realised Urma couldn't see her through the telephone. "Grief can affect people in different ways," Harriet said. "Tilly is probably still in shock. She was there when they found Bianca. It's going to take her some time to come to terms with everything she has witnessed and even then, it might be years before the true depth of her trauma begins to present itself. If ever."

"That's what the counsellor said."

The silence stretched out between them and for a moment, Harriet was reminded of the companionable silences she'd often enjoyed with Bianca.

"So, will you come?" Urma asked. The moment shattered and Harriet was thrust into the present with all of the pain and heartache it brought with it.

"Of course. When do you want me?"

"We're having a service on Thursday, but we'd love to see you anytime you'd like to drive up. You have my address, don't you?"

"You live in Kirkbridge too, don't you?" Harriet asked, wracking her brain for the information she needed.

"That's it."

"Well, I'll clear my lectures and—"

"I forgot, you teach, don't you? If you can't make it up before Thursday, that's fine. I didn't mean to put pressure on you. Bianca was always telling me I needed to think of other people more, that I was always allowing my own plans to run riot and now—" Urma choked off and the line dissolved into the sounds of her sobbing, leaving Harriet at a loose end.

There was nothing she could say to the woman on the other end of the line; at least nothing that would take her pain away.

"Bianca was always telling me I needed to get out more," Harriet said instead, choosing to share one of the few precious memories she had of her friend with the woman who had brought her into the world. "She reckoned I spent far too much time cooped up with my books. She was probably right. Bianca always understood just what other people needed to hear, even if they didn't want to admit it themselves."

Urma's sobs changed in pitch and it took Harriet a moment to realise the other woman was laughing, and not crying.

"She was a bit of a busybody, wasn't she? I used to tell her that not everybody welcomed or wanted her advice. But would she listen?"

Harriet smiled in spite of herself. "No, I don't think she ever took that advice on board."

"Thank you," Urma said.

"For what?"

"For sharing that with me. Everybody is so concerned with not wanting to upset me that they don't talk about Bianca at all; they avoid her, and it's started to make me doubt that the beautiful funny daughter I brought into this world ever really existed at all."

"She existed," Harriet said. "And she was much loved... Still is loved."

Urma cleared her throat and there was the tell-tale rustle of tissue paper in the background. "I'll see you soon," Urma said. "I won't pin you down to a day and I'll take Bianca's advice for once."

"I'll see you soon, then."

The line went dead, leaving Harriet alone in her kitchen again. She stared down at the phone for what felt like an age before she slowly replaced it on the cradle.

Without hesitation, her finger slid over to the voice mail recorder and she clicked it on. Her own dulcet tones filled the air and she quickly clicked through to the only message she'd saved.

"Hi, Harri, it's me. Just giving you a quick buzz to see how you're getting on. I'm hoping you're really out on a hot date and not on the couch with your head stuck in a musty old book." The message continued, and Bianca's vibrant voice filled the kitchen. The line clicked and Harriet's own voice joined Bianca's. The voicemail had managed to record the conversation they'd shared in its entirety.

She'd made the discovery shortly after Bianca's death.

As they both chattered away on the line, Harriet could almost convince herself that her friend was still alive.

Alive and well, taking Tilly to swimming practice and going about her daily business as though nothing had ever changed.

Tears dripped onto the counter in front of her and Harriet didn't bother to stop them. She'd knew it was good to cry, an important catharsis to shed some of the burden that emotional turmoil brought. But these days, it felt like crying was all she was good for. And for all of the salty droplets she'd shed, she was still none the closer to any sort of catharsis.

Before Bianca's death, Harriet had been sure of her convictions that there was no such thing as an afterlife. Well, as sure as anyone could be considering the lack of evidence either way.

But now she found herself wishing there was at least some kind of truth in the tales of a life after death, because then it would mean that Kyle and Bianca were out there somewhere, looking after her, and that brought with it a kind of comfort Harriet hadn't known she'd needed.

At least if it were true, Bianca wasn't gone. She was still somewhere, even if unseen, and perhaps one day they would see each other again.

The tape whirred as the message came to an end.

"I'll see you, then." Bianca's final words hung in the air and the recording cut off, leaving Harriet to sit in the silence of her kitchen and contemplate her friend's last goodbye, which in typical Bianca fashion hadn't been a goodbye at all.

CHAPTER SIX

TRACING his finger over the lines cut into the photograph, a deep sense of satisfaction swelled within him. The edges were crisp, just how he liked them, and once the puzzle was taken apart everything would come together beautifully.

Picking the image up, he raised it above his head before letting it fall onto the bench before him. The pieces scattered, breaking apart on impact.

The once perfect and complete photograph now lay in a thousand scattered fragments. In his mind, he could still see the finished piece, but to anyone else, it would take real effort to complete the puzzle.

A smile curled his lips as he glanced up at the newspaper clipping. He had no evidence to suggest she even liked jigsaws but that would all change. It would have to, if she was going to work this out.

His attention drifted back to the polaroid photograph that sat on the work bench next to the puzzle pieces.

Picking it up, he studied the smiling woman. The way she'd glanced over her shoulder, tantalisingly looking in his direction before turning away again. Soon, she wouldn't look away. Soon, all she would see was him. And there was only one person who could help her.

"Let the games begin, Dr Quinn."

CHAPTER SEVEN

A FEW HOURS LATER, Harriet hurried up the steps into the bustling building where Dr Baig and the others were waiting. She was late. Not that she really cared. In order to clear her mind after her short talk with Bianca's mother, she'd returned to her academic papers. Not that it was possible to concentrate. Every time she found her mind wandering, she'd been forced to return to the beginning. In the end, she'd read the same paragraph over and over at least ten times before she'd given up and decided to get ready.

Smoothing down the front of the red dress, she touched her hand to her hair nervously and took a deep breath before she pushed in through the double, mirrored doors.

The room beyond was filled with people, the

loud sound of their chatter droned into one big cacophony that threatened to overwhelm her senses.

How was she supposed to find anybody in here? Harriet found herself regretting her refusal of Dr Baig's kind offer to escort her to the event.

"You can do this, Harriet. Head up, shoulders relaxed. It's fine."

The words were little more than a murmured prayer on her lips but they worked, nonetheless. The tension she'd been holding onto slowly melted away as she spotted one of the waiters making his way toward her with a tray of what appeared to be fluted champagne glasses. Harriet gratefully took one of the proffered drinks and raised the glass to her lips.

Sparkling wine. It seemed that whoever had organised the event hadn't wanted to stretch to actual champagne. Not that Harriet minded. The sparkling wine, with its fruity aftertaste, was lighter than champagne and coated her palate with its sweetness in a way that champagne never could.

"Dr Quinn, glad to see you could make it," Dr Baig touched his hand to her elbow and Harriet nearly jumped out of her skin.

Ever since the incident with Robert Burton, she'd become more sensitive to physical touch, preferring to keep a distance from those around her. And Dr Baig's sudden appearance next to her unsettled her in ways she'd prefer not to admit to. Because an admission like that would suggest she wasn't as in control of herself as she wanted to believe.

"Of course. You didn't exactly give me a choice, Dennis," she said curtly, plastering a smile on her face so that anyone who passed would believe their conversation was a pleasant one.

"You know how important something like this is for the university," he said, under his breath.

"Not that long ago, you were the one berating me for splitting my time between the university and other things."

"That was before you hit the front page of every paper in the country," he said, referring to the painful images some journalist had managed to take directly after Burton's attack. The photographs showed Harriet on the stretcher being escorted from the house with a concerned Drew holding her hand as though afraid to let it go.

Every time she had to see the picture, Harriet was reminded just what her lies had cost her.

She sighed and turned to face him. "Why am I here, Dennis? I'm tired, and I've got a lecture to prepare for tomorrow that..." Harriet trailed off, the words caught in the back of her throat like a moth stuck in a spider's web as her gaze fell on Drew.

He stood on the opposite side of the large domed room, one elbow propped against the bar as his gaze flickered over the congregation.

"You didn't tell me he was going to be here,"

Harriet hissed, digging her fingers into Baig's sleeve as she ducked behind one of the large pillars dotted around the room.

"Christ, Harriet, get a grip of yourself." He extricated himself from her grasp and shot her a withering glare. "Of course he's going to be here."

"Why?"

Dr Baig sighed. "You didn't read the invitation I sent, did you?"

In the back of her mind, there was a vague recollection of an email invitational he'd sent but she'd sent it straight to the trash bin on her computer without reading it. Of course, once he'd cornered her and explained, in no uncertain terms, that the security of her job rested on her appearing at the function, Harriet had found herself with no choice but to attend.

"You already know I didn't," she said. "If I had, I'm guessing I wouldn't be here. Threat or no threat."

"Nobody threatened you, Harriet," he said. "Don't be so dramatic. You and I both know that shaking a certain number of hands and engaging in a certain amount of polite conversation with the people who provide the university with the funds it badly needs, is vital."

"So, if this is just a fishing expedition for more funding, then why is DI Haskell here?"

Dr Baig had the good grace to look ashamed. "We were approached about potentially setting up some kind of consultation style arrangements between the psychology department and the police force. There was even talk of setting up a dedicated task force for serious crimes in the UK but that's still hush-hush."

"No," Harriet said, shaking her head vehemently as though that one word alone would be enough to convince either Dr Baig or herself.

"No, what?"

"I lecture at the university and I'm happy there," she said, digging her fingernails into the palm of her hands as she fought to force herself to believe the lie. "I don't want another job, working with the police."

"This could prove useful for the university, Harriet. It would allow us to apply for more funding and—"

"Is that all you care about?" she hissed, lowering her voice so as not to attract the attention of the others in the hall. "The last time I worked with the police, I nearly died."

Dr Baig shrugged. "An unfortunate event, for sure, but Harriet, think about it. If we deliberately worked with the police, then we could improve on safe-guarding and other areas where yours or any other psychologist's safety may become compromised."

"You really don't care," she said, her voice flat.

"I care about turning our psychology department into a centre for excellence," he said. "I care about ensuring our future."

She shook her head and felt one of the pins holding her dark curls in place slide loose. A lock of hair tumbled across her face as she glared at Dr Baig.

"Harriet, you—"

"There you are!" Katerina's voice cut over Dr Baig's, and Harriet glanced up in surprise to find the other woman bearing down on them both with a broad smile on her face.

"I'd wondered where you'd disappeared off to." Katerina's smile wilted a little as her gaze found Harriet's. Halting next to Dr Baig, Harriet watched as Katerina placed a hand over Dr Baig's arm almost possessively.

"Nice to see you again, Harriet. I hope you're feeling much improved from earlier?"

"I thought you were going to dinner," Harriet said, ignoring the question entirely. She glanced from Katerina to Dr Baig who glanced sheepishly down at the floor.

"We did," Katerina said, patting Dr Baig's arm affectionately. "Dennis knows all the best restaurants around here."

"So, you two are an item now?" Harriet couldn't keep the surprise from her voice. She'd heard that opposites often attracted, but Dr Baig and Dr Katerina Perez were *too* opposite for that old adage to hold true.

Katerina's rich throaty laughter floated up into the air as she pressed her head down onto Dr Baig's shoulder. "I suppose. We haven't really discussed it, have we Dennis?"

Harriet glanced over at the man in question. His face was suffused with colour and he opened his mouth to reply but there was no sound. Was he actually tongue-tied?

It seemed utterly preposterous and yet there was no denying the truth.

"I'm pleased for you both," Harriet said, managing to sound a little less stiff than she'd feared she would.

"I was just explaining to Harriet here how important it is for the university to make this connection with the police," Baig said.

"It's a marvellous idea," Katerina said. From the corner of her eye, Harriet spotted the woman's fingers tightening on her companion's arm as she spoke.

"Yes, well, it's not arranged yet," he sputtered sounding somewhat flustered.

"I'm parched," Katerina said. "You wouldn't mind getting me another vodka tonic, would you?" She smiled down at the man next to her and the colour that had begun to recede from his face once again sprang into his cheeks.

"Of course," he said, unwinding his arm from her grip. Dr Baig glanced down at Harriet's half-empty glass of sparkling wine. "Same again, Harriet?"

Harriet glanced over toward the bar and caught sight of Drew again. "Yes."

Dr Baig moved toward the bar, leaving Harriet

with Katerina. They stood in companionable silence before Katerina finally broke it. "He means well."

"I'm not sure he can see past the potential for growth in the university," Harriet said stiffly as she lifted her glass to her lips and drained it.

"Ambition isn't a bad thing," Katerina said with a tight smile.

"And what do you think of all of this then?" Harriet waved her arm, indicating the room of people.

Katerina's smile broadened. "I've seen them engage in such things in America with great success."

"But do you think it's the right thing to do here? I mean, we're not exactly a hub of activity, are we? Criminal or otherwise."

"I might have agreed with you before your unfortunate run in with Robert Burton," Katerina said. "But now, I'm not so sure. I can't help but feel we would all benefit from such a working relationship here; think of the potential for case studies."

Harriet scoffed, an unpleasant sound that ripped from her throat before she could stop it.

"I see you don't agree."

Harriet sighed. "Look, I'm not immune to the idea that working with the police on certain types of cases wouldn't be beneficial to all involved."

"But?" Katerina smiled pleasantly.

"But I just don't think using Drew and I as the poster children for such a thing is a good idea."

"You are the epitome of a working partnership,"

Katerina said. "I would have thought you'd have wanted to preserve that at any cost?"

Harriet shook her head and glanced in the direction of the bar, only to find Drew gone. She glanced around the room, but he was nowhere to be seen.

"We ended on bad terms," Harriet said honestly. "I made a mistake and it destroyed everything."

Katerina tutted sympathetically and touched her hand to Harriet's. "Surely everything can be forgiven?"

Harriet stared down into her empty glass and shook her head. "There are somethings that I think are beyond forgiveness."

Dr Baig chose that moment to return. "Here you go," he said, passing a glass of clear liquid with one chunk of lemon which floated near the top to Katerina. "And for you." He presented Harriet with a second glass of sparkling wine, which she took gratefully.

"Thank you."

Dr Baig nodded and eyed her speculatively. "What were you two discussing just now?"

"Nothing," Katerina said swiftly before Harriet could reply. "There's Superintendent Burroughs; shouldn't we go and speak with him?"

Harriet was surprised that Katerina already seemed to be familiar with the Superintendent. Despite working with Drew and having spent time in the station, she'd never met the man, and yet Katerina appeared to know him by name.

Harriet looked in the direction in which Katerina was gesturing and felt her heart sink into her shoes. Drew's dark gaze met hers across the room and there was no escaping the pained expression that flitted across his features as he recognised her.

The sight of him was enough to confirm Harriet's worst fears. She'd been correct in thinking that some things should not be forgiven. It seemed that Drew felt the same way.

Before she could say anything, Katerina looped her arm through Harriet's and started to steer them both across the space to where Drew stood stiffly with a group of official-looking gentlemen.

CHAPTER EIGHT

"DR PEREZ, so lovely to see you again!" Superintendent Burroughs exclaimed, his booming voice managing to echo in the room. Drew cringed. There was no escaping it, the man was a buffoon. A well-meaning buffoon but a buffoon, nonetheless.

Harriet looked positively terrified as the glamorous woman next to her directed them both across the room. She ducked her gaze toward the floor but not before Drew had caught sight of the shame that lurked within her blue eyes.

She looked beautiful. The red dress she wore made it so that every man in the room had no doubt spotted her and imagined what lay beneath. Her dark hair was piled on her head, but a stray lock had fallen over her face and Drew contemplated reaching over to push it back behind her ear. Not that it would stay there; her hair was as unruly as she was.

The dress was high around her throat and Drew couldn't help but wonder if that was to hide the remnants of her injuries?

The memory of her with the rope around her throat, legs kicking frantically as she slowly strangled to death was a sight that still haunted his nightmares. But seeing her here now, so vibrantly alive, made the darkness that threatened to overwhelm his mind lessen its hold just a little.

What was wrong with him?

He'd thought about the moment they would meet again. Planned it over in his head and knew exactly what he was going to say to her. Of course, now that the moment had arrived, he found himself suddenly unable to form words like a normal human being. That realisation made him even more pissed off than usual and it was an effort to stay put and not stalk away from the group.

The Superintendent had continued to blather on, and Drew tried to pick up the thread of the conversation.

"This is Dr Dennis Baig," Dr Perez said as she gestured to a small lanky man with rounded glasses who stood awkwardly next to her. "He's the head of the department up at the university. And he's done a wonderful job of getting it to a point where everyone can benefit from the expertise he's managed to curate there."

Drew knew a hard sell when he heard one, and

Dr Perez seemed determined to sell the potential benefits of working with the university.

"I think everyone would agree that the last case you worked on would not have had such a conclusive, and dare I say happy, outcome had Dr Quinn not assisted in the apprehension of Mr Burton."

"Three children died along with a young mother," Drew said, unable to keep his thoughts to himself. From the corner of his eye, he spotted Harriet flinch. Undeterred, he added, "I wouldn't exactly call that a happy outcome."

"Of course not," Dr Perez said with a wide and disarming smile. "Forgive me. Perhaps successful would be a better way of putting it. You are the estimable DI Haskell, are you not?" She held her hand out toward him and Drew was left in no doubt that the woman had known who he was before she'd even crossed the room.

"If it weren't for this man and his nose for sniffing out criminals, Burton would still be out there preying on our young," Superintendent Burroughs interjected. "It's our duty at Yorkshire CID to recruit only the very best into what we hope is a nurturing environment for such talent."

"Of course," Dr Perez said, turning her hundred-watt smile on Burroughs.

The whole exchange left Drew feeling decidedly grimy and he went to take a large mouthful of his beer in an attempt to wash away the sugary sweet exchange that threatened to make him gag.

Finding the glass empty, he smiled apologetically. "If you'll excuse me," he said, holding the glass up as an indicator of his intentions.

The others barely registered his departure, but he could feel Harriet's gaze on him as he skirted the edge of the room.

He needed to get out of there. It had been one thing to think about seeing her again and something else entirely to actually see her in the flesh. The corridor beyond the ballroom was practically empty, and the dress shoes he'd managed to dig out of his wardrobe squeaked across the parquet flooring. Pushing out through the side door, he drank down a lungful of night air and closed his eyes.

Shit, why was it so painful to see her again? He'd thought his anger could insulate him against anything he might possibly have felt for her before but now...

Seeing her standing there had felt like the wound had been ripped open again.

It wasn't just that, though; seeing her again reminded him of everything he'd lost. If it wasn't for her and that meddling bastard Dr Connor, Freya would still be here.

Deep down, Drew knew there was no way of knowing if that were true or not. Freya had been ill and what she'd suffered from had been the kind of illness that could have blown up in their faces at any moment.

Mentally she'd been a ticking time bomb and the fact that she'd left him in the dark, and not told him just how serious it all really was, hurt far worse than anything Harriet had done.

But he couldn't let go of Harriet's betrayal. He'd trusted her and she'd lied to him. She'd known all along how painful Freya's death had been and still she'd kept the truth from him.

Even if he could forgive her for keeping the truth from him; how was he ever supposed to trust her again?

"I'm sorry," Harriet said, her voice making him jump. Drew turned to find her standing by the door, as though just by thinking of her, he'd somehow managed to conjure her from his imagination.

"What for?"

She looked shocked, her face crumpling a little as the harshness of his words settled in the air between them.

"For this," she said. "Turning up here. And for everything else..."

"Sorry won't bring her back," he said bitterly. "Sorry won't heal the rift."

She nodded and let her gaze drop to the ground. "I know that, and I'm sorry for that too."

Drew snorted, and felt somewhat chagrined for being so petty but he couldn't help it. Seeing her again, hearing the apology leave her lips, stung a little too much for him to bear.

He wanted to rage at her, to shout, and break things and yet, as he stood there and stared at her, he found himself wondering if it was Harriet he was actually angry at.

"I'm leaving," she said. "I just wanted you to know so you wouldn't feel like you had to..."

Drew shook his head and sighed. "You don't have to run off just because I'm here. This is your world too. In fact, it's probably more your world than it is mine."

Harriet smiled. "Honestly, I'm only too happy to leave. I've never liked these kinds of things."

Drew found himself agreeing with her.

"I always feel like an idiot," he said, staring down at the suit he'd pulled from the closet. "I end up feeling like one of the waiters when I'm wearing one of these things."

Harriet glanced at him and shook her head, a small smile curling her lips. "You look great..."

The beginnings of a heat Drew hadn't felt in what felt like forever curled in the pit of his stomach and he crushed it down. Feelings like that felt like too much of a betrayal against the woman he'd lost... the woman he still loved.

"Don't," he said, drawing a look of surprise from the woman standing opposite him. "Don't do that. Don't pretend everything is fine between us."

"I'm not," she said quickly. "I was just--"

"Because it's not, fine," he said. "It won't ever be fine between us. You threw all of that away when you decided to lie to me about Freya."

"I know," she said, managing to sound as miserable as he felt.

"I couldn't ever trust you again. No matter how much I might want to."

"I know that, too."

Anger bubbled in his veins, a brilliant white-hot rage that threatened to rob him of all reason. "You know, do you? Where was all this knowledge while you were lying, then? Where was all this wonderful psychological insight when you decided that keeping the truth from me would be the best way of dealing with it all?"

She stared down at the ground. "I wanted to tell you, but if I had, would you have wanted to work with me at all?"

"Probably not," he said smartly.

"And what would have happened to the case then?" She raised her gaze to his and he found himself pinned in place by her icy glare. "What would have happened to Robert Burton?"

"You think you're the only psychologist out there I could have gone to for help?" He snorted his derision.

"I think I was the only psychologist you knew

who specialised in suicidal ideation and the phenomena surrounding clusters. I think considering everything you knew about the person responsible for killing those teenagers, I was the only one qualified to give you the help you needed to keep investigating."

She sucked in a deep breath, her shoulders heaving, and Drew found himself wondering if the trembling was caused by anger or upset.

Shit, now she was getting inside his head and poisoning his thoughts. When had he ever wondered in the past whether a reaction was caused by an emotion or not? He'd never cared before, so why did he care so damn much now?

"Look, I'm sorry I lied to you," she said. "But I'm not sorry I protected our working relationship so that we could apprehend the man responsible for all those deaths. I'll always regret breaking your trust, it really wasn't my intention, but I won't ever regret the outcome of it all."

Drew balled his hands into fists but as quickly as the rage arrived, he felt it drain out of him; leaving him wrung out as though she'd somehow managed to suck all the energy from the air.

"I won't disturb your evening any more than I already have," she said, turning away.

"You don't have to go," he said.

"I know," she said, and there was no mistaking the tension that kept her shoulders rigid. "But I can't stay here either." She sighed. "I just wanted to let you know I was leaving."

He nodded but knew she hadn't seen him. "Fine."

She stalked back up the steps, leaving him alone outside.

Drew's hands automatically went to the pocket of his jacket and he searched for the cigarettes he was used to finding in his coat. The pockets were empty, and he stared down at the ground.

"Well, shit," he said softly.

"Do you want one?" The voice came out of the darkness and he spun around to find Dr Perez watching him from the shadowed alcove next to the building. In her hand, she held a cigarette and Drew felt the swelling of his addictive desire as it thrummed in his veins.

"Go on then," he said, pushing the voice in the back of his head away. The last thing he needed right now was another guilt trip to run on. He took the offered cigarette and leaned in close as the lighter briefly illuminated the planes of her face. The shadows danced across her high cheekbones, keeping her dark eyes hidden.

Drew pulled deeply on the cigarette. The taste of tobacco slid across his tongue like the sensuous first kiss from a long-lost lover. He drank deep of the cigarette and, closing his eyes, leaned his head back and let the swirling emotions inside slowly ebb away.

"Better?" Dr Perez asked, the slight hint of her accent coloured the words with new meaning.

Drew straightened up and met her dark unfathomable gaze head on. "How much did you hear?"

She smiled, a slow sensuous curling of her lips and he couldn't shake the feeling that she was flirting with him. But why? He'd seen the way she'd draped herself over the arm of the head of the psychology department. He'd thought they were an item. Now, however, he couldn't help but think that he was somehow missing something important.

"Enough to know you two have some unresolved issues," she said. The tip of her cigarette lit up as she closed her red-slicked lips around the end. "Do you want to talk about it?"

Drew's laughter was bitter and abrupt. "No, it's the last thing I want to do."

She nodded and stepped out of the shadows. "I think you and I could help each other," she said, each word carefully enunciated.

"Oh, right. And how do you figure that?"

"You've heard the talk of this task force and we both know that those in positions of authority will want you to continue on your charade of a relationship with Dr Quinn. You've already had such wonderful success so why change what isn't broken?"

She crooked a perfectly shaped eyebrow at him.

He couldn't argue with her logic. Drew knew how the likes of Gregson and Burroughs thought. He knew, only too well, that they would insist he rekindle the relationship with Harriet if it meant good press.

The thought of working alongside the psychologist again both thrilled and depressed him. Working with her made the job all the more interesting. She viewed the world so differently, and it opened his eyes to possibilities he'd never even have contemplated before meeting her.

Not to mention the fact that she was easy to work with. Harriet was the type of person who made you feel at ease, as though you could share anything with her. Which, considering the way she'd screwed him over, made her all the more dangerous.

"So, what are you proposing?"

"That we should work together," she said. Whatever she saw reflected in his face made her sigh as though he'd somehow managed to disappoint her. "I don't see why we wouldn't be able to come to some sort of mutual arrangement."

"And what if I have no interest in working with another psychologist?" Drew extinguished the cigarette on the top of the bin. The stale scent of smoke clung to him and the guilt he'd been trying so hard to squash returned with a vengeance. Freya would be so disappointed.

Dr Perez's smile was all predator. "I've got a feeling, DI Haskell, that you'll find yourself without a choice before too long." With that, she was gone, the sound of her wickedly high stiletto heels *click clacking* smartly across the cement as she disappeared into the building.

Drew sighed and flopped back against the wall. Christ, why was everything so complicated these days? If he'd thought working alongside Harriet again might prove uncomfortable, then he had no doubt that working with Dr Perez would be downright painful. She was sex personified, and she knew how to use it to manipulate those around her. Not that he had a problem with a woman who wasn't afraid to use her own sexuality. Freya had been that way. She'd known how beautiful she was and wasn't afraid to use it to her advantage.

But there had been an inherent honesty in Freya that seemed to be lacking in Dr Perez. She struck him as the kind of woman who would happily sell her partner down the river if she thought it would get her a better deal and that wasn't the kind of working relationship that flourished in the police force. You had to be able to trust your partner and colleagues. No matter what happened, trust was the first and last undying rule. Without it, everything else fell apart.

Closing his eyes, Drew let his head drop back against the cold stone wall. "Out of the frying pain and into the fucking fire," he said under his breath.

CHAPTER NINE

SITTING IN THE LIBRARY, he stared down at the Snapchat messages Michael kept sending, each one depicting an even more raucous scene than the one before.

It wasn't fair. Here he was trapped with the musty bloody textbooks while Michael was probably getting off with some other bloke. Picking up his notes, he shoved them into his bag and arranged the rest of the dusty tomes into a neat pile. Carrying the books up to the desk he pulled his card from his wallet and shoved it over toward the guy sitting behind the computer.

"Studying again?"

Michael glanced up and met the brown eyes of the man sitting behind the library desk. "Yeah, I've got exams coming up and I wanted to get a jump start on everything."

The guy reached out and took the first book off the top of the pile. "Criminal and Behavioural Profiling?" The guy cocked a dark eyebrow in Gabriel's direction. "That sounds pretty heavy."

"It can be," he said, trying to sound bored. "I don't mean to be rude but is there any chance we can speed this up. I've got to be somewhere." He glanced down at his phone as another message appeared. This one came from Taff and as Gabriel clicked through his heart sank as he watched Michael gyrate beneath the hypnotic lights as another much older man tried to grope him.

"Motherfucker--" Gabriel raised his face and smiled apologetically at the man on the other side of the counter. "I'm really sorry. I just..."

"No worries," the guy said. Gabriel glanced down and read the name tag on his shirt.

"I'm going to come back for those books tomorrow, Chris, if that's all right?"

Chris nodded. "Sure, do you want me to put them aside for you?"

"You're an absolute angel," Gabriel said as he reached over and swiped his card off the counter. "Seriously, I really appreciate this."

Chris shook his head and looked sheepishly down at the floor. "It's not a problem," he said, managing to sound somewhat endearing as a pink blush suffused his cheeks.

Gabriel found himself taking a more serious look

at the man in front of him. He was definitely hot, in that understated, nice guy next door kind of way.

Chris raised his gaze and stared up at Gabriel through his dark lashes. Definitely hot...

The moment the thought popped into his head he thought of Michael. He couldn't throw a relationship away on something like this. What if there was a perfectly reasonable explanation for what was going on with that guy. After all it wasn't as though he himself didn't have to fight off his fair share of creepers when he went out partying.

"I'll see you around," he said to Chris, who looked somewhat disappointed at his sudden departure. There was one good thing in all of this though; if it all fell apart with Michael, he'd found his rebound without even needing to try that hard.

CHAPTER TEN

HARRIET STOOD in front of the small window overlooking the university car park. The gunmetal grey sky overhead did nothing to lift her mood and the drizzle that beat down on the glass left much to be desired.

In her head, she played the conversation with Drew over and over on a loop. Exhaustion plagued her brain and Harriet knew her ability to think critically was impaired. It wasn't as terrible as she was making it out to be in her head. Or was she simply telling herself that in an attempt to lessen the guilt gnawing at her inside?

The whole situation was nothing more than a tangled knot, and as much as she wanted to pick at it, her schedule for the day wasn't going to give her the chance.

"Dr Quinn?" The timid voice that called to her

from the doorway caused Harriet to snap out of her reverie. She turned to find a petite blonde standing in the doorway. The girl couldn't have been more than nineteen. She was fresh-faced, but as she stepped into the room, Harriet could see the subtleties of the make-up she wore.

"And you are?" Harriet scanned her mind back through the appointments she'd arranged for the day.

"Rachel," the girl said. "Rachel Kennedy. You said you had an opening to discuss my essay."

Harriet smiled and gestured to the chair opposite her desk; as far as she could remember, there was no Rachel Kennedy on her list of appointments.

Rachel hurried inside and gratefully dumped her books on the edge of the already-crowded desk. The textbooks looked brand new, and as Harriet scanned them quickly, she caught sight of the sale price sticker still attached to one book on criminal profiling.

"I really appreciate this. I know how busy you are and—"

"I don't remember seeing you in my class," Harriet said, almost nonchalantly, as she dropped into a chair across from Rachel and continued her study.

The girl had the good grace to blush, colour spreading up into her hairline. "I'll admit, I've only just started..."

Harriet shook her head. "We're midway through

the year. I don't see how you could have." She cut off and studied the young woman a little more closely. There was something familiar about her, but Harriet was exhausted, and pinpointing exactly where she knew this Rachel from seemed an almost impossible task.

Rachel had paused, a look of unease spreading across her face.

"What was your essay about?" Harriet asked, surreptitiously clicking into her online calendar. She was almost positive this woman hadn't scheduled an appointment.

"I'm writing a piece on how offenders' backgrounds influence the crimes they commit."

"The nature versus nurture debate," Harriet said with a smile. "That sounds a little complex for somebody who has joined the course halfway through the year. We've only briefly touched on the subject in class. What makes you think you're qualified to write an essay on any of this?"

"Well, that's where I was hoping you'd be able to give me some pointers," Rachel said, settling into the chair opposite Harriet. "How do you decide whether society or genetic make-up has caused the offender to choose the path they're on?"

"Nothing causes an offender to commit a crime, not in the context you're referring to anyway. There are some societal factors that may play a part in predisposing an individual toward committing certain crimes but again, you cannot say with any certainty that a particular person will or won't offend based on evidence you find in their background."

"That seems like a roundabout way of telling me nothing at all." Rachel smiled but there was an edge to her voice that suggested frustration over Harriet's answer.

"And that's why I've questioned whether you really think you're capable of writing an *article* of this kind." Harriet deliberately emphasised the word but the woman across from her remained unmoved. Could Harriet have misread the situation? "Perhaps you'd be better suited to writing an essay on the early beginnings of psychology and how it has evolved in today's society."

Rachel smiled and ducked her gaze so she could stare down at her hands. "Isn't there anything in your experience with Robert Burton you can tell me about that might shed some light on this debate? I mean, by all accounts, he should have been a stand-up guy. There was nothing in his past to suggest he would act out the way he did."

Harriet's smile turned icy. She wasn't wrong. It was the typical line of questions thrown at her in the wake of the case surrounding Robert Burton.

"Rachel," Harriet said, as she leaned across the table to flick through the top books stacked on the edge of her desk. "If that even is your name." The odd shape pinned to the top of the woman's bag which leaned against her chair leg caught Harriet's eye, confirming her suspicions.

The woman across from her tried to look shocked and she opened her mouth, but Harriet cut her off with a shake of her head.

"Don't bother. I know you're not really here to discuss an essay you want to write for my course."

"That's not true. I—"

"In fact, we both know you're not enrolled in my class at all. And if you have somehow managed to get your name on the register it's because you just wanted to get in here to try and pick my brain over the Burton case."

The woman across from her frowned and leaned back in her chair. "What makes you think I'd be interested in that?"

Harriet inclined her head in the direction of the woman's phone sticking out of her bag. The microphone adapter which was clipped to the side of her bag was designed to blend in. Deep down, Harriet knew she probably wouldn't have spotted it if it hadn't been for the brand-new books—whose spines hadn't even been cracked yet—piled on the desk in front of her.

"We both know the real reason for your presence but I'm going to tell you the same thing I've said to every reporter who has come looking for a story where there isn't one. I have nothing to say about an ongoing case."

"My name *is* Rachel by the way," the girl said, folding her legs as she leaned back in the chair and gave Harriet an appraising stare. "I honestly thought you'd figure me out faster."

Harriet kept her smile in place and folded her hands neatly on the desk in front of her. "I know you from somewhere, don't I?"

"I've done a few news reports, freelance stuff," Rachel said, tossing her blonde hair back over her shoulder.

"You seem a little young."

Rachel snorted. "It's amazing what a dewy complexion can help you get away with."

"Well, if you don't mind, Rachel, I really do have a busy day ahead of me."

"Tell me what tipped you off about Burton."

The question caused Harriet to cast her mind back to the moment when she'd suspected the grieving father and his role in the deaths of his three victims.

"Didn't you want to get even with him for killing your best friend?"

"I think you should go now," Harriet said tightly. Her palms had started to sweat, and she could feel them sticking to the surface of the desk in front of her. "I've said all I'm going to say to you."

"If he was here right now, what would you say to him?" Rachel asked, showing no sign of moving from the chair she'd settled into.

Harriet pushed onto her feet and strode over to the door. She tugged it open. "Martha, could you ask security to escort Ms Kennedy from the premises?"

Martha Metcalf glanced up in Harriet's direction with thinly veiled hostility. She sighed and reached for the phone as though Harriet's request was somehow beneath her.

"No need to get all hostile," Rachel said pausing in the doorway. "I'll go. One last thing though."

Harriet folded her arms over her chest and glared down at the young journalist in front of her.

"Do you think your mishandling of the Freya Northrup case led to her committing suicide after she was discharged from your care?"

Harriet felt her throat constrict and the world shifted violently around her. Freya had never been under her care but that hadn't stopped her from feeling responsible for the young woman's behaviour.

"Why would you ask that?" Harriet said, her voice sounded alien to her own ears.

"Dr Jonathan Connor seems to believe it was with your insistence that Miss Northrup be discharged from the care facility she had been admitted to. He said he was simply following your advice that Miss Northrup was sufficiently recovered and capable of receiving outpatient care."

"That's not true," Harriet said.

"Shut up," Martha said. The anger in her voice

snapped Harriet out of the panicked state she'd slipped into. She glanced over at the other woman, who stood next to her desk. But Harriet found herself unable to tell if the furious expression she wore was aimed at Harriet or at the young reporter.

"Excuse me?" Rachel said, glaring at Martha. "And you are?"

"None of your damned business," Martha said. "You were asked to leave, so go now, before campus security gets here."

Rachel eyed Martha speculatively before she smiled. "Fine, I'll go."

"You've got a loyal one there," Rachel said, indicating Martha. "But you won't always have somebody there to protect you from the difficult questions we need answers to. There are enough problems in this country without allowing those we're supposed to be able to trust off the hook for poor judgement. Especially when that poor judgement leads to a young woman killing herself."

With that parting shot, Rachel turned on her heels and strode out of the door. It took Harriet a moment to compose herself sufficiently to give Martha a grateful smile.

"Thank you."

Martha shook her head. "I didn't do that for you," she said. "It wouldn't surprise me in the least to know you'd played a part in killing some poor girl who put her trust in you. But what I won't have is your poor behaviour bringing down the reputation of this university."

Martha's words were the slap of icy water Harriet needed. "You're absolutely right, Martha," she said as she retreated into the office and scooped up her bag and coat from inside the door.

"Where are you off to now?"

"I've got business to attend to."

"And what about your business here?" Martha asked. The frustration that dripped from her voice brought the ghost of a smile to Harriet's lips.

"You said it yourself; you wouldn't want my poor behaviour affecting the reputation of this university so I'm going to make sure that doesn't happen."

Martha stiffened. "Fine. I'll cancel your appointments."

Harriet stalked out of the office, leaving the older woman to smoulder in her own rage.

FORTY MINUTES LATER, Harriet pulled up in front of the *Hermitage Hospital* and killed the engine. The huge white elephant of a building stood out in stark relief against the backdrop of the moors.

Hurrying to the doors, Harriet pushed inside. Why was it that every time she drove up here, she found herself caught in the rain? Shaking the stray droplets from her curls, she hurried across the main foyer to the reception desk.

The man behind the counter was unfamiliar.

"I'd like to see Dr Connor please," Harriet said, hoping her voice sounded as professional and official as she wanted it to.

The young man glanced up at her, his handsome brow crinkled in consternation as he took her in. "I'm not sure if Dr Connor is taking visitors right now," he said imperiously. "If you'd like to leave your name and take a seat, I can find out if he's available to speak with you."

"Dr Quinn," she said and watched as the young man's face smoothed out into a broad smile. "Of course, Dr Quinn. I'll let him know you're here."

Had Jonathan been expecting her? As she moved over to the seats that lined the far wall, Harriet reached into her pocket and pulled the crumpled letter free. Smoothing it out, she stared down at the unbroken seal and, not for the first time, wondered if she'd made a mistake in ignoring his correspondence.

The grating noise of a buzzer sounding somewhere deep in the building caught her attention and she shoved the letter back into her pocket. She lifted her gaze in time to see Jonathan striding out into the reception area. He glanced over at the young man behind the reception desk who, in turn, discreetly inclined his head in Harriet's direction.

She pushed onto her feet as Jonathan turned to

face her. His face broke into a broad smile and he held his arms wide, as though he expected her to rush toward him for an embrace.

"It's so lovely to see you again, Harriet. Come this way. I've got a few minutes. We can chat in my office."

Alarm bells rang in Harriet's head. "If it's all the same with you, Jonathan, I haven't had lunch yet, so I was hoping we could speak in the canteen. You know, for old time's sake."

If he knew the hidden meaning behind her words, he showed no signs of it. His smile never shifted as he nodded. "Of course." He let his arms drop back to his sides. "Come this way."

He directed her to a small corridor that led away from the reception and took them deeper into the heart of the hospital. They walked in silence, but Harriet's scalp prickled with the awareness of Jonathan's presence behind her.

Despite the size of the hospital, there was no private canteen for the staff. Staff and patients—at least those deemed capable—shared the same space for eating.

Harriet headed straight for the food counter and chose a pre-wrapped salad sandwich from the display. She ordered a coffee as she paid for the sandwich and carried the two items back to a table in the far corner.

From her seat, she had a perfect view of Jonathan

Connor as he interacted with the few lingering patients in the canteen and the staff at the counter. His easy manner and broad smile seemed to make him a favourite among the staff and residents.

Not that Harriet could blame them. They didn't know the truth about him. Up until a few weeks ago, she hadn't even known the real Dr Connor. Now, she couldn't shake the memory of his cruel streak.

"Finally," he said with a bright smile as he joined her at the table. "I thought I was never going to get away." He set a bowl of chicken salad down across from her and a pot of strawberry yoghurt. However, he ignored the items and turned his full attention to Harriet.

"How are you?" There seemed to be genuine concern in his voice as he addressed her, but Harriet knew better than to take anything he said at face value.

"I would be better if I didn't think you were spreading misinformation to the press about me." Harriet kept her voice deliberately low, forcing him to lean toward her.

Jonathan reared back as though she'd struck him, a look of pure horror twisted his features and Harriet fought the urge to roll her eyes at his amateur dramatics.

"I would do no such thing as spread misinformation," he said.

"You're denying that you've spoken to the press?"

He shook his head. "I have spoken to the press," he said. "I mean, of course I have. This place doesn't get the recognition it deserves, Harriet, so when a journalist comes knocking, I'm going to take the opportunity to speak about the wonderful work we're accomplishing here."

"And what about the less than stellar work you achieved where Freya Northrup was concerned? How did her name come up?"

He looked chagrined and glanced down at the table. "I may have mentioned her because of your connection with DI Haskell. I'll admit to finding it a little strange that he would agree to work with you based on your *poor* treatment of his fiancée."

Harriet felt the anger in her chest swell until she was sure it would choke her. "*My* poor treatment of Freya? I think you've got me confused with yourself, Jonathan. I wasn't the one who treated Freya. You were."

He shook his head and glanced down at the table. The moment stretched and he pulled the lid off his chicken salad and stabbed his fork into the centre of the bowl.

Pulling several pieces of lettuce free he stuffed them into his mouth and chewed thoughtfully before returning his attention to her face again. "How long have these episodes been happening, Harriet?" His voice was all smooth concern and Harriet found herself caught a little off kilter by the sudden directional change of their conversation.

"What?" It was her turn to lean back and wear an expression of confusion.

"This is how your mother's illness began isn't it?" He jabbed his fork aggressively into the salad for a second time. "I mean, you said it yourself the last time you were here. You're worried you'll end up just like her. That her illness will have somehow wormed its way inside your head too."

"That's not true."

"Are you sure?" He raised an eyebrow in her direction. "I mean, you don't seem to remember that you were the physician in charge of Freya's treatment."

"That's because I wasn't," Harriet said, hating the way her voice rose in denial. Getting upset was not going to do her any favours. It would simply convince Jonathan that he was on the right path with his gaslighting behaviour. Clenching her hands into fists, she sucked down a deep breath and tried to compose herself.

"You were the doctor in charge, Jonathan. When we discussed Freya's treatment plan, I told you it was my belief that she wasn't 'cured' as you so aptly put it at the time. I told you that sending her home with medication wasn't going to cut it. I warned you, and you discharged her anyway."

Jonathan sighed. "It's so sad to see someone as

bright as you succumb to stress. But then you always did have a fertile imagination."

"Why are you doing this?" Harriet leaned across the table toward the man opposite her. What had changed so drastically between them that he would behave like this toward her? It couldn't just be her rejection of his advances, surely?

"I'm just concerned about you, Harriet. Everything that happened with Bianca and your encounter with Robert Burton has obviously affected you on a deep emotional level."

"I know you're lying," Harriet said, folding her hands in front of her.

"That's not what the discharge papers say."

Harriet felt the colour drain from her face. "That's not possible."

Jonathan smiled at her but there was something that lurked in the depths of his eyes that told her she was dealing with a predator.

"I can show you the paperwork if you'd like."

"You're going to have to," Harriet said. "Because I haven't signed anything in relation to Freya Northrup."

He nodded. "Very well." He pushed onto his feet. "I've got the paperwork in my office."

Unease settled in Harriet's stomach. "Can't you just bring it back here?"

He stared at her aghast. "You are kidding me?

Bring it here, where anybody could read confidential files pertaining to a potential negligence case."

Harriet opened her mouth, but she had no good answer to give him.

"You're not afraid of me, are you Harriet?"

She shook her head but there was a part of her that feared the depths he would go to, just to punish her for what he perceived as her poor behaviour. The quote went, "Hell hath no fury like a woman scorned." And while there was some truth to be found in that, Harriet had found down through the years that Hell paled in comparison to a man whose ego had been bruised and humiliated.

"No, Jonathan, I'm not afraid of you. But that doesn't mean I'm going to let you back me into a corner."

He opened his mouth to argue with her, but Harriet shook her head, effectively cutting him off.

"We both know you don't have any paperwork with my signature on it. At least none pertaining to Freya and if you do, then you've forged it. I'm telling you now that if you don't stop this little vendetta you've decided to launch against me, I'll be left with no choice but to take legal action against you."

"You don't have the guts," he sneered, towering over her. The tone in his voice drew the attention of the few scattered patients in the room and they stared over curiously.

"Be careful, Jonathan, your mask is slipping."

Harriet pushed onto her feet as she pulled his unopened letter from her pocket. "And while we're discussing things, please stop sending me letters. I don't want or need them."

He stared at her in surprise, and Harriet felt a wave of satisfaction wash through her. It felt good to take back some of the control for once.

"You've overstepped here," he said quietly as Harriet turned to walk away. "You're making a huge mistake, Harriet."

She glanced over her shoulder and Jonathan smiled at her. There was no warmth in his eyes and Harriet's stomach churned uneasily. But rather than let him see how uncomfortable he'd made her feel, she pushed her shoulders back and angled her chin upwards as she stalked from the room.

Following the corridor that led back to the main reception area, Harriet mulled over every word she'd spoken and the implications of his threats. As far as she was concerned, he wasn't a stupid man; if he was to make a move against her it wouldn't be something that could be traced back to him. At least, Connor would try to ensure it wouldn't be traced back to him.

He was clever, with an ego the size of a small country; no doubt he would come at her from every angle imaginable because she'd dared to question him. But it wasn't possible for him to have discharge papers with her signature on them. She'd never worked at *The Hermitage*, at least not in any official capacity, so he had to be lying when he'd suggested he had something worth holding over her.

As she reached the reception area, Harriet paused next to the desk and smiled at the young man on the other side.

"I'd like to make a visitor's appointment to meet with Allison Quinn," she said.

The sound of his fingers tapping on the keys filled the small space and Harriet felt the tension in the room climb slowly.

"I'm afraid there's a note here to say Allison is not receiving any visitors at the moment," he said apologetically. "If you leave your name and number, I can have a note put on the file asking that you be notified when she is up for a visit."

Harriet shook her head. "There's got to be a mistake. Allison is my mother. I've been visiting her ever since she got here."

He glanced down at the screen again and shrugged. "It says right here. Dr Connor has specified she is not to receive any visitors."

Tight lipped, Harriet nodded. "Does it give any specific reason?"

The young receptionist shrugged again. "Not on here, no. I can arrange an appointment for you with Dr Connor so you can discuss it with him."

Frustration gripped Harriet as she nodded.

"Fine. Make one." There was one thing she

detested, and that was being backed into a corner. Dr Connor had done just that.

The young man grinned up at her. "Great. I've sent that to your email and your phone."

Without saying anything, Harriet walked away and pushed out into the cold afternoon air. How could she have been so naive to think she could come here and just sort it all out the way an adult might?

Despite the years between them, Jonathan Connor was not above childish games. As she reached her car, she tugged the door open and slipped in behind the wheel and glared up at the blank windows of the hospital.

Punishing her was one thing but to punish her mother--his own patient--was beyond the pale. Harriet clenched her hands over the leather steering wheel.

This was the kind of thing she could talk to Bianca about. Bianca would understand.

The realisation that she would never again get to tell her friend about anything happening in her life hit Harriet like a ton of bricks.

The sudden onslaught of emotion sealed the air in her lungs, and she choked as a pained sob crawled its way up the back of her throat.

As she sat in the car outside the hospital, Harriet buried her face in her hands and let the tears overcome her.

CHAPTER ELEVEN

SCOOPING UP THE WHISKEY BOTTLE, Drew poured another measure and stared at the morning chat show hosts who were at that moment extolling the virtues of starting the day with a glass of fresh juice. An overly exuberant chef stuffed tomatoes and celery through a machine that sounded like a pneumatic drill. Bile threatened at the back of Drew's throat as he watched them sip delicately at the putrid-coloured concoction and nod and exclaim how delicious it tasted.

"Liars," he said, taking a scalding mouthful of his own drink.

Starting the day off with a whiskey definitely wasn't usual for him but he was on holiday, so there was nobody to hold it against him.

He flicked through the channels and found himself sucked into the drama surrounding a DNA test regarding the paternity of an as yet unborn baby. The woman screamed across the stage at the guy who--as far as Drew was concerned--looked barely old enough to shave never mind father a child.

He'd seen too many cases like this go down the tubes over the years and the thought of maybe one day getting a call out to that kid's house because of some domestic dispute made him want to throw the glass at the TV.

The phone next to him rang and he gulped down the whiskey before picking it up.

"DI Haskell," he said automatically. "Shit. Drew Haskell. I'm on holiday, so I'm not a DI for another week."

There was silence on the other end of the line and Drew glanced down at the screen to make sure the call was still connected.

"Are you drunk, DI Haskell?" Dr Perez's voice purred down the line.

"What do you want?"

"I was calling to find out whether you'd thought about my offer at all?"

"It's not down to me," he said, straightening up in the chair and flicking off the television. The last thing he needed was some head doctor picking apart his choice in morning TV and beverage choice.

"No, but if you were in agreement, perhaps I could help expedite the process."

"I'm not at work," he said. Shame welled in his

chest and he pushed it aside. Plenty of people took holiday leave and it wasn't as though he'd even been given a choice in the matter.

"Excellent. Then perhaps we could meet up and discuss our future together."

Drew shook his head and then realised she couldn't see him down the line. "Look, I don't know what you think you're playing at here, but I don't need another psychologist picking my work apart. I've got a partner."

"You mean Dr Quinn. I had thought you two were not getting along." The woman on the other end of the line sounded somewhat irritated and it made Drew smile to think of her pacing back and forth.

"I don't mean Dr Quinn," he said.

"There's another psychologist? Who?"

Drew sighed. "I'm not talking about a psychologist at all," he said. "I've a partner on the force. DS Arya and he's more than enough to work through cases with. He—"

"Thank you, DI Haskell. I won't keep you from your pastimes any longer." The line clicked dead and Drew felt his hackles rise.

He let the phone clatter onto the table next to his chair. There was no doubt in his mind that she would be on the phone hoping to wheedle her way around Arya just as soon as she got his number.

Grabbing the phone from the table, Drew scrolled through the dialled numbers and found

Maz's number near the bottom. Punching the call button, he waited for the familiar sound of the ring-tone but instead was greeted by an engaged tone. Well, he had to give it to the woman, she was fast.

He contemplated calling the station and decided against it. Settling back against the cushions, he picked up the bottle of whiskey and cracked the lid before he pressed the opening to his lips. The familiar tang of alcohol surged against his tongue and he sighed.

"Shit." Setting the bottle back down on the table, he pushed the lid on and climbed unsteadily to his feet. Perez would eat Maz alive and the poor bloke didn't deserve that.

Drew had brought the plague of psychologists into their house, and it was up to him to keep them at bay. Heading for the stairs, he paused next to the window and caught sight of a blonde-haired woman making her way up the footpath.

He shrank back against the wall as she rapped loudly on the glass. She was probably selling something.

"I can see you through the frosted glass," she called through the letter box, and Drew's heart sank. Busted.

Pushing away from the wall, he tugged open the door and glared out at her. The blast of cold air that swirled in around him was enough of a shock to return all of his senses to him. He stared down at the petite blonde on the doorstep, who grinned up at him.

"Do you mind if I come in?" she asked, attempting to push past him. Drew blocked her and leaned his shoulder against the door frame to prevent any further attempts to gain entry.

"You do know I could arrest you for attempting to make an unlawful entry," he said. The beginning of a headache soured his mood further.

"I think you're going to want to hear what I've got to say." She held a card out toward him. The name *Rachel Kennedy* was embossed in bold black lettering on the upturned side.

Drew refused to take it from her. Instead, he folded his arms across his chest. "What do you want?"

"I've just been to see your girlfriend," Rachel said. Her words were a punch to the guts and bile swept up the back of Drew's throat.

"Freya's dead," he said hoarsely.

"Not that girlfriend; although what I've got does pertain to her and her unfortunate end. You were in the car at the time, right?"

"What do you want?"

"I'm writing a story about your girlfriend." She grinned up at him. "The *other* girlfriend. Dr Quinn."

Drew felt his chest constrict. "She's not my girlfriend," he said gruffly.

"Well, to be honest, that's a relief. It seemed a

little weird to me that you'd start dating the woman responsible for your fiancée's death."

Drew shook his head. "I don't know what you're talking about. Harriet had nothing to do with Freya's death. Freya drove us both into a lake. She committed suicide."

Rachel grinned. "Just because Dr Quinn didn't have her hands on the wheel at the time of your fiancée's untimely end, doesn't mean she's not the one responsible."

Irritation flooded Drew's body and he straightened up as he started to push the door shut. Rachel jammed her foot into the doorway, preventing him from closing it all the way.

"Move," he growled.

"Just hear me out. You might not want to hear this, but Dr Quinn has a lot to answer for."

"What is that supposed to mean?"

"Freya wasn't the first person to suffer at the hands of Dr Quinn. There's another."

"Freya wasn't under the care of Dr Quinn when she was sick," he said. "So, I don't know what you think you know but Harriet wasn't involved. Now move." As though to emphasise his point, Drew pushed the door against her foot.

"That's not what Freya's discharge notes say..." Rachel said, the triumphant note in her voice grated on his nerves before her words sank in.

Drew felt the blood drain from his face. "That's

not possible. Freya was under the care of a Dr Jonathan Connor."

Rachel glanced down at the pile of papers in her hand. "The name on the discharge notes here say Dr H. Quinn." She held them out to Drew, and he took them with shaking hands. His eyes scanned down over the page and his stomach clenched as he read the name of the person who had signed off on Freya's discharge.

"This isn't possible..."

"It's right there, in black and white," she said. "Dr Quinn was the doctor responsible for Freya's discharge and her negligent actions directly led to Freya's death. And Freya wasn't the only one."

"What are you saying?" Drew asked.

"I'm saying that you hunt criminals every day, DI Haskell, so why haven't you arrested this woman for her reckless endangerment of the lives of others?"

Drew stared down at the papers and read the note attached to the sheet. *Patient does not pose a risk to their own life or the life of another. Dr H. Quinn.*

"You better come in," he said, pulling the door open wide.

CHAPTER TWELVE

SITTING across the road from her house, he watched as she parked on the street. Patiently, he observed as she gathered her belongings, the papers and the bag she seemed to always carry with her, before she climbed from the car.

She was careful, he noted, as she paused halfway up the front path and turned to lock the car. It showed a certain kind of methodical thinking pattern on her behalf and it was something he could admire. How long would it take for such an approach to break down when the game began?

Anticipation built inside him as she approached the front porch.

He knew the moment she found the package. Every muscle in his body contracted as her shoulders stiffened almost imperceptibly.

If he had a stethoscope pressed to her breast right

now, he would be able to hear the exact moment her heartbeat picked up its rhythm.

The slight hitch in her breath as it caught in the back of her throat, the dilation of her pupils as her gaze fixated on the item.

This was better than any sex. This game of cat and mouse. His tongue slipped out and he moistened his lips as she stepped forward and nudged the painstakingly wrapped box with the toe of her shoe.

Yes, he'd been right to think she was careful. After all, she had no idea who had left the package for her. He'd been careful to make sure there was no way to trace it back to him. The packaging was nondescript, the kind you could pick up in any chain store. Even the tape he'd used was the kind you found in most high street stores, therefore making it practically untraceable.

She nudged the box again with the toe of her shoe and he gripped the steering wheel, leaning forward as he watched her. She started to lean down and then at the last moment seemed to change her mind. She paused, glancing around at the street as though searching for the one responsible. The desire to leap from the car and wave his arms in her direction was almost overwhelming. Instead, he pressed back into the seat, secure in the knowledge that she couldn't see him.

Dr Quinn bent down and lifted the box from the

ground. He watched as she wrestled to pull her keys from the bag slung over her shoulder.

Disappointment gripped him. Why couldn't she have opened the box on the doorstep? The others had done just that, and he'd reveled as they'd realised what lay inside.

But Dr Quinn was different. It was the reason he'd chosen her in the first place, after all. She wasn't like the others. If anyone stood a chance of catching him, it was her.

The thought of coming face to face with her, of seeing the look of admiration and shock that would light up her face as she realised who he was, made him squirm.

She carried her belongings and the box into the house and the door slammed shut, leaving him out in the cold.

She would know him soon enough and when she did, he knew she would beg to face him.

CHAPTER THIRTEEN

HARRIET PEERED down at the box on the doorstep. The hairs on the back of her neck prickled as though she was being watched. Glancing around, she eyed the other cars on the street, but nothing looked out of the ordinary.

Nudging at the box with her toe for a second time, she was relieved to find it didn't automatically blow up in her face. The red wrapping sparkled in the fading daylight. The golden bow that held it all together was perfect and intricate. Whoever had sent her the parcel had obviously taken great pains to get it just right.

Of course, there was only one man who was interested in sending her things these days. Frustration welled in her chest and she bent down and scooped up the parcel from the step.

Wrestling with the zipper on her bag, she fought

to extricate her keys from within. Finally, she managed to free them, and pushed the key into the lock.

Once inside, the feeling of being watched finally faded and Harriet let go the breath she'd been holding onto and flopped back against the door.

With the parcel clutched in one hand, she carefully carried everything through into the kitchen and set her bag and papers down on the counter. Pulling out one of the chrome stools, she sat on it as she placed the parcel down in front of her.

There was no indication of who had sent it. Leaning over it, Harriet sniffed delicately at the wrapped box and found nothing beyond the usual scent of tape and paper.

Turning it over in her hands, she searched the package for any signs of who it might have come from. It seemed a little too complicated for Jonathan to have sent it, not that she could dismiss him out of hand either.

Pushing onto her feet, she hurried across the room and fished around underneath the sink. Pulling a pair of rubber gloves free, she slipped them on before she returned to the parcel with a sharp knife gripped in her hand.

Call Drew. The voice in the back of her mind prickled but she pushed it aside, ignoring it.

Drew didn't want to hear from her, and she wasn't about to impose on him, not now. Not after everything that had happened between them, anyway. He needed time, and perhaps with enough of it, there would come a day when the mere sight of her didn't antagonise him.

Picking the parcel up, Harriet carefully popped the tape with the tip of the knife. Working it beneath the packaging, she pushed the paper back and stared down at the small white box that sat inside.

Setting the knife down, she pulled the lid off the top and stared down at the jumbled pieces of card. As she stared at the pieces, she realised she was looking at a jigsaw.

Her skin broke out in a cold sweat. There was a familiarity to the puzzle that tugged at her mind, but her exhausted brain refused to connect the dots.

Carefully, she tipped the pieces of the puzzle out onto the paper and spread them out using the tip of the knife to move them around. A small card with a single gold star imprinted on the front stared up at her from the bottom of the box. Using the knife once again, Harriet popped the card free and scanned the carefully printed words on the inside.

DR QUINN, you'll forgive this intrusion into your life but after I saw your picture in the newspaper, I just knew you and I were destined for greatness together.

You do not know me yet. You may never know me

at all, but I hope for your sake that is not true. I hope you enjoy puzzles. I certainly do, and I've created one just for you.

I've crafted the pieces myself, each one precise in its size and shape. Complete the puzzle to save a life. Fail to put the pieces together and there'll be one more star snuffed out.

Good luck.

STARING AT THE PIECES, she began to separate them out before she started to put it together. It took her only a moment to realise that there weren't enough pieces to complete the jigsaw. Fear crawled up her spine and sank its teeth into the base of her skull as she realised what she was staring down at.

The photograph was incomplete but there was no doubt in her mind that it was a picture of a woman. Reaching for her bag, Harriet managed to knock it from the counter as she scrambled for her phone. The items inside scattered across the tile floor and Harriet dropped to her knees, scooping the phone from the pile.

She quickly dialled Drew's number and was met with the typical voicemail recording.

"Christ, Drew, for once why can't you have your phone on?"

Ending the call, she dialled the number for the station. She waited as the call connected and the voice of a young woman told her she was through to Yorkshire CID.

"I need to speak to DI Haskell," Harriet said.

"Just one moment."

There was a click on the line and then another voice cut in.

"DI Haskell's not here at the moment. Is there something I can help you with?"

"DS Arya?" Harriet asked hopefully.

"That's me. Who's this?" There was a gruff hostility to his voice. Harriet wondered if he'd learned that from Drew.

"Harriet," she said. "Dr Harriet Quinn."

"Oh, right, Dr Quinn. How have you been?"

"I've been better," Harriet said quietly as she studied the jigsaw. "Look, DS Arya, I've got a bit of a situation here that I think you and DI Haskell will want to see."

"Well, like I said, Haskell's not here. He's on leave at the moment so you'll have to make do with me."

The urge to ask the DS whether Drew was all right or not was painfully strong, but she pushed it aside and focused instead on the puzzle pieces. "I think I've got a message from the Star Killer," Harriet said.

"The who?"

"The Star Killer. He sends puzzles and then demands they're solved before he takes and murders the victims pictured in the puzzles."

There was silence on the other end of the line. "I don't understand," DS Arya said. "You're telling me there's a killer out there called the Star Killer and that he's been in contact with you?"

"Yes, there is. And yes, he has." Harriet chewed her lip nervously and stared down at the puzzle spread out on her kitchen counter. "And the more time we waste debating the issue, the more time he's got to take his first victim and kill them."

Harriet was only too aware of the sound of breathing from the other end of the phone line. "What do you want me to do about it?"

Harriet drew in a deep breath. "You have no idea who I'm talking about, do you?"

"Well, no, but—"

"I think you're going to have to get Drew off his annual leave."

"I don't think—"

"What choice have you got, detective sergeant? We've got a killer who kills in threes before he goes to ground, and the clock is ticking. If we don't act fast, we'll have three bodies and he'll go back into the hole he crawled out of."

DS Arya sighed on the other end of the line. "I'll talk to Gregson."

The line went dead and Harriet was left in the kitchen with the partially completed puzzle.

CHAPTER FOURTEEN

DREW STARED down at the discharge papers still gripped in his hands. Rachel had long since left but he hadn't been able to tear his gaze away from the words written on the piece of paper. How could something so seemingly innocuous be so devastating? He hadn't wanted to believe it, hadn't wanted to believe that Harriet could be so callous.

Carrying the papers into the living room, he dropped down into his chair and lifted the whiskey bottle from its place on the table. The thought of swilling more alcohol only made him sick to his stomach and there wasn't enough alcohol in Yorkshire to drown out the rage that hammered in his veins.

Balling the discharge sheets up in his hands, he tossed them across the floor and watched with a modicum of satisfaction as they bounced off the sound bar and slipped underneath the television stand.

Harriet wouldn't do something like this. It wasn't as though he knew her particularly well but there was something inside him that refused to believe she was capable of the kind of deception Rachel Kennedy seemed to believe of her.

Of course, if she was innocent, then there was something else going on. Something even more twisted.

Scooping up the television remote, he flicked on the TV and turned the sound up as loud as it would go in an attempt to drown out the anger that raged in his mind.

CHAPTER FIFTEEN

"SIR." DS Arya paused in front of the door that led to DCI Gregson's office. Swallowing back his unease, he tried for what felt like the millionth time to compose the speech he was about to give his boss in his head.

"Hey Sir, I've just had Dr Quinn on the phone, and she says she got some puzzle sent to her by some psycho..." Maz shook his head. That definitely wasn't going to cut it. *"Sir, Dr Quinn phoned, and she said someone called the Star Killer has been in contact with her..."*

Shit. Who in their right mind thought calling a murderer the Star Killer was a good idea? As far as he was concerned, it sounded like some kind of made up bullshit name the tabloids had dreamt up. Either that or it was a moniker that belonged to some serial working in Hollywood. Round these parts, there weren't many 'stars' to speak of.

"Hey sir, I've got—" The door swung open and Maz took an involuntary step backwards as Gregson appeared in the doorway.

"What the hell do you want?" Gregson barked, eyeing Maz up as though he'd just been scraped off the bottom of his shoe.

"Sir, I—"

"Well, spit it out, man, I don't have all day."

"Sir, I've had Dr Quinn on the phone..."

"Oh, Christ, what does she want now? I hope you told her Haskell's not here."

Maz nodded. "I did, sir, but you see the problem is—"

"What did she want then?"

"Well, sir, she said she got a parcel and—"

"A parcel? Who does she think we are, Royal Bloody Mail? Why is she calling us up to complain about a parcel? Christ, some people! I've just had Dr Perez on the phone giving me an earache about how I shouldn't be letting my best detectives sit at home withering away on the drink."

Gregson drew a breath. "And you know who she's referring to, don't you? Bloody Haskell is at home probably drinking himself into a stupor like a bloody child sent to his room. Most people would be only too happy to take their holidays but not Drew. Bloody hard-headed bastard that he is..."

Maz stared at the Monk, his tongue stuck to the roof of his mouth, and an icy bead of sweat slowly slipped down his spine. If he didn't tell him what Dr Quinn had said, then he had a feeling he'd be in shit up to his neck once the DCI found out what the true meaning of the call had been.

"Sir, I really think—"

"Now Dr Perez thinks she can come down here and get a *'feel'* for the potential working environment." The Monk used air quotes to emphasise the word *feel*, and Maz found himself feeling suddenly sorry for the man they'd dubbed the Monk. His job certainly didn't look easy, that was for sure.

"Sir, Dr Quinn..."

"Yeah, go on what did she want then, with her parcel?"

"She said it's a puzzle. She thinks it was sent to her by someone called the Star Killer—" Maz cut off as the Monk's face blanched and his gaze turned furious.

"She said what?"

"She said it was a puzzle sent by some guy she thinks is the Star Killer..."

"Jesus Christ, Arya, why didn't you lead with that instead of letting me waffle on about my problems..." The Monk pushed a hand back through his non-existent hairline and glared at Maz. "Have you sent uniforms around to her house?"

"No, sir, I brought this straight to you because—"

"Well, what are you fucking waiting for? Get uniforms over to her place now and then send a SOCO unit over there. Maybe this time the crazy bastard got sloppy and we'll find something to pin him down."

"Of course, sir, I'll get on it right away." Maz started to turn away and then changed his mind. "Sir, if I may?"

Gregson nodded and halted his progress across the office. "What is it?"

"Sir, she suggested we call DI Haskell back off his leave. She seemed to think he might be useful in all of this."

Gregson sighed. "She might be right, but I'll be damned if I give that smug bastard the satisfaction of calling him in tonight. We've only been without him a few days. Call him in now and he'll think we can't run the place without him."

Maz faltered. "So that's a no then, sir?"

Gregson sighed. "Send the SOCOs over there and some uniforms and then you and I will pay Ms Quinn a visit. In the morning, we'll reassess whether we need Drew back here or not."

CHAPTER SIXTEEN

MONTHS, weeks of preparation had culminated in this one perfect moment. He watched from across the street as she slung her leather bag back over her shoulder and proceeded toward the multi-storey car park.

Her schedule switched back and forth, but he'd followed her enough now to know that somethings never changed, and this was one of those things. The same coffee shop for a three-bean tofu salad. The thought of it turned his stomach but then again, it wasn't as though he had to eat that garbage.

Vegans. They were a strange bunch. He admired their desire to save the planet and protect the animals but what they failed to understand was that man's position at the top of the food chain was sacred. He'd rather pluck his own eyeballs out with a rusty spoon than subject himself to the faux meat-products many of them preferred.

Carrying her salad box across the street, she pulled her phone from her bag, her thumb moving quickly over the screen. She'd probably had another one of those wonderful epiphanies that seemed to strike her out of thin air every now and then. Perhaps, if he was lucky, she would share this one with him before they got down to the real business of the game.

Sliding his hands into his leather gloves, he flexed his fingers. The long hours it took to cut the intricate patterns in the puzzles tended to give him cramps in his fingers. It was delicate work, but he hadn't yet made a mistake. His mother had once told him he had a surgeon's hands. Perfectly steady, they never faltered, no matter what task he turned them to.

She disappeared into the darkened doorway of the garage and he followed; careful to keep at a safe distance. She'd never met anybody here before, but you could never be too careful about these things.

The sound of her boots clicking on the metal steps rang out in the stairwell and he followed at a slightly slower pace. He already knew where she was going. The second floor, third row down. He'd parked his van next to her car.

It would have been easier to wait for her inside the van but where would the fun be in that? This way, as he followed her, his heart rate slowly picking up its tempo as he closed in on his prey, he could practically taste the anticipation of what was to come on his tongue.

Plus, there was always the chance that she would see him in the van and then the game would be over before it had even begun.

Women had learned, over the years since he'd started to play these games, to be more cautious. Men, on the other hand, were easier because they always assumed that they were invincible. It was a stupid mistake to make.

Sure, they were strong, and many of them had been much larger than he was, but that hadn't stopped him from taking them down. That was the beauty in having a cause. Once he set his mind to something, he could plan for all possible outcomes. They, in their naivety, never even saw him coming. He used their strength against them, bringing them to their knees with only minimal effort.

She approached her car and he knew she'd spotted the van. She pointed her key fob at her Toyota and its lights lit up the space momentarily before dying again. He watched as she slipped the keys between her fingers and he couldn't keep the smile that slid across his face. He'd seen that move before but, just as it had then, it would prove useless now, too.

"You've got to be kidding me!" She exclaimed to nobody in particular as she reached the driver's door and realised how close the van was. Despite being slim, there was no way she would fit between the vehicles. He'd measured the exact distance between the cars and carefully parked the van next to her car. It had taken two attempts to get it exact, but he'd done it. The result had been worth it.

Her keys slipped from their place between her fingers as she forgot to be cautious and sidled up to the car.

"Who does that?" She set the salad box down on the bonnet of her car.

Closing the distance between them swiftly, he reached her as she pulled her phone from her bag. His hand snaked around her face, sealing the scream that fought to escape behind her lips.

With his other hand, he pressed the tip of the scalpel against her throat. She froze, and he could practically feel her muscles bunching up beneath her skin.

"It's a real pleasure to finally meet you, Rachel," he said, his voice little more than a whisper as he urged her forward. She whimpered, the sound barely making it past his fingers. He felt the sound reverberate against his palm.

He walked her toward the opposite side of the van and paused.

"Pull the door open."

She was like a deer caught in the headlights and his impatience spilled over into his hands as he pressed the tip of the blade against her soft skin. It split like hot butter beneath the wickedly sharp blade and the metallic tang of her blood hit the air.

"The door, Rachel, or I will open your carotid artery up here and now."

Her hands shook so badly that the first time, her fingers only managed to graze the door rather than grip it. He gave her a gentle shake and her hand closed around the door handle. She pulled it open, the metallic sound echoing in the silence of the car park.

Rachel whimpered again and he fought the urge to close his eyes and savour her suffering. There would be plenty of time for that later, when they were safely away from the prying eyes of the world.

"I'm going to help you inside," he said. "Once we're in, I'm going to have you secure your ankles with the cable ties to your right. Nod if you understand."

He felt the almost imperceptible shift of her head as she tried not to press her throat against the blade which had already tasted her.

"Good girl."

They climbed inside and he allowed her a small amount of freedom to reach for the cable ties. Twisting her around to face the door, he pressed his mouth against her ear.

"Now close the door."

She whimpered and tried to shake her head, but he tightened his grip; a simple but effective warning.

"You heard me before, Rachel. I will open you up here and now if you don't do exactly as I say. Be a good girl and everything will be all right."

He felt her sob as it vibrated through her body and she reached for the door handle. This was the part that mattered most, getting them to participate in their own downfall, it was a delicious kind of torture that he would use against them later.

At any time, she could fight back. It was a risk. She'd felt the knife, but he knew that if he was in the same position, he would rather take his chances there and then and run the risk of a quick death. It would have been easier than facing what he had in mind for her. Her fingers closed around the door handle.

"Good girl, Rachel. Now close the door, gently."

The door clanged shut, sealing them both inside. He kissed her ear.

"Good girl. Such a stupid, good girl."

As though she knew the mistake she'd made, she started to cry, the sound echoing in the soundproofed van as he removed his hand and reveled in her misery.

CHAPTER SEVENTEEN

A COUPLE OF HOURS LATER, Harriet sat on the couch in her living room, studying the SOCOs as they traipsed past her in their Tyvek suits. It was unnerving to watch them comb through her own home.

When in the white coveralls, with the hoods pulled up and the masks in place over their faces, they were completely anonymous; if she passed them in the station, she'd be none the wiser as to who each one was, and that didn't sit particularly well with her.

With difficulty, Harriet pulled her attention back to everything she knew about the puzzle and the note. Before the uniformed officers had arrived, she'd taken several pictures on her phone of the puzzle pieces and the note she'd received from the man who'd stalked Yorkshire for eighteen years and never yet been caught.

Why her and why now? The two questions had blurred into one another and the more she thought about them, the harder it got to separate them out.

Harriet glanced down at her watch and felt her heart sink. Where was Drew?

She knew the drill only too well. She'd studied it in university. From the time of receiving the first part of the puzzle and the note, they had twelve hours to identify the first victim. If they failed, Harriet knew the next puzzle would come with something a little more personal. Fear prickled at the base of her scalp.

Everyone the Star Killer had chosen to be his puzzle solver so far had failed and within each cycle, three victims had been taken. But it was the third victim that was particularly special. The Star Killer had a twisted sense of justice and each time his chosen puzzle solver failed to correctly rescue the victims, it led to only one outcome.

"Dr Quinn, it's nice to meet you again." DCI Gregson's voice filtered through Harriet's jumbled thoughts and she jerked as though he'd awoken her from a deep sleep and not just from the meanderings of her addled mind.

"Sorry, I was miles away."

DCI Gregson shook his head and smiled sympathetically. The juxtaposition of his behaviour now versus her first meeting with the man was like night and day. "That's understandable. I've seen others act the exact same way when faced with something similar."

He spoke as though he came from a place of authority on the matter and Harriet couldn't help but wonder if he'd been involved in previous iterations involving the Star Killer and his twisted game.

"I thought—" Harriet had to cut herself off before she called Drew by his first name. "I thought DI Haskell would be here."

DCI Gregson nodded. "I'm afraid DI Haskell is on leave at the moment. We'll assess the situation in the cold light of day but for tonight, at least, we've got this under control."

"Really?" Harriet couldn't keep the incredulity from her voice. "We've got less than twelve hours to figure out who the woman in the puzzle is."

"How do you know it's a woman?" Gregson asked, deftly changing the topic as he took a seat on one end of the couch.

"Because I've had time to study the pieces of the image," Harriet said bitterly. "It took you over two hours to get here. I had plenty of time to review everything he sent me."

"And how do you know it's a 'he'?"

Harriet sighed. "Please, DCI Gregson, don't play games with me. I've had quite enough of those now to last me a lifetime. We both know that the person known as the Star Killer is male."

Gregson glanced down at his hands. "Actually,

we've got no proof either way to suggest the gender of the person responsible. There was never any evidence to point in a definitive direction."

Shoving her hands back through her hair, Harriet closed her eyes. "Late thirties to late forties. Male. Judging by the complexity of the crimes committed, I'm going to say we're dealing with somebody who has an exceptionally high IQ. Probably a middle-class background that allowed him to work his way up in the world to some kind of position of power. But it's either not enough to satisfy him or when he applied for said position he was turned down. Most likely, he found himself rejected from something important and so now everything he does is to prove how much better than everybody else he is. Add to that a serious issue with people in authority, and you've got yourself a recipe for disaster."

"What makes you say that?" Gregson asked, his eyes glittered with interest and Harriet vowed to find out whether he'd played a role in previous investigations. Judging by his level of interest it certainly seemed more than possible.

"Look at the previous iterations of the game. In each one he has turned a member of law enforcement into his puzzle master. Tasking them with doing the one thing they do every day of the week."

Gregson shook his head. "I don't mean to be rude here, Dr Quinn, but we don't go around solving jigsaws for a living."

"No," she conceded. "But you do solve puzzles. After all, each crime you pursue is just a puzzle waiting for the pieces to be put together. You seek out clues and eventually it creates a picture for you."

Gregson inclined his head in agreement. "Fine, but that still doesn't explain why you think he's got an issue with authority."

"Everything he does is to prove that he's better than you are. Every time you've failed in the past, it has proved to our man that he's the superior hunter. That he deserves the recognition you all enjoy."

"You mean everything he does is driven by some kind of warped jealousy?" DS Arya piped up, managing to sound both curious and disgusted.

"Not exactly. Jealously is not inherently destructive. What we've got here is much more along the lines of envy."

Gregson and DS Arya stared at Harriet uncomprehendingly and she sighed. "If I'm jealous of something I don't have to choose a destructive path. I can turn that jealousy into something healthy and achieve the same goal as the person I was originally jealous of. In the case of our killer he envies what others have because he cannot have it himself. Are you familiar with the term *schadenfreude?*"

Both men across from her shook their heads and Harriet was instantly reminded of being in the lecture hall.

"*Schadenfreude* is a German word. There's

nothing in the English language that captures the true essence of its meaning but ultimately, it's used to describe the delight taken over the suffering of another human. Other languages can describe it somewhat. In French they call it *joie maligne*, or a perverse or malignant joy or happiness for the suffering of another human. There are other words in other languages that mean something similar but in all of these it comes down to the same thing."

Harriet glanced down at her hands clasped in front of her. "His envy drives him to destroy his chosen proxy by virtue of a game that cannot be won."

DCI Gregson pushed onto his feet, his face pale beneath the glare of the artificial lights overhead. "You're telling me that he's going to kill three people because we're too stupid to figure out who he plans to target?"

"I'm saying he's going to kill three people because the game he's forced us to play is ultimately rigged in his favour. It won't matter what we do, or how we try to beat him..." She scrubbed her hands over her eyes. "Look at the puzzle and tell me how we're supposed to figure out who he's targeting based on the minuscule amount of information we have?"

Gregson strode from the room and Harriet flopped back against the sofa cushions and closed her eyes. A headache had started to form between her eyes and all she really wanted to do was find somewhere dark to lie down. Instead, she had a feeling that her night was going to go from bad to worse.

"So, what are we supposed to do, Dr Quinn?" DS Arya asked, from his position across from her.

Harriet opened her eyes and met his gaze head on. "Unless he has somehow slipped up and left us something to work with forensically. All we can do is wait until he takes his next victim." Her stomach churned unhappily. This wasn't how it was supposed to be. She wasn't supposed to just sit back and wait for the killer to strike. She was supposed to help people, save them from the pain and anguish they found themselves in and instead... Instead here she was advocating that they do nothing at all.

It went against every fibre of her being and Harriet fought the urge to jump to her feet and begin pacing the room; something, anything just to feel as though she was in control. But wasn't that what he wanted?

"The other cases," she said. "The past case files, can I have a look at them?"

Gregson reappeared in the doorway. "I'm not sure that's such a good idea. You're technically a victim in all of this by virtue of him contacting you. I can't just—"

"Don't you see? That's what he wants. He wants you to cut me out of the investigation just like the others were every time in the past. The game is already impossible to beat because we don't fully understand the rules of engagement. If you do this, if you take me off the investigation then you're giving him exactly what he's hoping for."

Gregson shot her a pained expression and scrubbed his hand over the top of his balding head. "You don't know what you're asking of me here," he said.

"Yes, I do."

He glanced over at DS Arya and nodded. "Fine. But there's one condition."

Harriet nodded.

At that moment she knew she would have done anything to stay on the case; even if that meant jumping through whatever hoops the DCI hoped to place in her path.

However, as she waited to hear what he had to say next, deep down inside she had a feeling that whatever the stipulation happened to be, she wasn't going to like it.

Not one bit.

CHAPTER EIGHTEEN

CROSSING THE CAMPUS, Gabriel pushed open the door to his favourite coffee shop and spotted Michael already at the counter.

"You've got to be kidding me," he muttered beneath his breath as he started to turn around.

"Gabe, wait, please. Just let me explain."

"Explain what?" Gabriel said. "Explain why you had your tongue jammed down that stranger's throat? I'm pretty sure that's self-explanatory."

"You need to listen to me," Michael said. "I was drunk, and I missed you and--"

"And what? You thought you could replace me with just any old guy who happened your way?"

It brought him a little satisfaction to see Michael genuinely uncomfortable. Getting the messages from Taff, which turned out to be a blow by blow account of everything Michael had got up to that night, had hurt. He'd spent the whole day in bed yesterday nursing his bruised heart but there was only so much mint-choc-chip ice cream he could ram down his throat before he started to feel sick. He wasn't the one who needed to feel bad. He wasn't the one who should be lying in bed, crying into his pillow.

"That's not how it was," Michael said, reaching out to brush his arm. "It was just one kiss."

"Taff said it was more than a kiss," Gabriel said. "He said you left with that guy."

"That lying piece of shit," Michael said and Gabriel couldn't help but think he actually sounded sincere. Had Taff lied?

The sensation of being watched washed over him for the second time that morning and he lifted his gaze from the ground and scanned the coffee shop. The guy at the far corner table stared openly at him and Gabriel felt his discomfort levels rising.

"What is his problem?" He muttered beneath his breath to Michael, cutting the other man off mid-apology.

The man at the table was familiar but the more Gabriel glanced over at him, the more he struggled to remember where he'd seen him before.

"What's whose problem?" Michael glanced over his shoulder in the direction Gabriel was staring. The man at the table looked down at the magazine open in front of him in a poor attempt to pretend that he hadn't been openly eyeballing them. "Who? Him?" Michael asked, managing to sound more than a little irritated.

"Just leave it," Gabriel said. "This isn't the time or the--"

"No, I won't leave it. I saw him staring. I want to know why." Michael shrugged free of the placating hand Gabriel laid on his arm and strode over toward the stranger's table.

"What's your problem?" Michael asked.

"Nothing, I--"

"You were just what?" Michael asked, his voice rising to match his aggression. "Do you get a kick out of watching? Is that it?"

"No, I--"

His voice brought it back to Gabriel and he remembered the cleaner he'd bumped into outside Dr Quinn's office.

"It's fine, Michael," he said touching the other man's arm. "We bumped into each other the other day and this was probably just one of those weird where do I know you from moments, right?" He directed the last part of his statement to the guy at the table who nodded and shrank back from Michael.

"It's like he said, I thought I knew him and--"

"You're just a creep," Michael said.

Gabriel rolled his eyes. "You always have to do this, don't you? We were having a serious conversation and you just had to make this all about you and your heroics."

"Gabe, that's not it at all..."

Turning on his heel, Gabriel stormed out of the coffee shop, leaving Michael to call after him.

CHAPTER NINETEEN

DREW WOKE to the sound of his phone ringing next to his ear. Lifting his face from the pillows, he stared down at the blinking screen that lit up the darkened bedroom. Pushing upright, he scrubbed his hand over his jaw. The rasping of his stubble made him feel grotty, and the taste of yesterday's whiskey didn't help either.

Grabbing the phone as it went dead, he swore beneath his breath. With one flick of his thumb, the screen lit up again.

Freya grinned up at him. Her blonde hair danced in the warm breeze, which had lifted it away from her face that day on the beach. He could remember taking the picture as though it had happened only yesterday. She'd been so happy then. They'd both been happy, hadn't they?

Every time he looked back at the photographs of

their time together, he found himself wondering if everything he'd ever known, everything they'd ever shared, had been a complete lie.

The knowledge that she'd hidden her illness from him for almost the entire time they'd been together was more than painful. How could she? Why hadn't she trusted him with the truth? What was worse was knowing that he couldn't ever ask her to explain her reasoning.

She was dead and there was nothing more he could do. Nothing he could do to help her. It killed him to know that she'd been so close to him and he'd been unable to save her.

Of course, if she was here, she'd have laughed at him and told him not to be so ridiculous. She didn't need a white knight to ride in and rescue her.

Freya was the type of woman who had informed him early on in their relationship that she didn't need saving. If there was any saving to be done, she was more than capable of doing it herself.

Closing his eyes against the onslaught of emotion, he clicked out of the photographs and back to the blank home screen of his phone. As he reached for the call display icon the phone once again lit up in his hands.

"Go for Haskell," he said, his voice gruff and almost unrecognisable as he answered the call.

"DI Haskell, you sound as though I woke you up," Dr Perez said, her chipper voice made him want to grind his teeth. It seemed unnatural that there were some people out there who enjoyed rising early. People who cheerfully referred to themselves as 'morning' people, or early birds who always got the worm.

As far as Drew was concerned, they needed to be locked up, the whole lot of them. There was nothing good about the morning; well, except possibly a breakfast sandwich smothered in HP sauce. The mere thought of it made his stomach grumble.

"What do you want?" he asked, managing to sound both irritated and alert.

"I've got you a case," she said, sounding more than proud of herself. "It was my one stipulation for working with Yorkshire CID."

How the woman managed to make a situation she'd fought to create sound like it was some great big favour she was doing for Yorkshire CID was a serious skill. Most people would have been grateful for the opportunity, but it seemed Dr Katerina Perez was not one of them.

"Oh, right, and what's that then?"

"Well, you'll have to come to the station to see," she said managing to make it sound lascivious. She was definitely a piece of work; he'd give her that.

"I told you yesterday, I'm on leave. I won't be back—"

"That's been cancelled," she said. "I called in a favour and--given the circumstances--it was agreed that you returning to work early would be beneficial to everybody involved."

"What circumstances?" Drew asked, feeling his hackles rise.

"There was an incident involving Dr Quinn."

Drew felt all the blood in his body as it started to drain away from all the vital organs. He stood up abruptly and the world spun around him so that he was forced to sit back down on the side of the mattress.

"What do you mean there was an incident involving Harriet? She's all right, isn't she? What happened?"

"Come to the station DI Haskell and everything will be explained."

"Is Harriet all right?"

"See you soon." The line went dead and Drew fought to wrap his head around everything Dr Perez had said. Why would she toy with him like that? Why not just tell him whether Harriet was all right or not? A memory of her kicking and clawing at the rope wrapped around her neck filled his head and he scrambled to dial her number.

The seconds slipped by as he waited to hear her familiar voice as she answered the call. Instead there was nothing but the ringtone. The call disconnected and Drew clenched his hands into fists. She was fine. If something had happened to her, somebody would have called him; Gregson, or

Arya... They wouldn't have left him in the dark like this.

He called DS Arya's number and got him on the second ring.

"Yeah?" Arya said, sounding more than a little out of breath.

"Is Harriet all right? What happened to her?"

"What? Yeah, she's fine. She's in speaking to the Monk now. Why, what's the matter?"

Drew let go the breath he'd been holding onto in a loud whoosh leaving his entire body to feel like a balloon that somebody had let the air out of.

"Why is she at the station?" Drew asked, when he was finally able to control his voice.

"I don't know if you've heard of someone called the Star Killer," Maz said, sounding more than a little excited. "He's been operating for eighteen years now and—"

"I know who the bloody Star Killer is," Drew exploded. "Tell me what Harriet has to do with it all?"

"Keep your hair on. Dr Quinn was contacted by the killer."

"When you say contacted?" The strange feeling had returned, leaving Drew light-headed. Obviously, the whiskey on an empty stomach the day before had been a bad idea and now he was paying the price for it with the hangover to end all hangovers. The day was definitely not going as he'd planned.

"He left her a puzzle. Dropped it off on her doorstep with a note and everything. The whole thing is seriously creepy."

"And no one thought to call me in?" Drew asked. The beginnings of his anger started to churn, and he grabbed it with both hands, clinging to it as though it were a life raft cast adrift on a choppy sea.

"Well, you were on leave and—"

"So bloody what, Maz? The biggest case we're ever likely to see falls into our laps and you decide to leave me out of the loop?"

"It wasn't my decision," he whined.

"Well, I'm on my way in."

"DCI Gregson won't be too happy."

"I don't care what the Monk thinks," Drew said. "I'm coming in and that's final." He ended the call and stared down at the darkened screen. His breathing came in short hard gasping pants and he realised Maz wasn't the only one who sounded out of breath. What the hell was wrong with him? Why was he behaving like somebody on the verge of hyperventilating?

The voice in the back of his mind tried to answer him but he shoved it away. There was no way he had the time or the energy to unpack his reaction to the possibility that something had happened to Harriet. Right now, he needed to focus on the fact that she was fine. Caught in the middle of a sadistic game of cat and mouse but still for now at least, fine.

Dropping the phone on to the bed, he stood and waited for the sensation of light-headedness to return. When it didn't, he drew in a deep breath and headed for the bathroom. He suddenly felt as though he had a purpose again and that alone was enough to make him almost giddy. The water, when he switched it on, was cold, but he didn't care as he pressed himself beneath the spray.

He was going back to work. No more moping around the place feeling sorry for himself. There was a killer out there who wanted to be caught and Drew was more than willing to oblige.

CHAPTER TWENTY

HE PULLED his mind from the path it had meandered down. Dr Quinn was not behaving the way he'd hoped and while it had proved interesting for a little while that she would so completely buck the trend set by other professionals who had come before her, he found himself growing increasingly irritated by her lack of reaction.

He picked up the craft knife and doodled across the image of her he'd printed off the internet. Carefully, he cut her nose off, sliding the piece of triangular paper away from her face, leaving a tiny void where it should have been. Next, he set about carving out her eyes.

Under normal circumstances, being so creative brought him great joy, but not today, and it was all her fault. She was screwing everything up.

He'd expected the police to release a statement to

the press and instead there had been nothing but radio silence on the fact that he had reemerged.

What if they didn't believe it was really him? He'd read more than enough conspiracy theories on the internet—speculation that because it had been more than seven years since his last kill, he was either dead or incarcerated—to know that this was a possibility.

Raising his face to the jars that lined the wall, he studied the items within. Pushing up from his seat, he crossed the cement floor and lifted one such jar from its place and peered in at the contents. The greyish skin floated in solution, the pigment completely leeched away thanks to the chemicals used to preserve it.

Suranne didn't look as she had done all that time ago. None of them looked as they had done but he alone knew and remembered the moment when he'd acquired each piece of his intricate puzzle. There would be more pieces to add soon.

The thought of removing the piece of skin from the jar and securing it for transport made him queasy. Giving away a piece of his precious hoard wasn't a step he was willing to take. And anyway, it would be easier to prove his identity with the sending of a gift with the *second* part of the puzzle. Then they would know the truth. Then, they would be certain of who they were dealing with.

Perhaps then, Dr Quinn wouldn't be such a disappointment.

He contemplated the look she would wear when she opened the second puzzle box and it brought a smile to his face.

Glancing down at the watch on his wrist, his smile broadened. "Tick, tock." The silence closed in around him as he set the glass jar back on the shelf and crossed back to the image of Dr Quinn. With one decisive slash, he removed her head from her body and watched as it fluttered into the bin.

It was time to up the ante and he knew just what to do.

CHAPTER TWENTY-ONE

"I DON'T NEED another psychologist looking over my shoulder as I work," Harriet said through gritted teeth. She kept her legs crossed and her arms folded tightly over her chest as she sat in DCI Gregson's office. "I work better when I'm alone."

He shook his head. "I told you last night. You're a victim in all of this and if I were to just let you off on your own to go trawling through those files the higher ups would have my arse in a sling. This way, we can say you're assisting Dr Perez in looking through the old case files."

"What's the difference?" Harriet asked, struggling to keep her emotions in check. Tempers were definitely beginning to fray as the clock slowly wound down. Sooner or later, they would get the call they all dreaded.

"The difference is that I've got enough on my

plate as it is," Gregson said with a sigh. "Don't make this any harder than it needs to be, Dr Quinn. Please."

She sighed. "You're not exactly giving me a choice in all of this, but I want it noted that I'm not happy. Having another psychologist there is only going to distract me and I don't need that right now."

"I didn't think you would be so threatened by my presence." Katerina's voice cut through the tension in the room. Harriet half turned in her chair to see the other psychologist framed in the doorway.

"I'm not threatened. I'm merely stating how I work best."

"And I've heard that two heads are often better than one," Katerina said amicably.

From the corner of her eye, Harriet watched as she flashed DCI Gregson a bright smile and stepped into the room. "I must admit, DCI Gregson, I was surprised to get your call last night."

He ducked his gaze toward the desk and Harriet felt a knot of tension form in her stomach. The last thing they needed now was for Gregson's focus to be split away from the case by Katerina's flirtatious behaviour.

Was that really the problem though? Or was there some grain of truth to what Dr Perez had said? Was she feeling a little threatened by the other woman? Harriet wanted to dismiss the notion immediately out of hand but could she really in good conscience do that?

After all, there was plenty to be jealous and threatened by when it came to Katerina Perez. She was far more experienced. Her work with the FBI in America made her an obvious choice for a position working alongside the British police. However, all of that had never bothered Harriet before so why now? Why had everything changed?

"After Dr Quinn here let us know about the Star Killer contacting her, we thought it prudent to bring a second pair of eyes onto the case. I've got the utmost faith in Dr Quinn and her abilities. However..."

"However, you fear she may be compromised due to the killer choosing her as his puzzle master?"

Harriet dug her fingernails into the side of her ribcage and bit back the retort that hovered on the tip of her tongue. Her silence must have surprised Dr Perez because her patience was rewarded with a speculative look from the other woman, confirming Harriet's fears. Katerina was goading her. But why?

"Something like that," Gregson said, clearing his throat awkwardly as though Katerina's choice of words had bothered him as much as it had bothered Harriet.

"Look, I know this is unorthodox, but we've got a real chance to catch a killer that has been on the loose for eighteen years. He's got twelve deaths on his hands and anything you can tell me that'll help catch this bastard is a good thing."

Harriet had to agree with him. They were in a unique position. At no other time in the history of the Star Killer's prolific career had he contacted a psychologist. His preference for targeting high profile detectives in order to lure them into his twisted game was well documented. What was less well known was the fact that all of the detectives had later gone on to fall from grace. Their inability to catch their quarry and his subsequent taunting of them had devastated their psyches. And most had retired from the force long before they were due for it.

This time however he'd decided to play the game a little differently.

"Why do you think he contacted you?" Dr Perez asked, leaning against the wall next to Gregson's desk.

"Judging him by his past behaviour I'd say it's because I've been mentioned quite a bit in the paper lately. With everything that happened after the Burton case I've spent more time in the news than I have out of it."

"So, you think he's targeting you because you've become somewhat high-profile?" Katerina managed to make the question sound like an insult.

Harriet smiled. "I wouldn't say I was high-profile. Just that I've been linked to a high-profile case and I was helpful in bringing it to a close. When you look back through the files, you'll see a similar pattern emerge. He comes out of hiding whenever a high-profile case is closed, almost as though he's doing it to set the balance straight."

"You think he's got a problem with the police?" Dr Perez asked thoughtfully. "I mean, it's possible, but don't you think it's a little pedestrian for our perpetrator?"

Harriet shrugged. "Have you got a better idea as to why he's doing this?"

Katerina shook her head and smiled. "No, I just wanted to know a little more about your reasoning."

"When are we going to go public with all of this?" Gregson interjected.

"I don't think that's wise," Dr Perez said. "For all we know it's not really the Star Killer but somebody copy-catting his behaviour."

Harriet glared over at the other woman. "He isn't a copy-cat," she said. "This is the real deal."

"You cannot be sure of that," Katerina said. "Unless there is some form of forensic evidence to link him to the other crimes, nobody can positively say that it is the same person. And going public with this runs the risk of creating a sense of panic and drawing other copy-cats from out of the woodwork."

She turned her attention to Gregson. "Has there been anything come up from forensics?"

The DCI shook his head and glanced down at the open file on his desk miserably. "Nothing. Just like every other time. It's like these gifts or whatever you want to call them come out of thin air."

"They come from somewhere," Dr Perez said. "We just need to work our way backwards until—"

"And the best place to do that is with the old case files." Harriet pushed onto her feet. "I think that not making a public statement is a mistake," she said. "We've got a partial photograph of a young woman and there's somebody out there who might know who she is. It's a long shot but it could help us and to deny that is beyond foolish. In my opinion anyway."

DCI Gregson glanced from Harriet and over to the other woman standing in the room.

"If you want to incite panic among the people for something that is not yet confirmed, then by all means go right ahead." Dr Perez spread her hands out in front as though presenting the DCI with a clear choice.

He groaned and buried his face in his hands. "I thought having two of you here would make things easier. Why have I got the feeling that everything just got a hell of a lot more complicated?"

Shaking her head, Harriet made it as far as the door. "I'm going to look over the files. You'll know where to find me if you actually want my input."

She slammed out through the door and the sound of it hitting the frame gave her a perverse kind of satisfaction. Crossing the office, she made it as far as the conference room and dropped into the nearest swivel chair. Angling the seat, she watched as Gregson and Dr Perez continued their heated debate without her.

Ignoring the two of them, Harriet turned her attention to one of the boxes that sat on the desk awaiting her attention. Pulling it toward her, she tugged the lid off and stared down at the files. She was positive the answers she needed would be found among the pages gathered here. If it was a game he wanted to play, then she was willing to join in, but only as long as the playing field was levelled.

So far, he held all the cards and she had nothing. It was time to change that and there was only one-way Harriet knew of doing that.

She would need to know everything there was to know about the so-called Star Killer and she needed to know it fast.

CHAPTER TWENTY-TWO

FIFTY MINUTES LATER, Drew pushed through the swing doors into the office. His gaze automatically strayed over to DCI Gregson's office and he half expected to see Harriet sitting inside the glass box. Instead, he was greeted with the furious expression of his superior.

Before the other man could signal him, Drew turned his attention to the rest of the office. Maz's desk sat empty, as did a couple of the other officers'. Drew scanned the room and found the conference room occupied by several bodies.

His gaze fell on Harriet. The sight of her familiar, dark-haired head bent over a case file while she proceeded to chew the tip of a ball point pen she'd jammed into her mouth, spread warmth through his chest. When Dr Perez had suggested that something had happened to Harriet, it had felt as though his whole world had tilted off its axis.

The fear he'd felt had been all too familiar to him as the same kind of fear he'd felt when he'd woken in the hospital and asked for Freya.

But it wasn't the same, was it? It couldn't be the same. He'd loved Freya, had wanted to marry her. Harriet, on the other hand, was someone he barely knew. Not that it meant he couldn't feel something for her.

It just couldn't be the same kind of feeling he'd had for Freya, and he needed to remember that.

His gaze turned to Dr Perez. She sat at the head of the table, her hair pinned at the nape of her neck. Unlike the others in the room, she wasn't studying the case file open in front of her. Instead, Drew found himself pinned in place by her intelligent gaze. From where he stood, it almost felt as though she could see straight through him, as though she knew what he was thinking and feeling.

It was impossible, and he dismissed the thought out of hand.

"Haskell!" DCI Gregson's voice boomed through the office space making him jump. Turning toward his superior officer Drew cocked an eyebrow at him. "Get your arse in here now."

Drew knew better than to push the Monk when he was in this kind of mood and he crossed the floor without argument. Pausing inside the door, he pushed it shut behind him and then turned to face Gregson.

"What are you doing here?"

"I got a call."

"Fucking psychologists," Gregson muttered under his breath as he dropped into his chair behind his desk. "Take a seat, Haskell."

Drew took the offered seat and stretched his long legs out in front as he lounged in the chair.

"I take it she told you what we're dealing with here?"

"I'd prefer if you filled me in, sir," Drew said. Staying on the good side of his boss right now seemed like the smartest plan.

Gregson glared across the room at him and for a moment Drew wondered whether he would speak to him or send him on his way with a flea in his ear.

"Fine. Last night Dr Quinn received a package from what we suspect is the Star Killer." Gregson paused as though he expected Drew to interject. He wanted to but instead, he bit his tongue and simply nodded his acceptance of the facts.

"We attended the scene along with SOCOs who went over the place with a fine-toothed comb, but as of right now they've found nothing."

"Sir, you said you suspect it's the Star Killer. Is there some reason you feel this is just a suspicion and not a fact?"

Gregson scrubbed his meaty knuckles into his

eyes. "Honestly, I'd be happy to make a statement saying it's our man. It bears all the hallmarks of his previous crimes. From what I could see there's nothing to suggest it's anything other than legit and I should know. I'm going to have a word with the Super and if he agrees we'll make a public statement."

Drew nodded. "You worked the last one if memory serves me."

Gregson shifted somewhat uncomfortably in his chair and cast an uneasy eye over the office beyond. "I was one of many," he said. "The man I worked under was one of the best officer's I've ever had the privilege of working with."

"What happened to him?" Drew asked.

"It took a couple of months for the Star Killer's final victim to be found and when she was..." Gregson trailed off and stared down at his hands. "She was eighteen years old. She had her whole life ahead of her."

He gave himself what looked to Drew like a mental shake and glanced up. "Suranne was DCI Colridge's daughter. He stayed on only because he wanted to be the one to bring her home. It wasn't exactly official, and they actually promoted me so I could take over the day to day running of the CID. But the man never gave up."

Drew's chest tightened. "He always takes

someone close to the one he assigns as the puzzle master?"

Gregson nodded. "Every one of the files I've ever looked at says the same thing."

Drew fought the urge to chew his non-existent fingernails. "Then we need to put somebody on Dr Quinn's mother. She's the only close relation she's got."

Gregson glanced up. "Shit, you're right. I've been all over the place with people demanding to know our next move I completely forgot. I'll get a protective detail set up straight away. Is there anyone else close to her?"

Drew shrugged. "I don't know. I'll ask her..." He trailed off the thought of having to speak to her didn't exactly fill him with pleasure, but this was an active investigation now and he needed to set his personal feelings aside and do his god-damned job. If he couldn't do that then he was good for nothing.

"As much as I hate to admit it, I'm glad to have you back." Gregson's body was rigid as he passed the grudging compliment, but Drew took it for what it was.

"Thanks, sir, I can't say I enjoy sitting on the sidelines."

Gregson cracked a smile. "That makes two of us." He drew in a deep shuddering breath and his gaze dropped back to the desk. "Just do one thing for me, Haskell."

"Yes, sir?"

"Don't let this bastard get away this time."

"I don't intend on it happening, sir."

Gregson inclined his head. "You know, I felt the same way when I was in your shoes. Don't make the same mistakes I did."

Drew climbed to his feet and headed for the door, he paused with his hand on the door handle. "You know, sir, nobody blames you for not catching him." He glanced back at the older man behind the desk who before his eyes seemed to age several decades at once.

"You might not blame me but that doesn't stop me from carrying the guilt of all those people whose lives were snuffed out by that bastard. Before this is over, I want him behind bars, and I want just five minutes alone with him. DCI Colridge and his daughter Suranne deserve that much at least."

Drew gave an abrupt jerk of his head and pulled the door open. "Oh, do you have any issues with me pulling PC Crandell from the traffic division?"

Gregson shook his head. "I've already pulled all available personnel and I'm sure her name was on the list. Why her specifically?"

"I worked with her on the Burton case. She handled herself well, I think she'd be an asset to the team."

Gregson shrugged. "Do what you think is necessary. Just make sure you catch him."

"I'll see what I can do, sir."

Gregson didn't answer him as he slipped out into the office and pulled the door shut after him. Not that he really expected him to. Seeing the Monk as vulnerable as that didn't sit well with Drew and he couldn't help but wonder if by the end of the case would he carry similar scars to that of his DCI?

As much as he wanted to keep his promise and deliver the one responsible for such misery up on a platter to the world, he couldn't help but worry he wasn't up to the task especially when so many other officers—better officers—had found themselves in the same spot and they'd failed. What would make him any different?

He saw her then as he pushed open the door to the conference room. She raised her gaze to his as though she'd sensed him coming.

Harriet was the difference. The killer had made a mistake when he'd picked her to be the puzzle master, Drew was sure of it.

The only problem was, how could he make her see it too?

CHAPTER TWENTY-THREE

"I'M JUST NOT sure I agree with you, Dr Quinn," Katerina said.

Unable to contain her frustration any longer, Harriet rolled her eyes. "And why is that?"

"I just don't see where you are getting your assumptions from about his motives for the murders. Jealousy? Envy? *Schadenfreude?*" She quirked a dark eyebrow over the last one. "These are just words. They are meaningless in the context of our killer."

"So, what do you believe is his motive?" DS Arya asked, interrupting the flow of the conversation. It hadn't slipped by Harriet unnoticed that Arya seemed to have a bit of a crush on Katerina. He waited on her attentively, bringing her cups of black coffee whenever she asked for them. Even going so far as to nip to the local coffee shop when she'd complained over the state of the stations black tar.

Dr Perez smiled and leaned forward, placing her elbows on the desk. It was as though she'd been waiting for just this moment. Harriet knew a performer when she saw one and Katerina knew exactly how to play to her captive audience.

"It is my belief that we are dealing with somebody in their mid to late fifties. He is assured and confident in his abilities. I will concede that he is intelligent; although I won't give his intelligence as much credit as Dr Quinn here likes to do. When she speaks about him, she almost builds him up to be some kind of boogeyman and I just don't see that."

It was an effort to keep her expression neutral as she listened to Katerina.

Dr Perez smiled warmly. "I feel he lashes out as he does due to feeling impotent. Perhaps his wife has left him recently, or--"

"Wait, you think he's married?" Drew couldn't keep the incredulity from his voice and Harriet felt some of the tension she'd been carrying slowly leech from her body. Even if he refused to look at her, or even speak more than two words to her since he'd arrived it was nice to know somebody agreed with her.

"Yes, I do," Katerina said. "Especially as I'm not entirely convinced that he is this Star Killer. Why would he change his method of execution so drastically now after so many years?"

"What do you mean?" Harriet asked, sitting up a little straighter in her chair.

"He contacted you, did he not? That is quite the shift in method. Before now our killer has been rigorous in his choice of puzzle master. To choose you when you are not officially connected with the police in any way seems a little strange to me."

It was a difficult point to argue, and one Harriet had found herself sticking over more than once now. He'd never faltered in his selection before so why change now?

"I think you're ignoring the very real fact that Harriet's connection with the police was cemented during the last case," Drew said. "She's been plastered all over the papers as Yorkshire's profiler. One newspaper even went so far as to warn the criminals out there to get out of dodge before they were caught by her."

Harriet glanced over at Drew. "I haven't seen that one."

He nodded and stared down at the desk. "I spotted it here in the station. They've probably chucked it by now."

"You think our killer is using the newspaper's as his source for choosing the person he wants to solve his puzzles?" Katerina shook her head. "I just don't see it."

"Well where else then?" Harriet asked, fighting the urge to drum her fingers against the tabletop.

"Perhaps it is a disgruntled patient come back to teach you a lesson, Dr Quinn?" Katerina said. "Surely you like the rest of us must have some skeletons in your closet..."

"I'm going to get a coffee," Drew said abruptly pushing up from the table.

Harriet watched as he stalked out of the conference room and across the office toward the small room they'd converted into a make-shift coffee dock.

"You should go after him," Katerina said not unkindly.

"What?" Harriet swung her attention around to the woman sitting at the head of the table.

"You should go after him. Clear the air between you both. It's clear you're distracted, and it would be better for everybody involved if you were not."

Harriet felt heat spread up into her face as she glanced around at the others gathered at the table. They studiously ignored her, all of them keeping their gazes pinned on the desk and the work in front of them. But there was no getting away from the fact that they'd all heard what Dr Perez had said.

Pushing up from the desk, Harriet smoothed down her blouse as she made her way out of the conference room. No sooner had the door slid shut behind her than the murmured sound of conversation filtered out through the glass walls. Dr Perez had given them all something to gossip about. Great.

Heading in the direction Drew had disappeared

in, Harriet was surprised to find the kitchen empty. The mug he'd been using was gone suggesting he had told the truth when he'd said he was going for a coffee.

"You're, DC Crandell, right?" Harriet caught the attention of a young female officer standing at the sink washing out a cup that had seen better days.

"Yeah," the female officer glanced up in surprise. Have you seen DI Haskell?"

"I think he went outside for a cigarette."

Harriet smiled her thanks and retreated toward the back stairs. She'd seen enough of the officers disappear down this direction to make an educated guess it was the path they took to get outside for a nicotine break.

The fire door at the bottom of the stairs was propped open and Harriet stepped out into the cool afternoon air. At least it wasn't raining here. She wrapped her arms around her body as she scanned the area and her gaze fell on Drew who sat on the bottom of a set of stone steps leading away from the station.

"I had a feeling you'd follow me," he said quietly as she approached.

"I know I'm the last person you want to talk to--" she began before Drew shook his head and stood.

"Then if you know this why come out here?"

"Because we need to clear the air. We can't go on

working like this. Not with this elephant between us."

He looked as though he was about to argue with her and then changed his mind, his expression smoothing out until it was nothing more than a pleasant mask of indifference.

"Better?" he asked. "Because if you're asking me to just let everything you've done go, then you can forget it."

"That's not what I'm asking you. But I am asking for you to talk to me about it."

He sighed. "Fine, then tell me why your name is on Freya's discharge papers?"

His question caught her off guard and Harriet took a small step backwards. "My what?" It was all beginning to sound a bit too much like deja-bloody-vu to her.

"According to Freya's discharge papers you're the one who released her from the hospital, not Dr Connor."

"That's not true. I wasn't even working in the hospital at the time, at least not in any official capacity."

He nodded and scrubbed his hand up over his face. "Why is it that everything with you has to be so damned complicated?"

"I don't understand what you mean?"

"Why can't it be straight forward? Why do the

papers have your name on them? What has this Connor guy got against you?"

"It's complicated," Harriet said. "His ego is bruised because I rejected him."

Drew snorted, the sound harsh and unforgiving to Harriet's ears. "You know most men don't behave like that, right?"

She sighed. "I know that."

"But you sure can pick them."

Harriet bit back the words that longed to spill from her. She hadn't chosen Jonathan. He was her mother's doctor, nothing more and nothing less, or at least that was what she had assumed.

"Did you know Freya?" Drew's voice had dropped to a contemplative whisper.

"I met her once," she said honestly. "Jonathan asked me to sit with her, to speak with her. He wanted my opinion on how I thought she was progressing."

"And what did you think?" Drew asked. He met her gaze head on and there was a rawness to his emotions that haunted his eyes.

"I told him the truth," Harriet said. "I told him she wasn't ready to leave the hospital. I told him she needed more time and that I wasn't convinced the medication he'd prescribed her was actually doing what he seemed to think it was."

Drew sighed, the sound rushing out of him as he slumped back against the wall.

"You know when she came home that time, she seemed better."

Harriet nodded. "I know."

"I really thought we were going to get past it, that she would be all right, you know? She just needed time to heal." He scrubbed his hands over his face. "I needed time too I suppose but when I look back at it now it feels selfish."

"It's not selfish to want to preserve your own mental state," Harriet said a little more vehemently than she'd intended. "I mean, where would we be if we allowed ourselves to be dragged under by those already drowning? How would we help anyone if we became just another casualty?"

"I wanted to save her," he said, staring down at his hands. "I wanted to protect her, and I failed."

Harriet fought the urge to reach out and touch him. There was so much pain behind his words, so much heartache and guilt that he carried with him but there was nothing she could do to make that go away. He would have to find his own way to lay down his burden and until he decided he was capable of doing that no amount of sympathy from her would help.

"There was nothing you could do for her," she said finally. "She was ill, Drew. You couldn't have made her better no matter how hard you wanted to."

He shook his head. "I promised her. I promised I would stay with her." He raised his face to hers then and Harriet could see the wretchedness of his fear and self-loathing over everything that had happened to Freya. "How do I reconcile that? How do I accept that I failed her like that?"

Harriet glanced down at the ground. "I don't know," she said. "I haven't figured it out myself yet either." It was the honest truth.

Even now, after all these years she still carried the guilt of leaving her brother behind. The rational part of her brain knew it was foolish. She'd been a child; there was nothing she could have done to save him. Even he had understood that. He'd sent her away because he'd known that for her to stay would mean they'd both perish.

But all that knowledge. All the years of study and psychology. All the time she'd spent listening to other people and the terrible and devastating stories they had to tell her about their own life and struggles and not once had it ever helped her to understand the pain she herself carried deep down inside.

Instead, she'd learned that it was simply a part of her. One of the many facets that made up her personality. It wasn't wrong and she wasn't broken, no matter how many times the destructive voice in the back of her mind told her she was. She simply was who she was, and there was nothing she could do about that. Accepting it, learning to live with it, those things were in her control. Everything else was just white noise.

"I don't blame you for her death," he said finally. "I blame myself."

"I'm going to tell you that you shouldn't," Harriet said, cutting over him before he could interrupt. "But I already know you won't believe me. All I can offer you is this. Allowing that guilt and pain to consume you only prevents you from doing your job. You were born to help people, to protect them from people like the Star Killer, but letting your own emotions block you from doing that will destroy you."

He nodded. "I know you're right."

"But you don't know how to move past it?"

He smiled at her. "Something like that."

"One day at a time," she said. "It won't make it better and there's no magic bullet for the grief and the pain, but you have a choice to make. Either lie down in it and let it eat you alive or choose to carry on. Choose to live again."

"I can't let her go."

"And nobody is asking you to. But your relationship with her has changed. Honour her and everything she gave to you by carrying her with you."

"We should go back in," he said suddenly, and Harriet knew the moment between them was gone.

She sighed and pulled her phone from her pocket. "Oh, god," she murmured as she caught sight of the message from Urma.

"What is it?"

"I'm supposed to be somewhere..."

"What, now?"

Harriet nodded. "It's too important," she said. "I--
"

"What is it?"

"Bianca's memorial..." She swallowed past the lump in her throat. Here she was telling Drew to move on from his grief, to allow himself to heal but when was she going to take her own advice? "I can drive up in the morning and--"

"You should go," he said. "Anyway, officially you're not supposed to work on the case."

She dropped her gaze to the message. "Honestly, I'm afraid."

"What of?"

"What if he hurts them because of who he has chosen me to be?"

Harriet could see the realisation as it dawned in Drew's eyes. "You're worried about who the third victim will be?"

She nodded.

"Well, we've put a protective detail on your mother and the hospital where she is."

Harriet swallowed hard. "I didn't even think, I just--"

"It's fine," he said, touching her arm lightly. "This is what I do, remember? It's my job to think of the mundane tasks like protective details. It's your job to come up with the profile you think is going to help us catch this bastard."

Harriet allowed herself to smile in spite of the fear that rattled around inside her.

"We'll get something arranged for Bianca's family too if that'll help set your mind at ease?"

Harriet nodded. "Yeah, actually that would help. I can't bear to think of anything happening to Tilly, or for her to lose anyone else close to her."

Drew nodded sympathetically. "Is there anybody else you can think of?"

She sighed. "I'm not close to many people," she said. "I tend to just live inside my books..." She shrugged and a terrible thought occurred to her. "You don't think he'd target Dr Connor?" Drew's expression darkened. "I'm sorry, it's just up until I discovered what a complete asshole he could be, alongside Bianca he was probably the closest thing I had to family."

Drew closed his eyes and for a moment Harriet wished she'd never opened her mouth on the matter.

"I'm sorry, I shouldn't--"

"No," he shook his head. "You're right. We'll have to arrange something for him too. Christ what a clusterfuck." Drew turned away and scrubbed his hand over his jaw. "I'll say this though," he said, casting a look back over his shoulder. "You need to pick better friends."

There was a censure to his words that cut to the bone with Harriet. She hadn't chosen Dr Connor out of any kind of genuine affection for him. Her mother's illness and her being so young when everything had changed had set her on a collision course with the man.

If she'd been wiser, she would have kept her distance from him, but then again, she was beginning to learn she wasn't particularly wise or knowledgeable about anything.

"You two," DS Arya's shout brought them up short and Harriet turned to see him leaning out through the fire door. "We think we've got something in here."

"What is it?" Drew asked and he was already halfway across the space, his long stride eating up the distance to the door faster than Harriet could process everything that was happening.

"Someone just made a delivery for Dr Quinn..." Harriet's heart sank in her chest and she hurried after Drew. This was the moment they'd been dreading. The second part of the puzzle.

The Star Killer had his first victim and he wasn't hanging around with the puzzles. Which suggested a level of preparation and organisation Harriet had never encountered before.

"Are you all right?" Drew asked as she reached the door. He caught her arm and Harriet glanced down at the place where his fingers pressed through the fabric of her blouse.

"I'm fine."

"You sure?"

She nodded. "It's not as though I have a choice here. He's chosen me for a reason, and I owe it to the victims to uphold my end of the bargain."

Drew smiled at her, a brief flash of understanding that passed between them and then it was gone as though it had never been there at all.

"Let's get this over with," she said, moving ahead of him and up the stairs. She pushed the phone back into her pocket. "Sorry, Bianca..."

Of course, if Bianca had been alive, she would have understood.

Harriet had a feeling however, that Bianca's family would not be so understanding.

CHAPTER TWENTY-FOUR

"I DON'T SEE why we are standing around here waiting for Dr Quinn." Drew heard Dr Perez's protests as soon as he stepped into the squad room.

The woman was standing inside the conference room but with the door open, her voice carried to every corner of the place. "What does it matter if she opens it, or I open it?"

DCI Gregson stood next to her and he shook his head. "*Nobody* is opening it until the SOCOs get here."

"Sir, they've said they've been delayed on the way over and--"

"Bollocks," Gregson swore violently and then glanced sheepishly at Dr Perez, who ignored him entirely.

Drew paused in the doorway and glanced down

at the nondescript brown box which sat in the middle of the conference room desk.

"Who delivered it?"

"Some courier, we've got him downstairs in one of the interview rooms but he's not too happy about it."

"And we're sure he's not our guy?" Drew asked.

Gregson shot him a scathing glance. "Unless our bloke was a baby when he started murdering people, then the bloke in interrogation isn't our guy. What do you take me for, Haskell?"

Drew didn't answer but instead turned his attention to the box.

"We can't just stand around here and ignore it," he said finally. "Sir, so long as we wear gloves while it's opened what harm is there in opening it now?"

Gregson stared down at the box. "I don't like this."

"I should be the one to open it," Harriet said, stepping forward. Beneath the fluorescent lights she looked pale and Drew found himself wondering just how much of a toll all of this was exacting on her.

"Fine," Gregson said. "But wear gloves and a mask." He turned to the rest of the room. "I want everyone to clear out of here."

Drew glanced over at his boss. "You don't think there's anything dangerous in there, surely. I mean, he always follows the same pattern. He wouldn't change now."

DCI Gregson shrugged. "I'm not willing to take that risk. Everybody who doesn't need to be in here has to leave. I'll stay with Dr Quinn and the rest of you can—"

Drew shook his head. "Sir, with all due respect, I'm not going anywhere."

Gregson gave him a once over and sighed. "Fine. You can stay but you'll be gloved up and masked too."

Drew started to protest but the Monk cut him off with a stern look. "Gloves and a mask or you're outside the glass."

Drew glanced over at Harriet and nodded. "Fine."

DS Arya passed out the gloves and masks he'd dug out of the closet. From the corner of his eye, Drew watched Harriet take her pair of single use gloves. Her fingers shook but she smiled at Maz as though there was nothing unusual about the situation at all.

"Did the courier say anything?" Drew asked as the others filed out, leaving him with Gregson and Harriet.

The DCI shook his head. "Aside from moaning about us holding him when he should be out there delivering the rest of his parcels, no."

"Have you got something sharp I can open this with?" Harriet asked, examining the box from all angles.

Drew knocked on the glass door, drawing Crandell's attention.

"A knife."

She nodded and took off across the office and disappeared into the small kitchen. She returned a moment later and Drew opened the door and took the blade from her. With the knife in hand, he secured the door and Gregson inclined his head giving his assent to proceed.

Returning to Harriet's side, he noticed she hadn't moved but her eyes were locked on the package as though if she studied it hard enough it would somehow spill all of its secrets to her.

"Here," Drew said, holding the knife out to her. She took it gratefully and pressed it against the parcel tape holding the cardboard box shut. The only sound in the room was that of the tape separating as the knife bit through it.

She worked quickly, pulling the flaps on the box apart. She set the knife down on the table and reached into the box and withdrew another box. This one however was wrapped in the same red sparkly paper as the first package. The gold foil string that held it together was tied in a perfectly symmetrical bow that looked far too complicated as far Drew was concerned.

"Just as with the first package, I don't see anything written on the outside of this one." Harriet's voice was hollow, almost monotone. Using the knife, she popped the ribbons and slipped the flat edge of the blade beneath the tape holding the paper in place. The parcel unfolded quickly, and Drew felt the tension in his shoulders ratchet up several notches.

It was then he realised the bottom edge of the white box was discoloured. "It's leaking," he said, directing the attention of the others in the room to the box.

Harriet took a step backwards as though the box had suddenly become sentient and Drew watched as her eyes widened slightly at the sight of the damp patch that was rapidly spreading on the box.

Maz tapped on the glass. "It's not blood," he said, his voice only slightly muffled by the clear wall between them. The others glanced over at him and he shrugged. "Well, it's not. If it were blood it'd stain the box. That's more like water or something else that's clear."

"He's right," Gregson said. "Blood would leave a stain. Whatever is leaking inside the box is clear."

Harriet squared her shoulders and Drew was unable to tear his gaze away from her as she reached two trembling hands out toward the box. She popped the lid off and stared down into the parcel.

"What is it?" he asked, taking a step toward her.

"The puzzle pieces are here," she said, pulling what appeared to him to be pieces of a jigsaw free of the box. The puzzle pieces were wrapped in what looked to Drew like a clear sandwich bag which had been sealed along the top.

"Oh..." There was an audibly sharp intake of breath from Harriet as she set the puzzle pieces down on the table. Her gaze was fixed on the contents of the box and Drew moved up next to her and stared inside.

His stomach churned in response to the sight within.

What is that?" Maz's voice filtered through the glass but Drew ignored him.

The tongue lay inside a bag of ice which had begun to melt. Undoubtedly due to its time spent in the courier's van. It was the melting ice from the bag which had started to leak through the cardboard box soaking everything it had been transported in.

Drew glanced up and found Dr Perez had turned away, her shoulders were stiff, hand across her mouth. DCI Gregson looked a little green around the gills, but he cleared his throat awkwardly as he met Drew's stare.

"The jigsaw, we need to see what we've got there." Gregson jerked his head indicating Drew should take the puzzle pieces from Harriet.

Unlike Dr Perez, Harriet was still staring in at the contents of the box. Her eyes were a little too wide, and a fine sheen of sweat coated her brow.

"Harriet, we need to take a look at the jigsaw now."

She didn't respond to him and instead continued to gaze in at the macabre contents.

"Harriet."

"I think I know who it is," she said finally after what felt like an age.

"You do?" Gregson asked, casting a sideways glance in her direction. "How is that possible? It's just a tongue..."

"The stud," she said, and Drew found himself wondering if perhaps the stress of everything which had happened over the past few weeks was finally beginning to get to her.

"What stud?"

She pointed a trembling finger into the box. "The one in the tongue."

He glanced into the box again and sure enough embedded in the tongue was a piercing. The neon yellow stud looked to be more of a sickly shade of snot as far as Drew could tell beneath the harsh artificial lighting. How had he missed it the first time?

"It could belong to anyone," he said.

Harriet shook her head. "No, I had a reporter come to see me yesterday morning. Rachel Kennedy, I think her name was."

Drew felt the world drop away from beneath his feet as he stared into the box. She was right.

"She came to see me too," he said softly. "She had the exact same stud in her tongue."

Harriet met his gaze over the top of the box. "She fits the puzzle too," she said. "Rachel is a blonde."

Drew nodded and turned his attention to the little baggy in her hands. "We need to see the rest of the puzzle."

CHAPTER TWENTY-FIVE

PUSHING the forceps beneath the spray of water in the sink, he watched the water turn from a crystal clear colour to a pink. There was a moan and he glanced over his shoulder at the woman slumped in the chair. She was a fighter, no doubt about it.

The tongue had been almost too tempting to keep but sending it in with the next part of the puzzle would prove far too interesting. They wouldn't be able to sit on this a moment more. Just how long would it take them to figure out who he'd taken?

If they were smart--well as smart as anyone could be these days considering what the television did to the brain--then they would work it out relatively quickly.

She had friends and family members who would miss her but for now they were happy to believe she was off saving the world. Eventually they would make a call to the police to report a missing person but by then the game would nearly be done.

He let his mind wander to Dr Quinn. Would she see the significance in the tongue? Surely, she would know what it meant. She might even thank him for it, once she got over the shock of seeing it.

But would she know the timeline had changed. Allowances needed to be made. It wasn't easy to deliver packages safely on time, not to mention grabbing victims on a schedule. And then there was the small issue of Dr Quinn putting the pieces together faster than he'd allowed for. It was a risk, but it did make the game so much more thrilling.

Letting the forceps fall into the sink, he sauntered back over to his prey and stood back to admire his handiwork.

She'd used that tongue of hers to tell so many lies. Better to have it removed so as to take the temptation away. Sliding his hand beneath her face, he tilted her chin upwards toward the light. The lower half of her face was bruised and bloodied. She'd fought so hard he'd ended up breaking three of her teeth just trying to keep the forceps in place so he could get the tongue out.

Her screams still echoed in his ears.

The piercing had been a nice touch, he couldn't have picked a better specimen to work with.

When her eyes fluttered open, her confusion

slowly became abject horror as she realised who stood over her. He drank it down; her terror and fear. It fed him, consumed him, and he wanted nothing more than to make her scream again.

As her awareness grew, she bucked and thrashed in the chair. She whipped her head away and to the side in an attempt to get away from his hand. A slow grin crossed his face as he stood and watched her panic intensify.

Picking up the pliers from the tray next to the chair, he crouched down by her shoeless feet.

"Tell me, Rachel, do you know this one?" He tapped her big toe. "This little piggy went to market. And this little piggy stayed at home."

He glanced up at her and grinned as he moved the pliers along in time with the rhyme. "This little piggy had roast beef, but this little piggy had none..."

He came to a halt at her little toe. "But this little piggy went, wee-wee-wee, all the way home."

Her screams ripped the air and he drank them down as though they were the finest of wines.

CHAPTER TWENTY-SIX

STANDING in front of the mirror in the ladies' toilet, Harriet splashed water onto her face before returning her hands to the edge of the sink. Her eyes looked as though they had sunk into her face. Her skin was pale and washed out and her hair was nothing more than a tangled mess around her shoulders from all the times she'd dragged her fingers through the unruly curls.

"Why are you doing this?" She stared at the mirror as though the answers to all of the questions swirling in her brain would suddenly become apparent. "Why wait so long? Why now?"

"I used to talk to myself too," Dr Perez said. Harriet froze and glanced over her shoulder at the other woman who had entered the bathroom.

"Did it help?"

Katerina smiled and shook her head. "No, it only brought strange looks from those who didn't understand what it was I was trying to do."

Harriet nodded and switched off the tap. "I can see how that might happen."

"They've removed the note from the box," Katerina said. "It's just more of the same goading style as the first one. He doesn't give anything away."

"And he won't." Harriet turned to face the other woman. "Tell me why you think my profile is so off?"

Katerina shrugged. "I find them to be too restrictive. Police officers have a tendency to adhere to them a little too rigidly and that tends to create holes through which the killer can wriggle."

Harriet shook her head. "DI Haskell is not a fool. He wouldn't rule a potential suspect out just because it didn't fit a profile I gave. It's just not how he works."

"True as that may be," Katerina said. "You don't have a suspect right now. So, all your profile will achieve is a narrowing of the search parameters which, as I said, can lead to suspects slipping away."

"But you gave your own version of a profile. If you're so against them, why say anything at all?"

Katerina laughed, a rich throaty sound that made Harriet cringe. She stalked over to the sink and switched on a tap before she delicately splashed water up onto her wrists. Meeting Harriet's gaze head on in the mirror she smiled broadly. "I was right, wasn't I? Earlier I mean, when I said you were threatened by me?"

"This isn't about whether I feel threatened by you," Harriet said, feeling her frustration beginning to mount. "It's about whether we can work together to put a stop to the person responsible for this."

Dr Perez shrugged and turned, leaning on the sink she closed her eyes. "You could well be right where your profile is concerned, especially if this is the original killer."

Harriet nodded. "He's power orientated. Everything he does to his victims is to gain power over them. He enjoys hurting them, torturing them. According to the post-mortems carried out on all the previous victims as far as they can tell most of the injuries they sustained happened while the victim was still alive."

"So, he's a sadist?" Katerina said, pursing her lips. "A true sadist is not easy to find. Most wind up being a watered-down version of the true meaning of the word."

"I don't think he's watering anything down," Harriet said.

Grabbing a tissue, she proceeded to dry her hands. "There's something I need to check." She hurried from the room, leaving Dr Perez behind to stare after her.

Reaching the conference room, Harriet pulled

the file she'd been studying towards herself and scanned the page quickly. The box and its gruesome contents had been removed by the SOCOs and the room had been returned to some semblance of normality. But as far as Harriet was concerned the smell of Rachel's blood still clung to the air.

"I'm going to have a chat to our courier downstairs," Drew said, interrupting the silence of the room. "I was wondering if you wanted to sit in?"

"Do we know how he abducted his victims?" Harriet asked, glancing up at the man who towered over her.

Drew moved over toward the desk. "I presume any information we've got has to be in these boxes."

"I haven't found any."

"What are you getting at?"

"Well, if our guy is into power and control then the initial taking of the victim has to be special to him. He plans everything so meticulously, so I've got to assume he plans the abduction just as carefully. In order to plan a successful abduction--and he's done it over and over. I mean, Rachel makes lucky number thirteen--he knows their schedules, he knows their every movement, which suggests a level of familiarity with them."

"You think he's stalking them?"

Harriet nodded. "He has to be." She sucked in a deep breath. "We think he found me because of the news reports," she said. "But in order to know where I lived, where I worked... In order to know I was here today and not at home, or the university, then he has to be following me."

Drew raised his eyebrows. "That's a lot of assumptions."

Harriet shook her head. "Is it, though?" She pulled the last file from the stack and laid it open in front of Drew. "Suranne Colridge, her father was the DCI in charge of the case then. She disappeared into thin air on her way out of the supermarket, or at least that's what they think."

Drew nodded. "That was the last time she was seen on CCTV."

"But what if our killer knew something about Suranne that nobody else did? What if he knew her schedule so well that he didn't just grab her outside the supermarket where anybody could have seen him."

"Her car wasn't seen on CCTV leaving the carpark. That's why everyone assumed he'd nabbed her there."

"There's plenty of lighting there, not to mention CCTV around her car. If he'd tried to take her anywhere in this area, we'd have spotted him."

"So, what are you suggesting?"

Harriet sighed. "I'm saying, maybe we need to look into any reports of stalking the previous victims put forward. We need to know their schedules... It would be helpful to know what Suranne was really doing that evening at the supermarket and why she didn't head back to her car straight away."

Drew shook his head. "Do you realise what you're asking for here? There aren't enough hours in the day to go through everything you're suggesting. We need to narrow this down, somehow."

"We can start with Suranne and Rachel," she said. "If we can figure out their movements then maybe we can get a glimpse of how our guy found them and how he stalked them."

"Gregson isn't going to like this."

Harriet shrugged. "Have you got a better idea right now? We know he has Rachel, the only thing is, he doesn't know that we know. It's our only ace right now, Drew. We need to get ahead of this for a change."

"Fine, you're right I suppose." He closed his eyes. "I can put Maz and Olivia on the CCTV for now. At least that way we'll get a head start on it." He folded his arms over his chest. "What about Rachel though? Are we definitely sure she's the one he's taken?"

Harriet glanced down at the table and her mind conjured the memory of the tongue. "I don't see how it can be anyone else. He wants us to guess who the victim is, he's not going to throw such a broad curve-ball into the mix. At least not like that."

Drew nodded. "We still need to confirm it

though. I'll get some of the other officers to try and track her down and get in touch with the family and friends, find out when they last spoke to her. We need to know if she really is our missing victim or not. Otherwise we're just wandering down rabbit holes."

Harriet nodded. "You're right..." She glanced down at the file in front of her. "I guess we should speak to the courier first though."

Drew pinched the bridge of his nose between his index finger and thumb. "Not that I think the guy is going to tell us anything."

Harriet chewed her lip. "I don't know. How did our killer get the box onto the truck?"

"Well, obviously he—" Drew cut off and swore. "You think our courier had some connection with the killer?"

"It's the only thing that makes sense. We both know Rachel was fine yesterday and I didn't get the puzzle until yesterday evening. The game is always a little rigged but—"

"What is it?"

"He has to have taken her yesterday."

"What makes you think that?"

Harriet shook her head. "Because nothing else makes sense. What he did to her, that wasn't rushed. He spent time with her, spent time enjoying the process."

"What are you saying?"

"Just that I think the game is more rigged than we first thought. We always worked under the assumption that we got the puzzle before he took his first victim."

Drew nodded. "Right."

"What if this time he sent the puzzle after he'd already taken her?"

"Or maybe he dropped the puzzle off early in the day and you just weren't in?"

Harriet nodded. "You're right. It's all possible."

"Well, share with the rest of the class what you've got in mind."

She smiled at him. "Once I have my own thoughts sorted into something remotely approaching a useful train of thought, you'll be the first to know."

Drew eyed her and for a moment she thought she saw a flicker of suspicion in his gaze. It was gone as quickly as it had arrived, but Harriet couldn't shake the feeling that she had seen it and not imagined it.

"Let's get this over with then," he said, directing her out of the office.

Pushing onto her feet, Harriet followed a little more slowly behind him.

"Are you going to question the courier?" Dr Perez popped her head up from the file she'd been going over. Unlike the others, she hadn't returned to the conference room, stating she found it somewhat claustrophobic. "I'd like to sit in if I could?"

Drew glanced over at Harriet and she shrugged.

"Fine. But you're to keep your thoughts to yourself unless asked," he said.

She smiled up at him and Harriet moved ahead of them both. The last thing she needed to have right now was her focus splintered by Katerina's open flirting.

CHAPTER TWENTY-SEVEN

"YOU'RE TELLING me that you don't know how this package got on your van?" Drew asked for what felt like the millionth time.

The man across from him—all they'd managed to learn so far was that his name was Sawyer Lakin and he worked for Global Express, a parcel delivery firm which travelled all over the UK—shrugged and leaned back in his chair.

"That's what I said." His London accent was clipped, and it grated on Drew's nerves.

"Nobody asked you to add it to your route?"

"That's not how this works," Lakin said. He turned and eyed Dr Perez up, his gaze sliding up over her body in a way that brought Drew's already frayed temper to the fore. As soon as Gregson had found out where they were going to, he'd insisted that Dr Perez be the one to sit in on the interview which had only irritated Drew further.

"Then how does it work?" Dr Perez asked, her voice husky.

Drew glanced over at her, he'd told her to stay silent and let him lead in the investigation and instead, here she was taking it down a path he wasn't altogether comfortable with.

"I've never understood all that kind of stuff," she said, a sly smile curling her lips. "But I'm sure you could help me understand."

Lakin let the front legs of his chair hit the floor with a dull thud. He leaned his elbows onto the edge of the table and raked his gaze over Dr Perez's face as though searching for a trick.

"Well, I go to the depot and—"

"For fuck's sake, we know how it works," Drew said, unable to keep his temper under control. "Dr Perez, can I have a word?"

She stared over at him with a blank expression before she nodded. "Fine." As she climbed to her feet, Drew caught her as she gave a wide smile to the man opposite her. Now he wished he had pushed for Harriet to sit in on the meeting instead of Perez.

He let her go ahead of him and the sound of the door clanging shut brought him at least some pleasure.

"What the hell was that in there?" She turned on him with a temper that took him by surprise.

"I could ask you the same thing."

"Me? Detective, I'm doing my job. You, however, seem to think that antagonising our witness is the best path forward. How do you expect to open him up if all you do and say shuts him down?" Drew inwardly cringed at her phrasing. The last thing he'd ever contemplate doing with Lakin was opening him up.

"So flirting with the smug prick is going to tell us something useful? He clearly knows nothing and we're wasting our time here."

Perez shook her head and folded her arms over her chest. She glared up at him, her dark gaze furious.

"He would talk to me if you would let me do my thing."

Drew started to laugh, the sound filled the space and Perez's furious expression slowly faded. "You find this amusing?"

"It is amusing," Drew said. "Thinking we should interrogate suspects by flirting with them." His laughter spilled from him.

"But he's not a suspect," she said. Drew felt her penetrating gaze slid over him, studying him as though he were some kind of interesting specimen and she was searching for signs of intelligent life. "We need to know how he got his hands on that parcel. What does it matter if I'm nice to him?" She shrugged.

"Let her do her thing," Harriet said quietly, and Drew glanced up to find her watching their exchanged from the doorway of the observation room. She'd seen the exchange so far and she obviously agreed with Dr Perez's plan.

Drew gritted his teeth. "Fine."

"Be a good boy and stay out here. I need to go back in there alone."

He shook his head. "Absolutely not."

"And why not? He's not a suspect. He's a potential witness. It's not as though my having a friendly chat with him will do any harm."

"It's against protocol." Drew knew he was fighting a losing battle but the thought of letting this woman get any kind of upper hand just didn't sit right with him.

She sighed. "You have a better proposition?"

"Drew," Harriet said. "Let her do this."

Throwing up his arms, Drew sighed. "Fine."

Dr Perez smiled, looking altogether far too pleased with herself and turned back to the door. "Don't interrupt," she warned.

Drew rolled his eyes and let her slide past him into the room. Marching down the hall, he stepped into the observation room after Harriet and clicked on the speakers, allowing them to both hear and see everything that took place in the room on the other side of the two-way glass.

"Sorry about that," Dr Perez said. "You were telling me how it all worked."

"You don't really want to know how that works, do you?" he asked, raising an eyebrow in her direction.

Drew had to give him some credit for not falling for Perez's thinly veiled attempt at flirting.

"What makes you say that?" She asked, her voice was gentle, almost hypnotic and Drew leaned closer to the glass.

"I think you're more interested in me," Lakin said, leaning across the table to brush his fingers against Perez's sleeve.

Her smile made Drew's stomach flip, but she slipped out of Lakin's reach as though she were doing nothing more than playing hard to get.

Drew felt Harriet stiffen next to him and he cast a quick look in her direction, but the room was too dark to see her features clearly.

"I can't very well agree to that, now can I?" Perez said smoothly.

Lakin let his arms drop back by his side and returned to leaning back in the chair. The legs lifted from the floor and Drew imagined the chair disappearing out from beneath the arsehole sitting in the interview room.

However, he had to agree with both psychologists; Lakin wasn't a suspect and treating him as such wasn't going to win them any prizes.

"So, what do you want to know then?"

Perez glanced down at the table, her smile coy as she fiddled with the pen on top of her file. Never in the short time that he'd known her had Drew seen her behave this way.

During every interaction they'd shared, she had presented as a woman in control of every possible situation. From what he'd seen of her, she enjoyed being in control, but it amazed him now to see her so transformed.

The way she deferred to Lakin as though he were so much greater than she. Perez's actions proved one thing to Drew, she had the same skills as any chameleon and that she was capable of slotting herself into any situation.

She tilted her head and glanced up at him through her dark lashes. The perfect imitation of a femme fatale, Drew thought.

"Tell me how you got your hands on that package."

"And what will you give me in return?"

"What do you want?"

Lakin looked her over and laughed. "You're serious, aren't you?"

Perez shrugged before she glanced over her shoulder as though reassuring herself that they were both alone. She leaned across the table and lowered her voice to a theatrical whisper.

"Deadly serious."

Lakin's delighted grin lit up his boyish features and he let the chair legs hit the floor with another dull thud. "Fine, I got a call about a pickup from the university."

Perez's expression never faltered. "Is that unusual?"

He shrugged. "Not as unusual as you'd think. The university is a pretty big client for us."

"And that package was the only one you picked up from there this morning?"

He shook his head. "Nah, if you look through the log, you'll see I picked up a good thirty to forty packages."

Perez nodded thoughtfully and the carefully curated mask she'd worn slipped away completely. "Thank you for your time, Mr Lakin."

"You can call me Sawyer," he said as he reached across the table and attempted to brush his fingers against her hand for a second time.

Perez's smile was all predator as she slipped out of reach and moved gracefully to her feet. She gathered her files and started toward the door and Drew moved to do the same when Lakin called after her.

"Hey, I thought we had a connection?"

"We did," Perez said simply. "You had information I needed, and you were gracious enough to share it with me."

"And the other thing?" Lakin asked. "I mean, I didn't imagine it. You wanted me."

Perez's smile returned but this time it was nothing like the flirtatious one she'd used on Lakin only moments before. This was the smile Drew recognised as the Perez who would eat Lakin for breakfast given half an opportunity. It was unnerving to see her in action, but he couldn't fault her methods. Her ability to read the situation and pivot had taken him by surprise.

"No, do not mistake my need for your information as a need for you personally."

"You lying bitch!" he spat.

Perez shrugged. "This world is full of people who will use you up and spit you out, Mr Lakin. Take this as a lesson that has cost you nothing more than a little bruising to your more than healthy ego."

He started onto his feet and Drew was out the door, his legs pumping as he crossed the hall. He met Perez as she stepped out of the interview room.

"Lakin?"

She shrugged. "He's fine. Just a little upset." She cocked her head to the side. "But you already know that."

"It's my job, Dr Perez. I have to make sure things don't go pear shaped. Don't take it personally."

She nodded. "I don't." Her expression cleared and she glanced down at the notes held in her hands. "At least now there is somewhere for us to start."

"You think our guy is at the university?" Drew asked as Harriet joined them.

"It's possible." Harriet shrugged. "Although we can't rule out the possibility that this is just another aspect of his game. He might want us to believe that the university is part of his playground thus throwing us off the true scent."

Drew sighed. "We don't have a scent though. The university is the first lead we've had in—"

"Sir!" He turned to see DC Crandell hurrying down the hall toward them both.

"What is it?"

"Sir, we've received a call about a body..."

Drew's stomach sank and he glanced over at Harriet who had turned pale. "You think it's Rachel?"

She nodded.

"It's most likely," Perez said.

Harriet chewed her lip and straightened her shoulders. "I thought we had more time."

Drew glanced down at his watch. "We don't know what time the courier picked those packages up from the university. So our clock is already behind." Turning back to DC Crandell, he jerked his head in the direction of the squad room. "Has DCI Gregson been informed?"

She shook her head. "You're the first person I saw."

"Right, head up and tell him. He's going to be thrilled with the news." Crandell looked a little concerned but did as she was asked. Perez moved after the DC and Drew let them get a head start before he turned back to Harriet.

"This means he already has his second victim." Harriet leaned in toward him.

"We don't know that for sure."

Harriet gave him a sideways look.

A shiver tracked down Drew's spine as his mind conjured the crime scene photographs he'd been studying all day. Soon, there would be a new batch to add to the montage already playing in his head. Scrubbing his hand over his eyes, he tried to push the dark thoughts away.

"Are you all right?" Harriet asked. He noted the way her knuckles had whitened over the files she'd gripped to her chest. He should have been the one asking that question. After all, wasn't this his job?

"I'm fine. Tired."

She nodded. "You don't look like you've had much sleep, even if you did just come off leave."

Drew cracked a smile. "What can I say, Dr Quinn? I play hard and work harder."

Her smile lifted his spirits for a moment before it began to fade around the edges and he knew her mind had taken her to the same dark place his had just returned from.

"We should go," he said finally. "You were right when you said we needed to get ahead of this and we're not going to do it from here."

A COUPLE OF MOMENTS LATER, Drew stood in the middle of the conference room as DCI Gregson gave them a quick debrief.

"The call came in an hour ago, and when campus security went to check it out, they found the body behind the psychology building exactly where the caller had said it would be. We've tried to trace the call, but the trail leads to an old phone box on the outskirts of town."

"Do we have any CCTV in the area?" The question left Drew's mouth before he could stop it.

Gregson shook his head. "They're trying to bring the footage up now but there's a lot of it to go through."

Drew felt his heart skip and he glanced over at Harriet but either she wasn't listening or there was too much going on inside her mind and she didn't register what Gregson had said.

"As soon as they do, we might get lucky and get a glimpse of this bloke."

Dr Perez's expression was unreadable as she sat with her arms folded over her chest. Harriet on the other hand seemed to wear all of her emotions on her face. She bent over the pad she had on the desk next to her and scribbled down several notes and Drew found himself wishing he was standing closer to her so he could see what she was writing.

"SOCOs are already at the scene and they've agreed to let a couple of us go down there."

Before Gregson could volunteer people for the job, Drew put his hand up. "Sir, I think I should go."

Gregson nodded. "Fine, but take Arya with you."

Harriet's head snapped up. "I need to go."

Gregson shook his head. "Absolutely not, Dr Quinn. You're already only here as a courtesy. The fact that this bastard is now dumping bodies behind your place of work only serves to emphasise my point that you're a victim in all of this."

She shook her head. "He chose me to play against. You can't cut me out. Everything he's doing now is for my benefit, I need to see the body before they move it. I need the chance at least, to see inside his head and potentially get a feel for what he wants to tell me."

Gregson opened his mouth to deny her again but Dr Perez chimed in. "She's correct. She should see the body in its current state. Dr Quinn for whatever reason has been chosen by this killer. We deny him his prize now at the peril of this investigation."

Gregson's expression soured and he glanced from one woman to the next before he sighed. "Fine. You can go." He turned to Drew and glared at him as though this was all somehow his doing. "I'm holding you responsible for Dr Quinn, Haskell. If something goes wrong or she vomits on our body, it's your arse on the firing line. Am I clear?"

Drew nodded. "Crystal, sir."

"Good, then get out of here."

Drew didn't need to be told anything further and so he did as he was told. Harriet bent her head toward Dr Perez and the two of them seemed to be deep in conversation.

"You don't think she will vomit on the scene do you, Guv?" Maz asked as he paused next to him.

Drew shook his head. "Nah... Now getting sick on your shoes, well she might just do that."

Maz pulled a face at him and Drew struggled to suppress his laughter. Some people thought it was wrong or weird to have a sense of humour at such a serious time, but Drew had learned over the years that without it, you ran the risk of losing yourself in the darkness.

Still being able to laugh was proof that you were still human.

The moment that left you, it was time to hang up your hat.

CHAPTER TWENTY-EIGHT

ON THE DRIVE UP to the university, Harriet fought to control her emotions. Now, more than ever, she needed them under control or things would rapidly spiral out of hand. And then of course there was the small fact of seeing her first proper crime scene.

She'd been to Bianca's house directly after Burton had got to her but despite being in the vicinity, Drew had been careful to try and protect her from the worst of what had happened. This, however, would be different, and she needed to be ready for it.

Harriet sat in the back seat and fiddled with the pen she'd brought with her. The evening was closing in around them a little too rapidly and she found her mind wandering as she stared out the side windows.

Why had he chosen the university as his dumping ground for Rachel's body? If indeed it was Rachel he'd taken. The bigger question remained, why take Rachel and murder her? He had to know the kind of journalist Rachel was. He had to know the kind of story she'd been working on, why cut that short?

"We're here," Drew said, pulling up at the back of the psychology department. Harriet pulled on the door handle but found it wouldn't budge. Feeling foolish she was forced to wait for Maz to open her door before she stepped out.

"Thanks."

"Sorry about that," he said. "I forgot to take the lock off."

Harriet waved his apology away and turned to where the white vans were parked up next to an area of scrubland. There was a familiarity about her surroundings that triggered alarm bells in her mind.

"Where exactly is the body?" She asked, drawing level with Drew.

He pointed in toward a wooded area that sat in the centre of the scrubland. "Apparently it's over there."

"I guess that explains his anonymous tip."

"You think that was definitely him?"

Harriet nodded. "Just look at this place. Out here nobody would find her, at least not for some time.

The faculty members and some of the students come down and smoke around here but nobody strays out toward the woods."

"You need a suit!" A young man in a Tyvek suit pulled open the back of one of the white vans and pulled three packets free. He passed them over without a word and Harriet took hers.

Getting into the suit was an awkward affair and she was suddenly glad she'd chosen to wear trousers and not a skirt that morning. The idea of having to bunch a skirt up beneath the vaguely transparent material made her cringe and she made a mental note to make sure she wore trousers more often.

"You need to cover your hair, too," Drew said, pausing next to her. He reached out and tucked the stray strands of dark hair back beneath the hood of the white boiler suit. "There."

"Thanks," she said, feeling more than a little awkward. It was moments like that which made her question the kind of relationship that was growing between them. And it wasn't made any easier by the fact that Drew didn't seem to understand it any better than she did.

They passed her a mask and she slipped it on over her head before she pulled on her gloves and covered her shoes. She felt ridiculous, and judging by how the others appeared, she at least knew she wasn't alone in the feeling.

They followed the young man who'd equipped them with their suits across the scrubland toward the copse of trees sitting in the middle of it.

Vaguely, she remembered Dr Baig talking about plans for some kind of development to take place on the piece of land, but nothing had come of it. Now, she found herself wishing they'd made more of an effort to clear it up. As much as she'd disliked what the journalist was doing; the knowledge that this was Rachel's final resting place was an unpleasant one.

As she stumbled along behind Drew, it hit her why the place seemed so familiar.

She came to a juddering halt and Maz very nearly ran into her.

"Shit, sorry," he babbled as he jostled into her back, but Harriet barely heard him. She stood and stared up at the psychology building, her eyes scanned the floors quickly as she counted the windows. Her heart sank as she caught sight of her own office window. How many times had she stood there and stared out over the campus and the scrubland directly behind her?

"What is it?" Drew asked.

"The last place I saw Rachel was in my office," she said quietly.

"Right," Drew prompted but Harriet could tell from the frustration in his voice that he wasn't following along with her line of thought.

"That's my office there," she said, pointing to the third-floor window that sat in the centre of the red brick building.

The harsh intake of breath was the only indication that Drew's thinking had completely caught up to hers.

"He wants me to know every time I look out that window that I failed. He's trying to rub my nose in it."

"You can't know that for certain."

Harriet glanced up at the man next to her. "If this were you and somebody had done this; if they'd placed the body in the exact place where you happened to look every day you went to work what do you think they'd be trying to tell you?"

Drew's lips flattened into a thin line. "Fair enough."

"He's reveling in my failure."

"But we knew he'd taken Rachel," Drew said. "We just never had the chance to save her."

She nodded. "This isn't a game we're supposed to win." Harriet drew in a deep shuddering breath. She'd been wrong, not entirely but wrong enough to make her feel more than a little uncomfortable.

"We knew that already, didn't we?"

She shook her head. "No. Every time he's played this game in the past, the police officers involved have behaved as though this was a game they could win.

He's trying to tell me that I won't win. That no matter what I do, no matter how clever I am, or how quickly I solve the puzzles, I'll never beat him."

Her stomach churned uncomfortably. "Your DCI was right about one thing," she said softly. "Our killer sees me as one of his victims."

She caught the concern in Drew's eyes, and she flashed him a bright smile. "I'm not saying I am. I'm just saying what our guy thinks. He wants me to feel helpless, out of control. He feeds on power and control. To him it's as important as breathing. And just like all good sadists he gets off on the pain and suffering he causes to his victims. Dropping Rachel's body here is his version of leaving me a calling card. A kind of 'f-you' to me and the world in general."

"Do you think Dr Perez was right then?"

Harriet tilted her head upwards to meet Drew's gaze.

"You know, she suggested it might be a former disgruntled patient?"

Harriet shook her head. "I don't think it's quite as personal as that. And anyway, there's no one I've treated clinically who fits this level of violence or who suffers from such a deep sense of persecution."

"Are you coming?" The forensic officer who had moved ahead of them paused close to the entrance to the trees.

"In a minute," Drew snapped.

"It's all right," Harriet said. "We can go on.

There's no point in delaying the inevitable. If I'm going to feed his ego, then I need to see Rachel. I need to see what he's done to her, the punishment exacted on her for my failure."

"This isn't on you, Harriet," Drew said.

"I know that..." She drew in a deep breath and closed her eyes. She hated lying to him but there was no way she could look at everything that was going on and not feel somewhat responsible for it all. It was a flaw within her own personality but no amount of recognising it would ever truly fix it. "Come on, the sooner we get this over with." The rest of the sentence hung unspoken, but she knew he'd understand.

Drew nodded and they continued forward. The bracken grew thicker to either side of them and Harriet found herself studying the ground. What path had he taken into the woods? It was obviously an area he was familiar with. She glanced over her shoulder at the building where her office sat.

"How many times have you stood here and watched me?"

"What was that?" Drew asked.

"Nothing. Just talking to myself again."

He smiled an acknowledgement, but Harriet could see the strain on his face. His desire to protect her would eventually get in the way of them working together. The knowledge hit Harriet like a sledgehammer, and she stumbled over a stray branch that hadn't been cleared from the path.

DS Arya caught her arm before she fell into the bushes and made a complete fool of herself.

"You'll have to stand out here at the observation point," the forensics officer was speaking to Drew as she came to a halt next to them. "Because of the area we thought it best to bring in the palynologist first and let her go over the area."

Harriet glanced past Drew and caught sight of a woman crouched near the ground. She combed through the area, moving quickly and deftly as she swept indeterminate items into vials and gathered samples from the ground water and bracken.

"What can she tell us?" Drew asked the question hovering on Harriet's tongue.

"Professor Briggs focuses on the pollen and other particulate evidence picked up at the scene but mostly the pollen." The forensic officer spoke as though what he was saying should make perfect sense to them.

"I'm sorry but what good is there in knowing what kind of pollen is here? The place is covered in grasses and trees, there's bound to be thousands of pollen spores."

"She can tell us about where the body came from."

Harriet glanced over at the woman again, dressed head to toe in the same kind of suit she wore. She shook her head and watched the woman's slow progress.

"I don't get it," Drew said, sounding more than a little irritated. "This whole place is pollen heaven. All she's doing is wasting time we really don't have."

Harriet wrapped her arms around her body. "Look, it wasn't too long ago that you dismissed what I did as psycho-babble bullshit and now look at us?"

Drew snorted. "What makes you think I don't still think it's all psycho-babble?"

"But not bullshit," Harriet teased, drawing a smile from him. His eyes crinkled up at the corners and Harriet's chest clenched.

"Can you see the body?" Harriet asked, straining to see above the head of the woman crouched on the ground.

Drew nodded and his expression turned serious once again. "Why, can't you?"

She shook her head. "I need to get higher."

The forensics officer glanced over at her and then jerked his thumb in the direction of a small platform they'd set up to one side of the site. "Try the viewing platform. The forensic pathologist was short too."

"It's not Dr Jackson?" Drew asked.

The forensics officer shook his head and Harriet crossed the uneven ground to the platform. Stepping up onto it, she felt the metal stand sway gently beneath her before it settled. She glanced over at the scene and her stomach dropped into her shoes.

"Oh, Rachel..." The words slipped out of her mouth before she could stop it.

"She's in a mess all right," the SOCO said, leaning against the side of the platform. "Until we get in there we won't know if the disarticulation was due to animal interference or if she was dumped here like that."

Harriet nodded, her eyes skimming over the surface of the crime scene. He'd set Rachel out on her back; or at least what Harriet assumed was Rachel. The more she stared at the scene, the more it reminded her of the jigsaw puzzle he'd sent her.

"Something doesn't look right," Harriet said. She stared at the remains of what had been the vibrant young reporter in her office what felt like only moments before.

"Yeah, she's all jumbled up." The SOCO jumped onto the platform next to her, causing it to wobble beneath them both. "There, where her arm should be, that's actually her shin. And he's put her toes where her fingers should be."

"Could animals have done that?" Drew asked.

The SOCO shrugged. "Theoretically. Although, to be honest with you it looks too deliberate to me but until we get in there we can't say for sure."

Harriet swallowed back the bile that coursed up the back of her throat.

"Did he do that to her when she was alive?" Drew looked a little pale beneath the hood of his Tyvek suit, not that Harriet blamed him. She wasn't feeling particularly perky either.

The SOCO stared out at the scene. "Like I said, until we get the go ahead to go in there we won't know for sure and even then, it'll be down to the forensic pathologist to make the call."

Drew held his hand out to Harriet, but she ignored it and hopped down off the platform herself. He gave her an irritated glance and she found herself wondering if perhaps he saw her desire to be independent as a form of her snubbing him? It was entirely possible that a situation like this sent his desire to protect into overdrive. And if her assessment was correct then the fact that she didn't want or need his protection wasn't something he'd even thought of.

"I'm going to go back to the car," she said quietly. "I've seen enough."

Drew nodded. "Maz can take you back."

Harriet shook her head. "I'm fine. I don't need a babysitter."

Drew gave her a once over appraising glance before he inclined his head. "Fine." He fished the keys from his pocket and passed them over to her. Harriet took them gratefully and started back the way they'd come.

As she traversed the uneven terrain, her mind insisted on flashing back to the scene. If she'd had to go up to it Harriet wasn't sure if she would have managed to keep her emotions in check. Perhaps DCI Gregson was correct, and she was too close to this. But how else was she supposed to be considering the situation? Wasn't this where the killer wanted her to be? Wasn't this what he had in mind when he'd sent her the first puzzle.

Reaching the car, Harriet almost got into the backseat when another forensic officer jogged up to her. "We need the suit back," he said.

"What?"

"The suit, the white coverall. We need it back. It has to be returned so it can be logged into evidence."

Harriet glanced down at the suit and nodded. "Sure." She hastily stripped out of the suit and shoved the items into the waiting evidence bag provided by the SOCO. He jerked his head in thanks before he took off back to his post.

Sliding into the backseat Harriet tried to imagine the scene as the killer had wanted it to appear. His deliberate misplacing of the body parts intrigued her but just what was he trying to say? Was it just an extension of the jigsaw as she'd first thought?

Perhaps it was just another way for him to mock her. After all, in his mind, she hadn't figured it out, she hadn't guessed who the victim was.

Was that what this was really about?

Harriet flipped open the file next to her and scanned the notes she'd already made. What if this had nothing to do with his chosen victims? What if they were nothing more than a means to an end. A chance to send her a message.

Everything he'd done so far screamed of a level of narcissism that couldn't be ignored.

Glancing up, she spotted the groups of people gathered behind the police tape and her heart crawled into her mouth. Was he here now? Was he watching the whole sorry event unfold?

It made sense that he would hang around. After all, how would he get his kicks from her reaction if he wasn't here to see it?

Climbing from the car, Harriet moved toward the tape and the people gathered on the other side of it. Would she know him if she saw him? As her eyes fell on him, would a moment of recognition pass between them? If this were a movie, she already knew what the answer would be, but this wasn't a movie.

"Harriet, where are you going?" Drew called to her and she glanced over her shoulder only to see him jogging toward her. She paused and glanced back at the crowd. Who was she kidding? Even if she laid eyes on him right now, she wouldn't know him.

"Are we keeping tabs on the people coming to have a look at the scene?"

He nodded. "A uniform will gather their names. Why?"

She shook her head. "Just a hunch I had."

"Which was?"

"That he's here somewhere. He has to be otherwise how is he feeding his desires?"

"How do you know?" Harriet watched as he automatically clicked into a state of vigilance.

"It's just a hunch. I haven't seen him." She sighed. "But it makes sense, doesn't it? I mean, he has to be here or how else would he get to see our horror over the scene."

"Why would that matter to him."

"He's a sadist, he gains power and pleasure from the suffering of others and that doesn't just apply to physical suffering. For a true sadist they garner just as much pleasure from the suffering of the loved ones and the police involved. Death isn't a barrier to feeding their proclivities, it just increases the potential victim pool."

Drew shuddered. "I've come across a lot of sick bastards but nothing like this."

Harriet smiled up at him. "Count your blessings then."

"Is this the first time you've ever come across it?"

She glanced down at the ground and her mind conjured an image she'd tried to bury. "No. This isn't my first sadist, but this is a first at this level."

As though he could read her thoughts, Drew nodded. "We should go. It's getting late here and there's nothing more we can do for Rachel."

"And the other victim he has?"

"The puzzle is all we've got to fall back on."

Harriet sighed, frustration spreading in her core. "He's holding all the pieces. Without them we just keep chasing after him and I don't like being so far behind."

"You and me both," Drew said as he held open the car door for her and Harriet slipped inside.

CHAPTER TWENTY-NINE

SHOVING the headphones into his ears, he hit *ignore* on the ringing phone and turned the music up. Bending down, he tightened the laces on his trainers before he tugged the door to his apartment open and jogged down the stairs.

Out on the street, he let the sound of the music thrum in his veins as it carried him down the pavement. Reaching the gym, he ducked inside and logged in with his card before he dumped his excess jumper into the locker he'd been assigned.

He glanced down at the phone, only to find the screen littered with messages from Michael. All he'd done since that day in the coffee shop was apologise. Not that Gabriel cared. He was done and moving on. Michael could take his cheating ass and shove it.

Moving through the rows of machines, he paused at the first free treadmill and hopped on. Turning up the speed and incline he let his muscles warm up before he really started to push his body. It wasn't easy but forty minutes later he slipped off the treadmill. His legs felt like jelly and his heart was still hammering in his chest as he headed for the showers.

"Hey!" The voice tugged at something in the back of his mind. Pulling the earbud out, he turned and found himself face to face with the guy from the library.

Gabriel felt a warm smile slide across his face as he let his gaze roam down over the slightly built man in front of him. He had the physique of a long-distance runner, his body hard and honed for stamina and Gabriel could already imagine what he'd use that stamina for if given half a chance.

"Fancy seeing you here," Gabriel said, propping his shoulder against the door jamb.

Chris grinned at him. "Perks of working in the library," he said. "They let me use the campus amenities as much as I want."

"You don't study here?"

Chris shook his head and glanced down at the floor sheepishly. "No, I actually moved back from London. I spent some time down there but it's so expensive to live in the city."

Gabriel nodded. "Tell me about it. I'd love to go to London but like you said it's so expensive. I just couldn't afford it."

Chris smiled ruefully. "Well, I suppose I should

let you get cleaned up... And I need to get a run in before my shift starts."

Gabriel grinned. "I think I feel a study sesh coming on."

Chris' face lit up. "You know I thought the other night you weren't really interested..."

Gabriel's smile slipped. "It's complicated but I'd rather not talk about it."

Chris gazed at him sympathetically. "I can understand that. If you ever want to talk about it, you know where I am."

Gabriel straightened. "I might just take you up on that."

He watched as Chris turned and strode purposefully into the gym. Chris wasn't exactly his usual type, but he could totally see himself getting on board with the other man. If he was lucky, they might even get a little hot and heavy among the stacks. As he sauntered into the locker room Gabriel couldn't keep the grin off his face, it was a total cliché, almost as bad as being hot for teacher.

Slipping out of his clothes, he wrapped the towel around himself and headed for the showers. Beneath the scalding spray he could hear the sound of somebody else in the locker room and couldn't help but hope that it was Chris done with his workout.

Soaping himself up, he washed quickly and wrapped the towel around his waist before he stalked back into the changing room. As he rounded the corner he froze.

The cleaner, the one he'd bumped into at Dr Quinn's had his hand buried in his locker.

"Oi!" Gabriel's voice bounced off the tiled walls of the locker room. The other man looked up, his expression terrified as he found Gabriel bearing down on him. "What the hell are you doing? Get your hands out of my fucking locker."

"I'm sorry, I was just--" The cleaner held the driver's license up as though that card alone could ward Gabriel off.

"Were you trying to nick my licence?"

"No, I was trying to put it back--"

"You fucking scumbag!" Gabriel snatched the card from the other man's hands, and rammed it back into his locker before he turned on him.

"I was trying to put it back."

"You'd only have to put it back if you stole it in the first place," Gabriel shouted, jabbing his finger into the other man's chest.

"I found it the other day. You dropped it--"

"Have you been following me this whole time?"

"No, I wanted--"

"You have, haven't you? You've been following me. That's why you were in the coffee shop the other day too."

The man opposite him shook his head and dropped his hands down by his sides. "I'm telling you.

I was only trying to give it back. You dropped it and--
"

"Get the fuck out of here," Gabriel said, gesturing toward the door. "And if I see you snooping around my things again, I'm calling the police."

The cleaner shook his head, his salt and pepper hair falling into his eyes as he turned and stalked toward the door. "You try to do one good fucking deed--"

His voice faded as the door slammed shut behind him, leaving Gabriel alone in the locker room.

Turning, he opened the locker again and quickly checked through his wallet. There was nothing else missing. He slipped the driver's licence back into its slot and stared down at it. He had taken it out of his wallet... It was entirely possible it had fallen from his pocket that day and maybe he'd just overreacted.

Shaking his head, he gathered up his clothes and dressed as quickly as he could, his heart rate thudded uncomfortably in his chest. What if it wasn't so innocent? What if the guy had been following him?

There had been a vague mention on the news about some killer, but he'd dismissed it out of hand because the last victim had been a female. The police were appealing for any witnesses and Gabriel couldn't help but feel sorry for her family.

As he was pulling on his trainers, the sound of the locker room door flopping shut drew his attention.

Chris slipped inside. "I'd thought you'd be gone by now."

Gabriel shrugged. "I would have but--" At the last moment he changed his mind. Telling the guy he'd just met that he'd been spooked seemed ridiculous.

"What is it? Are you all right?" Chris' face was wreathed in concern and Gabriel felt some of the unease he'd been suffering from lift away.

"I'm fine." He plastered a grin on to his face.

"You don't fancy getting a coffee, do you?"

Chris pulled a face. "I'd love to, but I can't. I've got to make a quick trip into town and then I'm starting my shift at nine."

Gabriel felt his face fall and tried to cover it with a shrug. "Of course, sorry. I shouldn't have--"

"Don't be sorry," Chris said, taking a step forward. "Look, I can't go out for coffee, but you could always come with me. I know it probably sounds cheesy but if you'd like we could get a takeaway coffee from the drive through at McDonalds or..."

Gabriel glanced down at his phone and the messages from Michael that sat there. The thought of leaving the gym and potentially bumping into him just wasn't how he wanted to end his day. Not to mention the thought of seeing the creepy cleaner again. Drawing in a deep breath he nodded.

"Go on, then."

Chris' face lit up. "Perfect, I'll grab my stuff and we can get going."

"Don't you want to have a shower or...?"

Chris grinned at him. "I'm feeling wild so I'm going to skip the shower."

Gabriel leaned in toward him and inhaled the musky scent of his skin. "You still smell good to me."

Chris' laughter filled the changing room and Gabriel returned his attention to his own stuff while Chris got ready.

"Ok, I'm good to go." Chris paused next to him and waved a set of car keys in the air.

Pushing up onto his feet, Gabriel fell into step beside the other man as they headed for the door.

"DO you want to wait here while I get the car?" Chris asked. "It's a bit of walk, otherwise."

Gabriel glanced down at his phone and felt his stomach lurch a little uneasily. Was he really going to do this? Was he really going to get into a car with a veritable stranger?

All the childhood stories warned you about taking candy from strangers and allowing them to lure you into their cars. What they failed to mention was what did you do when the stranger was the candy?

"You know what, I think maybe I'm just going to head home for the night. I've got to be up early in the morning for a lecture."

Guilt crawled up the back of his throat as he watched Chris' face fall.

"I can drop you home, if you'd prefer?"

Gabriel shook his head. "As tempting as that sounds, I think I'll just jog home."

Chris nodded. "Yeah, sure. Of course."

Gabriel reached over and touched his arm. "I'd really like to get that coffee someday soon though, yeah?"

Hope lit in Chris' eyes and he nodded. "I'd like that too."

"Do you have a pen?" Gabriel asked suddenly.

Chris shot him a curious glance but pulled a biro from his backpack. Taking the pen, Gabriel felt his fingers brush against Chris'. Long sensuous fingers like those of a pianist and Gabriel could already imagine just what those fingers could do given half a chance.

Closing his hand around Chris' wrist, he tugged the other man closer and proceeded to print his phone number onto the back of Chris' hand.

"Whenever you want to get that coffee," he said. "You know how to reach me now."

Chris grinned up at him and it took every ounce of Gabriel's control not to close the gap between them and kiss the other man.

Releasing him, he took a couple of steps backward.

"Hey, what about my pen?" Chris asked, raising an eyebrow.

"You'll just have to call me to get it back."

Chris' laughter followed him down across the campus and filled his chest with a warmth he'd been lacking ever since everything went to shit with Michael.

TAKING the short cut towards the park, Gabriel picked up his pace. The evening had closed in and darkness had fallen leaving everything coated in muted shades.

The blow when it came knocked the air from his lungs and he went to his knees, his hands hit the hard tarmac, the grit digging into his skin as he struggled to get his sluggish brain moving.

The second blow knocked him for a loop and stars burst behind his eyelids.

When he came to, he felt the cold press of something sharp against his throat.

"Get up, slowly..." The whispered voice pressed against his ears and his head started to pound as he struggled onto his knees. It was then he realised his hands were bound.

"Slowly."

He did as he was told, the blade on his neck was wickedly sharp and he knew that it would cut him open from ear to ear before he could ever hope to get a word out.

"Over to the van."

He got to his feet and the hooded man next to him kept the blade at his throat.

"You can take my--"

"Sshh," the man said, pressing the tip of the blade a little harder against his neck.

Shit, why had he decided to take the short cut home? He'd blown Chris off because he'd been concerned about getting into a car with a stranger and then he'd thrown it all away by choosing to cut through the park. If he could have his time back, he'd have climbed into the car with Chris. If he'd done that, he'd be safe and warm right now with a cup of steaming coffee in his hands.

They reached the van and Gabriel's heart beat practically out of his chest as the man behind him nudged him toward the back door.

"Open it..."

His head was really beginning to pound and the stranger's voice was distorted. Warmth trickled and tickled down the side of face. The blow had caused his eardrum to rupture, he knew the feeling because it had happened to him when he'd been younger whilst playing rugby. He'd received a kick to the head that had ruptured his eardrum and resulted in a pretty serious concussion.

He reached out with his bound hand and

fumbled against the door handle. The world swam around him but a sticker from the university on the inside of the van door caught his attention.

Gabriel tried to turn then but the blade bit into his neck and he halted his movements. "Get in."

"No."

"Get in the fucking van."

The voice was familiar. His gaze fell on the mop and bucket on their side in the back of the van and his stomach flip flopped.

"Get in the van now."

"No." Something Dr Quinn had once said in a lecture she'd given swam back to him but as he tried to grasp onto the memory it swam out of reach.

"Do it the hard way then."

Something heavy slammed into him and he fell forward into the van. He tried to put his arms out to break his fall, but his body refused to cooperate, either because of the disorientation or the simple fact that his hands were bound.

Gabriel hit the floor of the van hard. He tried to lash out, but the stranger bundled him inside and slammed the door shut.

It was then the memory came back to him. Getting into the back of a van was definitely a bad idea. He was trapped now and at the mercy of his captor. Was there something he was forgetting?

Hands grabbed his ankles, forcing them together.

The cable ties bit into his legs as they were cinched tight.

"I know who you are," he said hoarsely.

"Good," the man said. "That'll make this far more interesting."

Gabriel lifted his head and the world shifted and moved around him.

The stranger's face swam slowly into view.

It was then that Gabriel started to scream.

CHAPTER THIRTY

HE'D BEEN SO close to her that he could have practically reached out and touched her. Her gaze had swept over him and for a moment, he'd wondered if she'd recognise him. Instead, she'd looked through him as though he wasn't even there. He didn't matter to her, didn't matter to any of them. It was a useful ability to have but it didn't exactly sit well with him.

How could they be such idiots? How was it that he could stand there within touching distance and nobody knew?

Deep down he knew the answer. It was easy to him, blending in was something he excelled at.

Not to mention that when you were as clever as he was, fitting in with those around you became infinitely easier.

But he wasn't here to prove he could stand in

front of Dr Quinn and go unnoticed. No, he'd come for a completely different reason.

They'd gone onto the scrubland, their ease with one another insulating them from what awaited them there. It would have been perfect if he could have crept closer, to really watch her when she saw Rachel.

If he could just have seen the look on her face as she realised what she was looking at...

It was the kind of emotional response that could have kept him satisfied for months, maybe even years. She felt it all. It was what made her so perfect for the task ahead. Her deep-seated empathy both a weapon and a curse. She would try to use it against him, and she would fail because emotion and feelings failed in the face of superior intellect and rational thought. Dr Quinn should of course know this but at every turn she seemed to falter.

Perez on the other hand was a far more intriguing piece of work. He'd recognised a kindred spirit of sorts in her. Not that he thought she was capable of the mastery he'd so far achieved in his life but there was something about her that called to him. Her desire for control, for power, it was almost as strong as his own.

She would never achieve everything she had in mind though. While she embodied the ambition needed for climbing, she was much more suited to climbing horizontally and that would never take her to the heights she desired. The men around her would always look at her as nothing more than a hole to fill and satisfy their needs.

Pushing open the door to the sound proofed shed, he flicked on the lights and stared at the young man tied down in the chair. His eyes were swollen shut but that could be remedied. Gabriel needed to see what was coming next. Not that he didn't get a kick from the element of surprise. He'd screamed so beautifully the night before when he couldn't see where his knife would strike next.

Crossing the floor, he turned his attention from his captive audience and took the newest jar down from the shelf. The star shaped piece of flesh floated in the preservative. Already, it had started to lose its colour. Not that it mattered. There would be others, and the memory was so fresh, so vivid in his mind, that he didn't have to reach very far to grasp it.

Rachel had been perfect, his best yet. But the best was yet to come, and he hugged the jar to his chest as he carried it over to where Gabriel sat. He set the jar down on the table next to his workspace and picked up the bloodstained remote, clicking quickly through his selection of music he settled on what he considered the perfect song for his next session.

Music blared from the speakers as Carly Simon's iconic song began to play and Gabriel stirred in his bonds.

"Why are you doing this?" Gabriel's voice was hoarse and almost ragged.

"Because I can..." He leaned in close and sang along to *You're So Vain*, his words causing Gabriel to shrink away from him, at least as far as the cable ties holding him in place would allow.

He picked up the scalpel from the tray and twirled it around his fingers as the music really started to ramp up. And pressed the cold blade against Gabriel's chest. The other man started to tremble.

"Don't hold back, Gabe, we can make such sweet music together."

The knife sank home and he gloried in the sound of Gabriel as he started to scream.

CHAPTER THIRTY-ONE

BACK AT THE STATION, Harriet buried her face in her arms and closed her eyes. They'd been staring at the files for hours now and were still no closer to working out just who was behind the killings.

She crept into the room where DS Arya and DC Crandell had taken up residence to go through the CCTV surrounding the college. As yet, there was nothing out of the ordinary to report.

"If he has another victim, why hasn't anyone reported him missing?" Katerina asked.

Harriet glanced up at the other woman who'd stepped into the room and shrugged. "I guess it depends. Our guy is clever so he's probably picked someone who would be relatively isolated."

Perez dropped into a chair opposite Harriet. "But how isolated are we talking about here because

Rachel wasn't what I would consider isolated and yet she wasn't missed..."

Harriet nodded. It was true. Nobody had called in Rachel's disappearance as suspect which in itself seemed odd. She was a well-regarded journalist working her way up from the bottom, so why hadn't she been missed?

"Drew wants to speak to the boyfriend before the press gets a hold of the story," Harriet said. "He doesn't understand why she wasn't reported missing either."

"And the ID is positive?" Perez asked, as though hoping Harriet would tell her they'd made a mistake.

"The forensic pathologist confirmed it this evening. Plus, he dumped her bag and other belongings along with her body in the woods. They found her car in a parking garage at the edge of town. They seem to think she'd gone there to pick up lunch and we have her on CCTV doing that but once she enters the parking complex she disappears."

"There's no tape?"

Harriet shook her head. "The cameras have been blacked out. Drew thinks maybe youths in the area are responsible, they spray painted over the lens of the camera making it useless. It's becoming more common."

"So, he knew about that in advance?" Perez for the first time since the case had begun actually sounded interested.

"He follows them, stalks them. He's probably been planning this for weeks, months maybe?"

"That's why I don't understand why he chose you?"

Harriet tried to fight the urge to roll her eyes and failed. "Like we said, I've been in the newspapers and--" She cut off abruptly.

What if Perez was right? She was one of the only pieces that didn't truly fit. And if he'd been stalking his victims for months then it didn't make sense as to why he'd chosen her at all.

Perez cocked an eyebrow in her direction. "Well?"

"Maybe you're right..."

"Hallelujah," Katerina said with a smile. "Finally, we can agree on something."

"If he's been following his victims for months then it only makes sense that he would follow his puzzle master for an equal amount of time. Everything is so meticulously planned, he wouldn't leave that to chance, would he?"

Katerina shook her head. "No, I do not think he would."

"But I've only been in the paper over the last few weeks. A couple of months ago I was a nobody."

"So, you think somebody else was supposed to play the part of the puzzle master?"

Harriet nodded and glanced down at her notes. "That's exactly what I'm saying. He always chooses police officers so if I wasn't the initial target, then who else could he have chosen?"

Katerina shook her head. "We are supposed to narrow the pool not widen the net."

Harriet stared glumly down at the desk. "I know. It's just everything about this doesn't quite add up. I feel like we're constantly missing something, and I don't know what it is."

"You like being in control, don't you?"

Harriet shrugged. "Who doesn't?"

Katerina gazed over at her. "If you were to put yourself in the killer's shoes, why do you think he chose you, over all the other potential people he could have chosen?"

Harriet picked up her pen and chewed the tip. "Without knowing who his intended target was, how can I possibly know?"

"But that's the point isn't it? That's the question you need to ask yourself. Why you? What do you offer him that his original choice no longer does?"

Closing her eyes, Harriet tried to block out the images that danced in her head. "I don't know."

"Think about it."

Harriet's eyes snapped open as Katerina climbed to her feet. "There's no need for me to stay here tonight," she said. "I think I'll go home and come back in the morning. Perhaps a fresh set of eyes will help me see things a little more clearly."

Harriet started to answer and then stopped

herself. She couldn't come in the morning; she'd made a promise to Urma and the thought of going back on that now just didn't sit right with her.

"What is it?"

"There's somewhere I need to be in the morning," Harriet said, setting the pen down on the files. "I think I'll stay a little while longer and see if things get any clearer."

Katerina smiled kindly at her as she shook her head. "You'll soon learn that things don't get clearer the more exhausted you become; they only grow muddier."

Ducking her head, Harriet smothered a yawn. "Call me stubborn."

"Stupid is another word that comes to mind," Katerina said as she slipped her jacket on. "But I was young once too."

Harriet glanced over at the other woman and shook her head. "You're still young."

Katerina's laughter was a welcome relief from the seriousness of the situation. "I am not old," she said. "But that is not the same as being young. You will understand this important distinction with time."

Harriet chuckled as Katerina swung her bag onto her shoulder. "Good look with your situation in the morning."

"Thanks."

Katerina nodded and left.

Alone, Harriet stared down at the papers in front

of her. When had everything become so disorganised? Climbing to her feet, she started to sort the files into orderly piles. She gathered each set of crime scene photographs and carefully arranged them into their respective case files.

"How are you choosing us?" Harriet asked herself as she glanced down at another mangled body.

Despite feeling exhausted, she knew if she went home now sleep wouldn't come. Every time she closed her eyes all she saw were the bodies of those he'd murdered doing the Danse Macabre on the inside of her eyelids.

She glanced up as Drew entered the room. "Anything on the CCTV?"

He shook his head. "No but I have tracked down Rachel's partner if you're up for one last trip out?"

"Yeah actually. Getting out of here is the best thing I've heard all evening. I think if I have to sit here with these pictures scattered around me any longer, I'll go mad myself."

Drew nodded. "I know what you mean. This won't be easy. Breaking news like this is always the worst part of the job."

"But you said it yourself, the fact that he hasn't reported her missing is too strange to ignore."

Drew grabbed his coat from the back of the chair and slipped his arms into it. "It is strange. I'd have expected to hear some kind of word from somebody by now but there hasn't been a peep."

From the corner of her eye, Harriet watched him move around the space. How could he do this day in and day out? She wanted to ask him but couldn't find the right words without making it sound utterly ridiculous.

As he paused at the door to wait for her, she couldn't keep the question to herself any longer.

"How do you do this?"

"Do what?"

"This," she said, gesturing to everything laid out. "I mean, how do you keep going and not let it make you jaded?"

Drew shrugged. "I don't know," he said honestly. "I guess some days are better than others. You hold onto those days for when it gets dark."

"You mean like now?"

He gave an abrupt nod. "We should go." Harriet was left with the distinct impression that he'd deliberately ended the conversation and that more than anything he'd said intrigued her.

CHAPTER THIRTY-TWO

HE PARKED the car in front of the block of flats and killed the engine. Harriet studied their surroundings carefully before she climbed out of the car.

"So how did you pick her?" she muttered.

"What?" Drew got out of the car and placed his elbows on the roof of the BMW.

"I'm wondering how he chose Rachel," she said quietly. "I mean, did he stand here one day and pick her out of the crowd, or had he seen her somewhere else?"

Drew shrugged. "I don't know. That's why you're here to figure it out."

Harriet sighed. "Katerina raised a good point earlier."

When Drew didn't interrupt, she took it as a sign to continue. "She questioned again why our killer chose me."

Drew blew out the breath he'd been holding and corrugated his brow with frustration. "She really isn't keen on you."

"I don't think that has anything to do with it," Harriet said. "And I happen to agree with her. Choosing me doesn't make any sense."

"I'm not following," Drew said. "I thought he chose you because of your appearance in the papers and your connection to a high-profile case."

Harriet shoved her hands back through her hair. "It's possible. But look at everything he's achieved so far? We've got to assume he spends some serious time following his chosen targets. Weeks, maybe months. He's meticulous, and he wouldn't leave anything to chance, so it makes sense that he would have chosen them months ago."

Drew pursed his lips. "Fine. Say we go along with this theory. Where does that leave us?"

She shrugged. "Nowhere, really. Unless we can work out who he'd originally planned to use as a puzzle master, it doesn't change anything."

"Come on, then," he said. "We should go and see Paul before the news gets out."

Harriet followed Drew as he led the way up to the apartment where Paul Benson had shared a life with Rachel Kennedy.

Drew sat on the buzzer until the telltale click that somebody had lifted the receiver on the other end sounded.

"Mr Benson, my name is DI Haskell and I'm here with Dr Quinn. I was wondering if we could come up for a chat."

Static sounded on the other end of the intercom. After a couple of seconds, the door clicked and Drew tested it, the door swung inwards, leading into a bare looking foyer.

"Second floor," Harriet said, noting Drew's indecision over whether to take the lift or the stairs. "It's not far up, we can walk it."

His shoulders loosened, and Harriet let him move up ahead of her. There was a distinctly nervous energy about him as he took the steps two at a time, leaving Harriet struggling to keep up. Nobody liked to be the bearer of bad news, but Drew seemed to take that to heart.

She reached him as he paused outside Paul Benson's apartment and then rapped on the door. It swung inwards and a tall thin man greeted them with a broad smile that quickly died on his lips.

"Who are you?" He barked, the irritation on his face evident as he tried to glance past Drew into the hall.

"Where's Rachel?"

"Like I said on the intercom, my name is DI Haskell and this is Dr Quinn..." As Drew said her name Harriet noticed the immediate recognition that flickered across Paul's face.

"What do you want?"

"We were hoping to have a word with you inside," Drew said softly. "You know a Rachel Kennedy?"

Paul's irritation never faltered. "I'm her partner... Look, if you're here because that bitch is prosecuting Rachel then you're wasting your time." He jabbed his finger in Harriet's direction, confirming her initial suspicions that he knew exactly who she was.

"That's not why we're here," Drew tried again. "Like I said, we'd like--"

"Yeah, Rachel isn't here so don't waste your breath with me. I--"

"Mr Benson, we already know Rachel isn't here."

The last caught Paul's attention and Harriet felt her heart clench in her chest as the blood drained from his face. "Yeah, I know she's not here either. I just told you that."

"Can we come in, please?" Harriet asked as gently as she could.

"What is this about?"

"Mr Benson..." Drew said. "Paul, let us in."

Paul stepped aside and Drew moved past him into the hallway. Harriet followed into the small, almost cramped apartment. The living room contained a small two-seater sofa with a multi-coloured throw tossed haphazardly across it.

"You might be better off taking a seat," Drew said.

"Not until you tell me what this is about? Did you arrest Rachel? Was she trespassing again?"

He rattled off the questions as though this wasn't particularly unusual to have police on his doorstep.

"When did you last see Rachel?" Drew asked.

Paul closed his eyes and counted the days off on his fingers. "Tuesday morning," he said. "She was working a big story." He cast a speculative glance in Harriet's direction. "About you actually."

Harriet nodded. "I'm aware."

"Then why are you here?"

"Mr Benson, I'm afraid we've got some bad news regarding Rachel."

"What's she done now? Just tell me."

"I'm sorry to tell you this, Mr Benson but Rachel is dead." Drew clasped his hands in front of his body.

"Nah, you're wrong, mate," Paul said. He shook his head as though that alone could confirm his thoughts. "She's just out on a story is all. You've got this wrong."

Drew shook his head. "We're not wrong."

Paul backed up and shook his head again. "No. She's not dead, she can't be..."

"When we first arrived," Harriet said. "You thought it was Rachel coming home, didn't you?"

He nodded, the look of confusion and panic on his face pulled at her heart. "What made you think it was Rachel?"

"She's always forgetting her keys," Paul said. "I thought she must have forgotten them again and--"

"The intercom doesn't work, does it?" Harriet kept her voice gentle.

Paul shook his head. "No. It buzzes but you can't hear anything the person on the other side is saying. We've been asking the super to fix it for months now, but he hasn't..." He swayed on his feet. "She's not dead."

Harriet filed the detail away. It was such a small thing but perhaps it wasn't as innocent as it first appeared.

"Maybe you should take a seat," Harriet suggested. "I can get you some water..."

His eyes widened and he lunged into the living room. Drew went after him but pulled up short as Paul lifted his phone triumphantly from the small coffee table in the centre of the room. "She's not dead. She texted me, said she was coming home soon. That's why I thought you were her--"

Drew shot Harriet a look of confusion but she was as in the dark about the whole situation as he was. "Can I see her message?" Drew asked, moving further into the living room to where Paul stood with the phone clasped in his hands.

He held the phone out and Drew's gaze scanned down over the screen before he passed the message to Harriet.

"Be home soon, babe. Things going better than I could have hoped. I'm really going to nail this bitch! xoxo"

Harriet scanned the messages above and noted the similarity in them, but it was the time and date stamps that caught her attention and her heart sank.

"Drew, he's been texting him the whole time."

Paul glanced between them both and shook his head. "You're wrong. She texted me. I know Rachel. We've got a code, you see, and I'd know if it wasn't her."

Drew nodded. "You did it so you'd always know she was safe?"

Paul swallowed hard, his Adam's apple bobbing in his throat. "People don't always like what she uncovers. About two years ago, she got into something bad. They roughed her up and it really unnerved her. So now we text regularly. When she's deep into something, she sends me the word apple blossoms, so I know it's her and that everything is all right."

Harriet's stomach lurched as she caught sight of the message he was referring to. "Apple blossoms! I got a new piercing today, can't wait to show it to you when I get home." Harriet turned the message so Drew could read it. "That was sent this morning."

The colour drained from Drew's face as realisation dawned on him, too.

Closing her eyes, Harriet tried to block out the mental images. How could he have done this? Deep down she knew why he'd done it. Keeping in contact with Paul had ensured he wouldn't think anything was amiss by Rachel's absence.

"Tell me where she is." Paul's voice lifted as Harriet opened her eyes again only to find Drew struggling to keep Paul calm.

"She's been taken care of," Harriet said. "I promise you, we're taking the best care of her."

He shook his head. "Stop it. Rachel is alive. She's alive. She's texted me and--" His voice choked off. "You're liars. She said you were a liar and she was right."

"Is there somebody we can call for you?" Drew asked. "Somebody who can come and be with you?"

"You're fucking lying. Where is Rachel? I want to see her! Rachel!"

"Paul," Drew said firmly. He caught the lanky young man by the shoulders and swung him around to face him. "I wish I was lying. But she's gone."

Paul stared at him before his legs buckled beneath him and he hit the ground. From her vantage point, he looked to Harriet like a puppet whose strings had been abruptly severed. As he collapsed, he started to cry, the pitiful sound rising in the room until it was the only sound that echoed in the space.

"Is there someone I can call for you?" Drew asked again.

Harriet glanced down at the phone she still held in her hand and clicked over into the recent contacts.

Paul sobbed and Harriet handed the phone over to Drew who helped the distraught young man to select several of the most recent calls. She watched on as Paul dialled them.

She moved around the flat, pausing at the fridge to stare down at the photograph of Paul and Rachel. He had his arms around her, and judging by the background, they seemed to be somewhere in Thailand. Their smiles lit up the picture, and Harriet felt her heart knock against her ribs again.

Their happiness had been taken, ripped up, and destroyed. And the entire time, the killer had made Paul complicit in Rachel's disappearance.

How had he forced Rachel to give up her secrets? The fact that he'd known to force a passcode out of her suggested a familiarity that went beyond just stalking. Had he interacted with her before? Had they spoken?

It wasn't impossible and his level of knowledge about her life and her movements supported the theory that he was more than just a passive observer.

It didn't take long for the place to fill up and Harriet found the overflow of emotion too much for her already frayed control to handle. Stepping out of the apartment, she found a young woman crying gently outside in the hall.

"I'm sorry," Harriet said, suddenly feeling as though she'd intruded on a private moment.

"No, don't be."

"I'm Harriet." She extended her hand to the woman next to her.

"Alyssa." She swiped her hand over her eyes before she took Harriet's hand and they shook. "I just can't believe she's gone."

Harriet nodded. "How did you know, Rachel?"

"We'd been friends since school. We did journalism together in college, but I wasn't cut out for it, not the way Rachel was."

Harriet smiled sympathetically. "How did Rachel seem to you lately?"

Alyssa screwed up her face. "She was fine. Same old same old, really..."

Squaring her shoulders, Harriet prepared to give her condolences and leave but Alyssa swiped at her eyes again.

"That's a lie."

"What is?"

"Rachel wasn't happy. She was trying to get this big story off the ground, but it wasn't going very well for her."

Harriet fought the desire to ask too many questions. There was so much she wanted to know, so much the other woman could potentially tell her, but she knew that too much now would cause her to clam up.

"Something changed though, didn't it?"

Alyssa smiled through her tears as she sniffed. "Yeah, how did you know?"

"It was just a guess."

"She got a new lead. Some guy who said he could help her get the information she needed. They met up a few times."

"Did she ever tell you who he was?"

Alyssa shrugged. "I think she said his name was Nathan something or other, but it turned out to be bogus in the end. He didn't know anything about the case, Rachel thought he was the one pumping her for information, so she cut off contact with him."

"Why would he have been pumping her for information?"

"Rachel had her suspicions that he was working for a rival magazine. She thought he was trying to scoop her."

Harriet sucked in a deep breath. "She didn't happen to tell you what magazine this might have been?"

Alyssa shook her head. "No, I'm sorry..." She started to cry again in earnest. "She's really gone, isn't she?"

Harriet nodded. "I'm afraid so."

"Shit..."

WHEN DREW APPEARED a couple of minutes later, Harriet was still comforting Alyssa at the door.

The other woman sobbed, her small petite body shaking as the emotion poured out of her.

"We should go," Drew said quietly.

Harriet nodded and tried to extricate herself from the woman's tight grip.

"I don't know what I'm supposed to do without her."

"All you can do now is be there for each other. Paul needs your support more than ever."

Alyssa nodded and sniffed loudly. "I know."

"I've got to go, Alyssa," Harriet said. "DI Haskell and I are going to do our best to find and bring Rachel's killer to justice."

Alyssa reluctantly let her go, allowing Harriet to take a small step backwards.

"You'll catch him though, yeah?"

Harriet nodded. "We're going to try."

"But you've never managed to get him before, what makes you think this time will be different?"

Harriet cast a quick glance over in Drew direction, but he was on the phone. "I can't make promises, Alyssa, it wouldn't be right or fair of me to do that. But I can say this. I'm not going to give up until I get Rachel's killer."

Alyssa studied her face for a moment and Harriet found herself wondering if maybe the other woman had succumbed to shock.

"Good," she said finally, after what felt like an age. "I hope you nail him to the wall."

Pulling away, Harriet smiled and crossed the hall to where Drew stood waiting for her.

"What was all that about?"

"That's Rachel's best friend," she said. "She said that Rachel wasn't particularly happy lately."

Drew cocked an eyebrow at her as they made their way down the stairs. "She's not the only one saying that," Drew interjected. "Paul said something similar inside."

"That's not all Alyssa said," Harriet added. "She said Rachel had been in contact with somebody that she thought had come from a rival publication."

Drew cast her a sideways glance as they pushed out into the crisp night air. "How does that help us?"

"I don't think he was from another magazine," Harriet said. "I think she met with her killer. I think he used his time to get close to the victims in the lead up to his abducting them."

Drew started to shake his head and then paused. "Wait, so you don't just think he's been stalking them?"

It was Harriet's turn to shake her head. "No. Look at the text messages he sent to Paul. He knew Rachel."

"Or he tortured her for the information."

"Look," Harriet said. "I'm not saying he didn't torture her to get the passcode from her, but the fact remains that he knew she had one in the first place. I mean, think of it logically would you have thought to ask her if she had a secret code that she shared with her boyfriend so they both knew they were safe?"

Drew glanced down at the ground. "I suppose not, no."

"No," Harriet said. "I think he spends time with them. Gets to know them and their lives. He inserts himself into their world and when that ultimately fails because it always will that's when he turns to stalking them."

"What do you mean it ultimately will fail?"

Harriet shrugged. "There are some excellent actors in this world, but I don't think our guy is the best one out there. It takes real effort to know somebody, to befriend them and get to know them and that's a ruse he could only keep up for so long before it would fall apart."

"You mean you don't think he's capable of fitting in with other people?"

Harriet shook her head. "Enough to skate by on. But anyone with such a deep-rooted sadistic streak as he's got, it's not something you could hide from people who were too close to you. Plus, I don't think he'd want people close to him, all that would do is cramp his style. He needs time alone so he can spend it with his victims."

"So, he's just your regular joe weirdo then?"

Harriet smiled. "I never promised you a perfect profile, DI Haskell."

"But it sounds like every other one out there. We need something to narrow this down."

Harriet chewed her lip. "We need to find out what his connection is with the university."

"You mean, aside from you?"

A cold shiver raced down her spine. The thought that their killer's connection with the university was all because of her didn't sit well with her.

"Yeah, aside from me."

Drew nodded and then glanced over at her a little more deliberately. "You should get some kip. You look as good as I feel."

"Thanks," Harriet said with a rueful smile. She stifled a yawn, he was right about one thing, if she was going to drive to Kirkbridge then she needed at least some sleep.

"I can drive you home?"

She nodded. "That'd be great, thanks."

Drew ducked his gaze toward the ground and Harriet climbed into the front seat next to him. As he started the engine, she cast another look up at the block of flats and suppressed a shiver. Just how many lives was he willing to ruin in order to get his kicks? It seemed difficult to believe there could be somebody so callous out there, but Harriet knew it was true.

There were those in the world who tried to make it better for all concerned; people like Drew who strove to protect those he perceived as vulnerable. And then there were those like their killer whose soul mission in life seemed to be the complete and utter annihilation of everything good.

As she pressed her head back against the seat, Harriet couldn't let the image of Paul and Rachel smiling and happy together go from her mind.

The more she thought about it, the more she knew she wasn't wrong when she'd first described his motives as being driven by a kind of *schadenfreude*.

He'd seen Rachel's happiness and envied her for it and that envy had created only one driving force in his mind.

The desire to destroy it.

To rip her happiness and joy away and leave nothing but a gaping void in its place.

CHAPTER THIRTY-THREE

DREW PULLED up outside the house and spotted the unmarked police car parked on the other side of the road before he turned to look at Harriet. It hadn't occurred to her to ask for a protective detail, which seemed to be pretty typical of her. She spent so much time lost in her own thoughts that the day to day occurrences that went on around her all but went over her head sometimes, or at least that was how it looked to him.

And that was where he came in. Things like having an unmarked car sitting on her residence were his job. Not that it felt like enough.

The thought of waving her into the house now and driving off filled him with dread.

He studied her face in profile beneath the glare from the streetlamps that filtered through the car windows. She'd fallen into a fitful sleep on the drive over and as he sat there, he found himself not wanting to wake her up. Tentatively, he reached over and brushed a strand of hair back from her face. She stirred and scrubbed her hand over her nose. Her eyes opened, and she glanced groggily up at him.

The moment was broken as her gaze focused and she sat up suddenly. "Sorry, I didn't mean to fall asleep."

He shook his head. "Don't worry about it. I don't blame you."

She stifled a yawn behind her fist. "I didn't think I'd sleep to be honest. I can't get it all out of my head."

Drew nodded. "I know how you feel."

He stayed silent as she grabbed her bag from the footwell and gripped it in her lap.

"Do you want me to come with you tomorrow?" His question hung between them and Harriet's silence worried him. Turning his head he glanced over to find her studying her hands in her lap.

"As much as I'd love that, I think you need to stay here. At least one of us needs to be here to keep things progressing forward."

"Right." He swallowed past his injured pride and tried to see it from her point of view. She was right, of course. They had an active case. He couldn't just go swanning off to do other things, no matter how well meaning they might seem.

She pressed her fingers against his arm, causing the hairs on the back of his neck to stand to attention.

"It's not that I wouldn't want you there. I just think we both need to focus."

"You're right," he said, plastering a smile onto his face. Christ but he needed to get a grip, one minute he couldn't bear to be around her and the next he didn't want to be apart from her. "Somebody needs to keep them on track at the station."

She glanced down into her lap and he fought the urge to break the amicable silence.

"I'll be back tomorrow afternoon," she said. "As soon as I can get away."

"Take your time, there's no rush." He shot her a sideways glance. "You know what I mean."

She smiled and pushed on the door. "I do." He watched as she got out and fought the urge to go after her. The uniforms had done a sweep of her house already and given the place the all clear. There was no reason for him to hang around.

Reaching her front door, she turned and lifted her hand in salute. *Just drive away, Drew. Leave now before it gets weird.*

He waved back and started the engine. Harriet pushed open the door and stepped into the dark hall, all but disappearing from sight. His heart skipped in his chest as the door slammed shut and he was left outside in the car.

"One, two, three," he counted aloud. It wasn't that far into the living room; shouldn't she have clicked on a light in there by now? It wasn't as though she could see in the dark.

He pushed open the car door and prepared to climb out as a light in the upstairs clicked on. His heartbeat returned to something approaching a normal tempo and he pulled the door closed after him.

He was letting his imagination get away from him and it was causing him to worry unnecessarily. But he couldn't help it. The case brought it all back to him. He'd failed Freya, failed to protect her from her own demons and that had ended in tragedy. He couldn't let the same thing happen to Harriet. The last case had very nearly caused it all to fall apart and now every time he closed his eyes all he could see was her panicked jerky movements as she'd fought with the noose.

He definitely needed to get a grip.

Drew sat there, the seconds ticking by, until the light in the upstairs room in the house clicked off plunging the house into darkness. Only then did he put the car in gear and drive away.

CHAPTER THIRTY-FOUR

THE ALARM BLARED NEXT to her head, and Harriet shuffled to break free of the nightmares that plagued her. Pushing up out of the comfortable blankets and pillows she'd buried herself in, she grabbed the phone and switched off the alarm.

Six-thirty am. The time blinked up at her, unrelenting and utterly unforgiving of the little amount of sleep she'd managed to get. But she *had* slept, which seemed like a miracle in itself.

Pulling herself to the edge of the bed, she let her feet hit the floor with a dull thud as she scrubbed her knuckles into her eyes. The photographs on the floor drew her eye, and she slipped from the bed and sat on the wooden boards as she picked them up and tried to arrange them into something approaching a neat pile.

The image at the bottom snagged her attention,

and she scooped it up. The date on it told her it was a crime scene photo from one of the first murders the Star Killer had committed; if not the very first murder.

It was sloppier than Rachel's had been, a point of fact that stuck out to Harriet. Where Rachel's had been meticulous and organised in its presentation, the photograph of this murder scene showed just how much more haphazard it was.

He'd been learning and honing his skills.

Scrabbling through the other papers, Harriet searched for the corresponding documentation which would tell her the name of the first victim. She pulled the file out from its hiding place underneath the chair next to her bed and flipped through the forensic pathologist's report of the gruesome crime.

Words like *tentative*, and *hesitation*, stuck out. He was definitely learning the ropes with this first kill. But the report also told her something else about his crime.

Had he found the murder so difficult because this was somebody he knew?

Scanning down through the notes, Harriet found the sheet she'd been looking for and pulled it free of the stack.

Valerie Rosen had been the first victim to have been claimed by their Star Killer. Harriet glanced over the report and found it to be difficult reading. The attack had been almost animalistic and frenzied in its nature. It bore none of the hallmarks they'd come to associate with the Star Killer.

Not only that but all the mutilations had taken place after the victim was dead which didn't completely fit with the idea that this was a deeply sadistic individual.

She read a little further and dug out the images for the second victim. Ben Kingslow had not suffered the same level of brutality that had been inflicted on Valerie. According to the pathologist's report, he'd died of a traumatic vascular injury to the neck as a result of repeated attempts at strangulation.

It had been posited by the pathologist who had conducted the examination that Ben had slipped into a state of unconsciousness shortly after the ligature had applied the pressure to his neck and he hadn't regained consciousness.

"What were you trying to do? Was this just you learning to find your way in this world?"

Considering the level of sophistication used on their most recent victims it stood to reason that the killer had been quite young when the first murders had been committed. But it also suggested that their perpetrator couldn't possibly have slipped by unnoticed by society.

Somebody who possessed this level of rage wouldn't be able to keep it hidden. It would spill out into their everyday lives.

Control would come later with experience.

"So where were you hiding?"

A sentence further down the page drew her eye and Harriet felt her heart lurch in her chest. The third victim had definitely been a step outside out of his usual pattern which supported her theories about the killers age and experience.

Murdering the puzzle master set the first cycle of deaths outside the methodology of the cycles that followed later.

Harriet flipped through the pages of statements and reports and found the written account submitted by the woman who had been the puzzle master. Her initial interview after she'd received the first note from the killer was cogent and well put together.

The next statement seemed, at least to Harriet, as though it were a little more haphazard but that was to be expected. Receiving the kinds of packages that the Star Killer enjoyed sending would cause anybody distress, and that had fed through into the statements.

However, there was something about the name Rosemary Cline which stood out. As she sifted through the corresponding images which accompanied the statements, Harriet felt her chest constrict.

The final crime scene photograph she came across sent her stomach plummeting into her boots. The first cycle of three had been imperfect in many ways. He had been a novice, unsure in his ability to kill his victims.

And not only that but in the first cycle he had murdered his puzzle master. Harriet sat back against the edge of the bed and closed her eyes.

Why murder Rosemary? Was he punishing her for failing to complete the puzzle?

Or had the motivation been something much more personal?

Pushing up onto her feet, Harriet snatched the phone from the bed.

Seven thirty am. A whole hour had just slipped by without her even noticing. Panic stirred in her chest as she called Drew's number.

The call clicked into voice mail and Harriet groaned in frustration. When she next saw him, she was definitely going to give him a piece of her mind over the full bloody mailbox.

Grabbing a pen from the pile next to her bed, she scribbled a few notes down on the back of an envelope, at least with it written down she wouldn't forget any of the pertinent information.

She dropped the pictures back onto the bed and hurried into the shower. As she stood beneath the spray of water, she struggled to remember where she knew the name Rosemary from.

There was something terribly familiar about it but no matter how hard she tried to get her exhausted brain to remember it refused.

In the end, she closed her eyes and enjoyed the scalding spray that beat down on her from above.

IN THE CAR later that morning, her phone started to ring but Harriet ignored it as she directed the car around the twisting back roads that led to Kirkbridge. Pulling into a farmer's gateway she lifted the phone from the passenger seat and flicked open the display. Drew's name appeared on the screen and she quickly called him back.

He answered on the second ring. "I was going to send you a message," he said, sounding as exhausted as she felt.

"What's wrong?"

"Nothing," he said. "We went over the CCTV from the time the call was made, and we think we've got our guy caught on camera." Harriet's heart stalled in her chest.

"You've seen his face?"

"No," Drew said, blowing out a harsh breath signalling his frustration. "He knew where the cameras were positioned. He kept his head down, and the hood pulled up on his jacket."

"What about putting out a call to the public with a still from the CCTV?"

"I'm telling you, Harriet, it would be pointless. He's dressed all in black. You can't see anything other than the fact that he's white."

"I suppose fingerprints are out of the question?"

Drew's barking laughter told her everything she needed to know. "He wore gloves."

"Of course he did." Harriet pushed her hand absentmindedly back through her hair, causing her curls to stand to attention on her head. "So, we're back to square one?"

"Not exactly," he said, sounding somewhat more upbeat. "You're never going to guess what's looking hopeful?"

"You know I don't like guessing games, so you may as well tell me."

"The palynologist thinks she might have a rough profile of where he is."

"What? How?"

"She reckons she has several samples which she took from the body that don't match where Rachel's body was dumped. She thinks she can narrow down a geographical area."

Harriet felt the tension in her shoulders slowly loosen. "You mean we might get to him before he kills his second victim?"

"Don't get your hopes up, but it's looking a lot more positive."

Gripping the steering wheel with one hand, Harriet pressed her face down against the back of her hand and closed her eyes. It was the best news she'd had all morning.

"You tried to ring me earlier," Drew said.

"Yeah, I had a thought after I woke up."

"Go on."

"The first murder cycle. It's the only time he broke his pattern."

"What do you mean broke his pattern? There wasn't a pattern to speak of then."

"I know but hear me out. We can see the pattern he was creating now because hindsight is twenty-twenty and all that."

Harriet took Drew's silence as a sign she should carry on. "But in his first cycle he was just learning the ropes. But what if that's not all he was doing. What if, because he was so inexperienced and young, he murdered someone close to him as a kind of practice?"

"And you think one of the first three victims was a kind of dry run?" Drew didn't sound as convinced as Harriet would have liked.

"You think I'm barking up the wrong tree, don't you?"

"I'm not saying your theory doesn't have merit."

"But?"

"But, would he be so sloppy? I mean this guy has been around a long time. Would he make such a huge mistake?"

Harriet sighed and pinched her fingers against the bridge of her nose.

"I posited originally that I believe him to be somewhere in his mid-thirties to late forties. Eighteen years ago, that would have made him a teenager if we say he's thirty-five now."

"He would have been seventeen, Harriet, that's very young for something so brutal."

She shook her head before she realised he couldn't see her. "Go back and look at the files. I'm telling you it's all there. With the first victim, the wounds were proceeded by hesitation marks and the worst of the mutilations were inflicted after she'd died."

"You think he was experimenting?"

"Yeah, I do. And for his second victim he chose a man, but I think he underestimated the strength required to restrain a man the size of Ben Kingslow."

Drew sighed. "Right, but wouldn't it make sense that his very first murder victim was the trial run? Making that one the person he knew?"

"You could be right." Harriet said, she couldn't shake the feeling that they were missing something important. "He chose a female police officer to be his puzzle master, a Rosemary Cline."

"Why is that name so familiar?" Drew asked.

"It's familiar to me too," Harriet said but I'm sure how I know the name.

"What's so special about this Rosemary? Don't tell me you want me to track her down and bring her in for questioning? Because I'm honestly not sure if going back that far is going to help us find our guy. Rosemary could be anywhere by now."

"No, I don't want you to track her down," Harriet said. "I already know where she is."

"How do you know where she is?"

"Rosemary is dead. When he first started killing, he murdered his puzzle master. Now, I don't know about you, but that sounds to me like it might have been personal."

Drew was silent on the other end of the line and Harriet drummed her fingers against the dashboard as she waited for him to answer her.

"Do you think you're at risk, Harriet?"

"No," she said. "He has moved on since then. All of his puzzle masters survive, that's not why I tried to ring you."

"What then?" Harriet couldn't be certain, but it sounded to her as though there was a hitch in Drew's voice, as though he was strained.

"I'm saying, I think he knew Rosemary somehow. There was something different enough about her, different enough that he murdered her because of it."

Drew sighed. "If Rosemary was a police officer, do you know how many cases she was probably involved in? How are we supposed to trawl through all of that?"

Harriet felt her body slump in the seat. "Drew, I'm feeling really positive about this. Looking back over the photos this morning, I really think we need to look into Rosemary's life. Maybe she reported somebody stalking her or?"

"Fine, leave it with us here. You've got a tough morning ahead of you. Stop worrying about the case and say goodbye to your friend."

She knew he meant it with kindness, but she couldn't help but feel the sting of the dismissal in his words. "We've got this under control here, I promise."

"I'm not doubting your ability to work the case without me," she said, a little more abruptly than she'd intended. "I'm just trying to help."

"I know," he said. "And we appreciate it. But we need to focus on moving forward."

Harriet bit her tongue and nodded before she realised he couldn't see her through the telephone. "Fine. I'll speak to you later."

"Don't rush back," he said. "I mean it. We've got this."

"Okay." She hung up and dropped back against the seat. It was hard not to take it personally. Was he still holding his grudge toward her over Freya's death? She couldn't blame him if he was; it wasn't exactly something you could just get over.

As she sat there in the car in the middle of the North Yorkshire Moors, she suddenly wished she was back at the station. Even though she'd made little to no progress there the day before, it had still felt as though she was in the thick of things. She hated feeling as though she was behind on things and being so far away amplified all of her fears.

The killer had chosen her to be his puzzle

master. Everything that had happened to Rachel--no matter what Drew claimed--was on her. And whatever the killer was at that moment doing to the next victim was also on her.

"This is what he wants, Harriet. Don't give into it." That was definitely easier said than done. Indicating, she pulled out of the gateway and back onto the road. Gripping the steering wheel, she let the familiarity of her surroundings draw her toward Kirkbridge as she struggled to affix a smile to her lips. The last thing she needed was to turn up at Bianca's parents with a dark cloud hanging over her. Urma wouldn't appreciate it, and neither would Tilly.

"They've got this, Harriet. Just let them do their job."

She sucked in a deep breath and fought to settle her mind. Not everything was her fault and not everything was her responsibility but that, as she was beginning to learn, was definitely easier advice to give than it was to take.

CHAPTER THIRTY-FIVE

DREW KILLED the call and fought the urge to hop in the BMW and follow her up the road. The last thing she needed right now was to have him hanging over her like some sort of brooding cloud. Better to stay here and focus on the task at hand. If there was a problem, then the protection detail which had gone with her would be able to handle it.

"Everything all right?" Crandell asked as she paused next to him. Drew glanced over at her and tried to hide his surprise. The others didn't need to know how distracted he was by Harriet's absence; there was enough gossip floating around in the station without his behaviour adding arms and legs to it.

"Fine," he said. "That was Harriet. She has a theory."

Crandell sighed. "Another one?"

Drew glared at her, but she met his gaze head on. "Come on, guv, we're drowning in theories here. We need something concrete we can act on, not more opportunities to chase our tails."

He couldn't fault her; whether he wanted to admit it or not, she was right.

"This one is worth looking into," he said. "She was looking through the old reports..." Drew ignored Crandell's long suffering sigh. "She says that when the Star Killer first emerged, he didn't stick to the pattern the way we know it now."

That seemed to get Crandell's attention and she cocked an eyebrow at him. "You mean he did something different?"

"Specifically, he murdered his puzzle master."

"I don't remember seeing that," Crandell said, sounding somewhat chagrined. "I must have missed it."

"Well, you weren't the only one. We all missed it."

She nodded. "What does Dr Quinn think it signifies?"

"She thinks our killer must have known his puzzle master. Harriet, I mean, Dr Quinn seems to think murdering her signifies a personal relationship of sorts."

"Please don't tell me this victim was another police officer."

Drew nodded. "I'm afraid so, which means the

suspect pool, if Dr Quinn is correct in her suspicions, just grew exponentially."

Crandell blew out a long breath. "Shit. Is there any way for us to narrow the field?"

"Start with whatever Rosemary was working on at the time. Once we've got a brief overview, I think we can start narrowing it down pretty quickly. You know, ongoing investigations, offenders who were locked up, etc."

Crandell nodded glumly. "Guv, can I ask you something?"

Drew hesitated, the tone of her voice concerned him, conversations that began with; 'can I speak to you,' or 'can I ask you something'? tended to never end well. But if he was to get a chance at joining the task force as Burroughs and Gregson had mentioned then he was going to have to learn to lead a bit better than he was.

"Go ahead?"

"Are we going to catch him?"

"What do you mean?"

"I mean, look at all the officers who tried and failed in the past. What makes you so sure this time we'll catch him?"

Drew shrugged. "I could ask the same question of myself every day of the week that I came into work. Nothing is ever guaranteed but I've got to believe in the strength and the fortitude of the men and women I work with. So long as we each put our all into the cases, we get results. That's all that matters."

"But how do you stop yourself from feeling disappointed when you don't get the result you want?"

Drew shrugged. "I don't. But disappointment is a part of life. Without it we don't learn or grow. I might not like it but it's necessary and so I don't let it slow my overall progress."

Crandell stared at him. "You know, you're beginning to sound a lot like Dr Quinn."

Drew shrugged. "If she's rubbing off on me, that's not a bad thing." His face broke into a wide smile which caused Crandell to shake her head as she strode away.

Her question was simply the same kind of question he'd been asking himself over and over. Would they catch him? And why would they get lucky when the others had failed?

It was a sobering experience and he did his best to push the thoughts from his mind as he headed for the conference room.

CHAPTER THIRTY-SIX

"IT'S SO good to see you again, Harriet," Urma said as she pulled her in for another bone crushing embrace. It was the second one she'd been subjected to since she'd arrived at the house after the funeral service.

The moment Urma had laid eyes on her, she'd insisted on getting her coffee and something to eat. No matter how much Harriet protested, the other woman wasn't interested in her excuses. She'd been forced to consume two slices of Victoria Sponge.

Until she'd put the first piece into her mouth, she hadn't realised just how hungry she actually was. The case, which had consumed her every waking moment, hadn't exactly left her with the time or the inclination to have an appetite, and perhaps breaking her forced fast with a rich, cream and jam stuffed, slice of cake hadn't been the best idea.

"I'm so glad you asked me to come," Harriet said quietly, as she carefully extricated herself from the hug.

"Of course I asked you to come. You were Bianca's best friend. Not having you here would have been a travesty."

Harriet glanced down at the floor as the guilt began to claw its way up the back of her throat taking the form of a half-digested bite of sponge cake.

"She'd have really loved the service," Harriet said, struggling for something suitable to say.

This was one area where she always tended to falter and fall apart. It was also the place where Bianca would sweep in and rescue her from putting her foot completely into her mouth. But Bianca wasn't here to rescue her now. "I'm sorry I couldn't say something."

Urma nodded and glanced away which only heightened the guilt Harriet felt. Just another aspect where she'd failed Bianca.

The moment she'd arrived at the church, she'd known standing up in front of the congregation to give a speech was out of the question.

Her mind was far too scattered and fragmented, and her memories of Bianca were all blurring into one another, making it almost impossible to differentiate one from the other.

Getting up there would only have led to disaster,

and that was the last thing Harriet wanted to put the family through. They didn't need to see her babbling to herself or see her breaking down in tears. She should be the one comforting them, not the other way around.

"Bianca always did understand that your job was a complicated one," Urma said not unkindly. "She told us you were working at a university, now."

Harriet nodded. "I am, but I do a little consulting with the police on some of their more complicated cases."

Urma nodded. "I can't imagine how difficult that must be. All those poor people..." She sniffed and pressed a tissue to her nose. "When we saw you'd almost lost your life to that monster too..." Tears glistened in her eyes, and Harriet felt a pang of regret. Had she misread the situation?

Perhaps they would all have been better off if she'd never come at all; after all, her presence was nothing more than a reminder that she had survived, when their child had not.

"The police were very good after Bianca passed," Urma continued, her voice gaining a little strength as she changed the direction the conversation had taken.

"I'm glad to hear it," Harriet said.

"You might tell them that we appreciate it," she said. "The police, I mean, and how they were..."

"Of course I will," Harriet said.

"You spoke to her," Urma said softly. "I mean, before it happened."

"I spoke to her a couple of days before," Harriet said.

"How did she seem to you?"

Harriet glanced over at the other woman in surprise. "She was happy."

"Was she?"

The last thing she wanted to do was begin to pry into Urma's business, but Harriet couldn't ignore the hope and pain reflected in the woman's face.

"She was. She'd met someone new."

Urma closed her eyes and pressed her hand to her mouth. Her shoulders shook gently as her body was slowly wracked with sobs. Harriet waited until she got herself back under control before she spoke.

"She loved you, you know?"

Urma stared down at her hands and shook her head. "We'd had a falling out."

"What about?"

"Tilly, of all things," Urma said with a smile. "We wanted to take Tilly with us in the summer. We're going to France so we thought we could make it a real family trip. I happened to mention to Tilly that Disneyland might be on the horizon, if she was a good girl."

"But you hadn't mentioned it to Bianca, first?"

Urma shook her head. "It was stupid of me, and I didn't think that Bianca might already have plans."

Harriet nodded and stared down at her own hands folded over in her lap. "She would never have held it against you, you do know that don't you?"

"She was so angry. She told me I was constantly trying to control her life, that I was always showing her up in front of her own daughter... I wasn't trying to do that. I was only thinking of how nice it might be."

Harriet took Urma's creased hand in her own. "She knew that. She was just angry. We both know Bianca had a temper and when she lost it, she really lost it."

Urma nodded.

"Do you remember the time I borrowed her top in high school and it ended up with a hole in the end of it?"

Urma started to laugh in spite of herself. "Oh, she wouldn't speak to you for days after that."

Harriet nodded ruefully. "I tried to tell her it was an accident, but she'd decided I'd done it deliberately."

Urma dabbed at her eyes with the tissue, which was slowly beginning to disintegrate. "She really knew how to hold a grudge."

"But I know she loved you. That was unwavering, no matter how angry she might have been. Given the opportunity she would have come around."

"I know that," Urma said softly. "Deep down I know that, but I can't shake the guilt. I didn't get to say goodbye to her. My last words to her were spoken in anger and I'm not sure I can ever forgive myself for that."

Harriet sighed. "It's not my place to tell you how to feel and I wouldn't even begin to try at this time, but I can tell you that Bianca wouldn't want you being so hard on yourself. It would hurt her to know you felt like this."

Urma swallowed hard. "I pray to her now. Every night. I just want a sign, one sign from her that she forgives me."

"You were already forgiven."

Urma smiled but it was tinged with sadness and pain. "I just wish I could go back and tell her I loved her."

"I know," Harriet said. And in her own way she did know. If she could have had her time back, there would have been so much she might have done differently. She'd have driven up to see Bianca that week rather than waiting for the weekend when it was too late, but those were her regrets to carry with her.

There was no changing the past, only moving ahead into the future and if Harriet had learned anything from her time as a psychologist, carrying guilt with you led to nothing but destruction.

"She loved you like you were her own sister," Urma said suddenly.

"She was my sister," Harriet said. "At least in every way that mattered."

Urma nodded and pushed onto her feet. "I suppose I should go and speak to a few of our other guests or they're going to think I'm deliberately ignoring them."

Harriet let her go and sucked in a deep breath. Closing her eyes, she pressed her head back against the cushion on the back of the chair. Being back in the house where Bianca had grown up, where they'd spent time together in their youth was a blast from the past and Harriet wasn't entirely sure if she was comfortable with all the feelings it had conjured up for her.

Climbing to her feet, she slipped from the room unnoticed and headed for the garden.

The patio steps were rain slicked as she made her way down them carefully. The familiar creaking of the old swing behind the garden shed drew her forward.

Tilly sat on the rotting wooden seat, her short legs barely touched the ground and Harriet caught sight of the tufts of mud the little girl had dug into furrows with the tips of her patent black shoes.

Her hair was pinned back in a neat plait and with her gaze cast down toward the ground Harriet couldn't help but see Bianca in every line of her small rounded face.

Harriet's gaze fell on the bear lying face down in

the dirt and fought the urge to pick him up before he was ruined by the mud.

"Hi, Tilly."

The little girl shrugged as though that action alone could rid her of the greeting.

"Can I sit with you?"

Tilly gave another small shrug of her shoulders, and Harriet settled onto the edge of the wall next to the shed. It was strange to sit with Tilly, as though someone had come and snatched the real little girl away and left behind this strangely silent doll in her place.

"How are you feeling?"

"Sad..."

Harriet nodded. "I'm sad too."

Tilly lifted her chin and gave Harriet a quick once over before she returned her gaze to the ground. "Nana says Mummy isn't going to come home."

"Nana is right." Harriet hated that this was the conversation she had to share with Tilly, but she also understood the truth no matter how painful it might be was better than a lie right now.

"She says Mummy has gone to Heaven," Tilly said. "But I don't want her to go to Heaven. I want her here with me."

"So do I." Harriet shuffled a little closer on the wall. "I wish your mummy was here more than anything else in this whole world." Harriet glanced down at the bear in the dirt.

"Do you want me to pick your bear up?"

Tilly shook her head so hard her plait rattled from side to side. "No."

"He's going to get dirty."

"I don't care."

Harriet remained silent and waited for the little girl to explain her reasoning.

"Nana says I'm being silly, but I know I'm not."

"Silly about what?"

"She says I shouldn't blame him..."

Harriet cocked her head to the side as Tilly lifted her solemn brown eyes and met her gaze head on. "It's Gruff's fault you see."

Pretending she knew what Tilly was talking about, Harriet nodded. "Do you want to tell me what he did?"

"He was supposed to look after Mummy, and he didn't."

It was a simple and straight forward explanation, but it served to break Harriet's heart into two pieces. She watched as Tilly proceeded to kick more mud onto the defenceless bear's back.

"Tilly, I'm afraid there are somethings that not even Gruff can do. I don't think he meant to let you down."

Tilly shook her head and glared over at Harriet. "I hate him. I hate him so much because he let Mummy die." There was such emotion in Tilly's small voice that Harriet had to fight her desire to go to the small girl and wrap her in a tight hug.

But that wasn't what she needed now. What she needed now was somebody to listen to her, commiserate with her but not smother her volatile emotions.

"I can see that you would."

Tilly looked down at the ground again. "You don't think I'm silly for hating him?"

Harriet shook her head. "No, love, I don't think that's silly at all."

Tilly sniffed loudly and hopped down from the swing and before Harriet could even prepare, Tilly threw herself against Harriet's chest. Her tears soaked through Harriet's blouse and her small body trembled and shook as she let go the terrible emotions she'd been holding inside.

Wrapping her arms tightly around the little girl's fragile form, Harriet rocked her slowly from side to side and stroked her hand down over the back of Tilly's silky hair.

"Your mummy is so proud of you, Tilly. She loved you so much."

The little girl sniffed loudly. "Will I get to see her again?"

Harriet's heart stalled in her chest as she contemplated what she should say to her. In the end she chose to give her the hope she seemed to be looking for. "I'm sure someday you'll see her again, but it won't be for a very long time."

"Why not?"

"Because it's important to Mummy that you grow up to be a big girl. She wanted you to be happy, Tilly. To have a good life, a job you loved, friends; lots and lots of friends. And maybe when you were old enough if you wanted, a family of your own."

"I don't think I want that," Tilly said softly. "In case I have to go to heaven like Mummy did and then they would be alone like I am now. I wouldn't want them to be sad like me."

There was nothing Harriet could say to the little girl's quiet confession of her fears. Nothing that would quell the unease and pain that throbbed inside her.

Instead, Harriet did the only thing she could and that was offer comfort to Tilly. She kept her wrapped in her embrace, rocking her until Tilly's breathing grew slowly more even and measured and her body limp.

The air grew chilled and Harriet stood and lifted the girl into her arms. Carrying her gently back to the house, she left the bear where Tilly had thrown it.

When Tilly wanted Gruff back, she would go and fetch him but until then it was better for her that she be allowed to vent her confusing emotions, even if those actions only made sense in the mind of a troubled little girl.

CHAPTER THIRTY-SEVEN

WHAT WOULD he think of him now, if he knew the truth? He'd been so blind then. So stupid. Short-sighted, even.

If he could see everything he'd achieved, what would it do to him to know he'd been so wrong?

He lay back on the camp bed and stared up at the ceiling. The metallic smell of spilled blood hung in the air. It wasn't his favourite scent--far from it, in fact--but it was a reminder of his success.

Turning his head to the side, he stared over at Gabriel, who sat slumped in the chair. He wasn't half as much fun as Rachel had been.

But that was the problem, wasn't it? The ones who were particularly fulfilling never lasted as long. Their suffering fuelled his vengeance, as though he could actually gain strength from every one of their pained sobs.

But Gabriel, while strong in body, was less so in spirit. It just wasn't as much fun to work with such inferior material.

He contemplated ending the game early but decided against it.

Instead, he rolled onto his feet and shook his body out like a boxer before a prize fight. There was still so much he could achieve. Gabriel wouldn't keep him from achieving his means. And there were more ways to inflict suffering on another being.

Smiling, he crossed the room to where Gabriel sat, unresponsive.

Grabbing him by the hair, he jerked his head up. "Wakey, wakey, rise and shine!"

Gabriel moaned and spat blood out onto the floor next to his bare feet.

"The game's not finished, Gabriel. There's work to be done. And miles to go before you sleep."

Grabbing the blade from the table he pressed it to the other man's face. "You always were such a pretty boy but I'm sure we can change that."

Gabriel bucked in the chair, and he felt the first stirrings of excitement thrum in his veins once again. Perhaps he wasn't such a lost cause after all.

CHAPTER THIRTY-EIGHT

"SIR, we received a call from a Michael Barrows."

Drew raised his face from the computer screen and glanced over at Maz, who'd poked his head in through the door of the conference room.

"Who's Michael Barrows?"

"He said he wants to report a missing person. He saw the appeal on the news and called in right away."

"Where is he? We should pay him a visit."

Maz nodded. "I asked him to come in, Guv. He says he only lives twenty minutes away, so he'll be here ASAP." Maz sucked in a deep breath. "Do you think his friend is the Star Killer's next victim?"

Drew blew out his cheeks and pressed his hands behind his head in an attempt to stretch the kinks from his neck. "It's possible. At the very least it's worth looking into. Did you get who his missing mate is?"

Maz nodded and glanced down at the notepad in his hands. "Says his name is Gabriel Hopkins. Attends the university..."

Drew pushed onto his feet. "I'd say we're definitely looking at our newest victim. Right, I want a picture of him and every bit of information you can dig up about him. We need to find out what his last movements were so you and Olivia head over to the university and ask them to pull the CCTV footage for the last few days. That way, when we get more information from Michael, we'll have somewhere to direct it."

Maz nodded. "Right-O." He disappeared from the room and Drew watched him cross the office to the room where he and Crandell had been tucked away watching the other CCTV footage they'd scraped from the town centre, near where Rachel had gone missing.

"You think this boy is a victim?" Dr Perez asked, leaning back in her chair.

He shrugged. "Have you got a better idea?"

She shook her head. "Would you mind if I sat in on the interview with Michael Barrows?"

Drew shook his head. "That's fine, so long as this time you actually let me do the questioning."

Dr Perez raised her hands in mock surrender. "You are the boss."

Striding out of the office, Drew couldn't decide, if she was being genuine or just taking the piss out of him. She'd been quiet all day, hardly speaking more than two words to anyone in the office. Drew was pretty sure Gregson had even forgotten she was here.

He stepped into the kitchen and filled a paper cup with water. The urge to slip down the back stairs and outside for a quick cigarette before Michael got here was almost overpowering, but he fought against it. He'd slipped up the other night and given in to temptation, but he wasn't going to do that again. No matter how much harder it seemed to be now.

Swallowing back the water in two gasping gulps, he crushed the paper cup in his hand and tossed it into the bin before he glanced up at the wall clock. Despite trying not to think of her, he found himself wondering what Harriet was up to.

A SHORT WHILE LATER, Drew sat on one side of the interview table. Michael Barrows sat on the opposite side, his leg bouncing nervously beneath the table as he pushed a hand back through his fair hair.

"I just don't know where Gabriel is," Michael said.

"And when did you last speak to him?" Drew asked.

The other man glanced down at his hands. "You see, that's the thing. We had a falling out."

"When you say a falling out," Dr Perez said smoothly. "You mean an argument?"

Michael nodded. "Yeah, an argument. It wasn't serious. We didn't get into it, or anything, but--"

"You were lovers?" Dr Perez asked the question before Drew could get a word in edgeways.

Michael nodded and swallowed hard. "I loved him."

"What did you argue about?" Drew asked, finally managing to take back control of the interview.

"I went out on Monday night and he found out that I wasn't as good as I should have been."

"You mean he found out you cheated on him?" Drew asked, his discomfort levels rising. The way it was beginning to look, Gabriel Hopkins wasn't missing, he was just ignoring his cheating ex.

"I didn't actually cheat on him," Michael said before he sighed. "I mean, I kissed another guy, but it didn't mean anything."

"And Gabriel saw you kissing this other man?" Dr Perez asked.

Michael shook his head. "No, not exactly. He wasn't there. But Taff--he's a mutual friend of ours-- sent him a video and..." Michael trailed off. "I just had too much to drink. I would never intentionally cheat on him."

"Is it possible that Gabriel is just hurt and doesn't want to speak to you because of what happened?"

Drew asked, feeling like one of those TV agony aunts.

"No way. Gabriel hasn't been to uni. I asked around. There was this guy Taff thought he liked, and, well...."

"There's someone else?" Dr Perez asked, leaning forward as though Michael had said something genuinely interesting.

"Yeah, he met him in the library on Monday. So, I mean it's not as though he can hold it against me all that much when he was shopping around too."

"This man in the library; did you meet him?"

Michael shook his head. "No, I asked him this morning if he'd seen Gabriel, but he said he hadn't heard from him since Wednesday night."

Drew glanced over at Dr Perez, but she had eyes only for Michael. "And you're sure this is the young man Gabriel was interested in?"

Michael nodded miserably. "You don't think he'd hurt him, do you?"

"We can't say with any certainty," Drew said. "But if you could give us a list of Michael's friends and the name of this guy from the library."

"There was something else weird too," Michael said suddenly. "On Wednesday morning, I waited for him in his favourite coffee place on campus. But he was acting all freaked because some guy was eyeballing him. When I confronted the guy about it, Gabriel blew me off like it was nothing at all."

Michael screwed up his eyes. "He mentioned something about bumping into the guy before."

"Did the man appear at all familiar to you?" Drew asked.

Michael shook his head. "Maybe. I don't know. I only take notice of the really hot ones."

Drew dropped his gaze to the notepad in front of him. "What time would this have been?"

Michael stared down at the table as though all the answers he sought would somehow magically appear there. "I think it was around eleven, but I can't be sure."

Drew nodded and made a note of the time. They could always pull the CCTV from the coffee shop to get a look at the man Michael had mentioned. Someone had to know him.

"Would anyone have any reason to hold a grudge against Gabriel? Anything at all, no matter how small?"

Michael shook his head. "Everybody loves him. He's one of those popular, happy go lucky types." He brushed his hand over his designer stubble. "Do you think something bad has happened to him?"

Drew pushed onto his feet. "We can't speculate Mr Barrows but if we need to speak to you again can you leave your details at the desk."

"Is that it?" Michael asked jumping to his feet. "You're not going to tell me anything at all? I mean, I just told you the love of my life is missing and you're just going to give me the brush off?"

Dr Perez shook her head. "Mr Barrows, we know this is stressful for you but getting upset is not going to help Gabriel."

Michael glanced down at her. "Then what am I supposed to do?"

She pushed onto her feet. "I suggest you go home and try to remember any details that may be pertinent. Nothing is too small."

Michael let his hands drop by his sides. "If anything happens to him, I'll never forgive myself."

"That is a burden you will have to carry," she said. "But it is a waste of an emotion." With that she strode out of the room, leaving Drew to clean up the mess.

A couple of minutes later, he cornered her in the hall. "What was that all about?"

She glanced up at him blankly. "What was what about?"

"The way you behaved toward Michael Barrows. The bloke is obviously upset that his boyfriend has gone missing."

"Ex," she said.

"Excuse me?"

"Gabriel is his ex-boyfriend. They split because Mr Barrows is incapable of keeping his dick in his pants. Do you really expect me to waste my sympathy on someone like that?"

Drew stared at her, and suddenly felt as though

he was way out of his depth. The way she swung hot and cold was giving him whiplash.

"He's clearly distraught; that alone deserves our kindness. Not to mention the fact that he's a human being who, at the very least, deserves our respect. He didn't come here today to be berated for being a bad boyfriend; I'm sure he already feels bad enough about it."

Dr Perez stared at him. There was curious expression on her face, and Drew suddenly felt utterly self-conscious. "You are a strange man," she said cryptically. "But I suppose that is your prerogative."

With that final remark, she turned on her heel and stalked off down the corridor leaving him to stare open-mouthed after her.

CHAPTER THIRTY-NINE

HARRIET POKED her head around the door as Drew slipped his coat on.

"You're back," he said, sounding almost relieved.

"Yeah," she said. "I drove straight back. Urma asked me to stay the night but I didn't want to impose." She left out the part where she hadn't felt right staying there when she knew the case was ongoing. The longer the killer was allowed to carry on, the more damage he was doing to whoever his new victim happened to be, not to mention the fact that he was planning his next move.

Of course, deep down, she knew the case was just a convenient excuse to escape. Everything in the house had reminded her of Bianca, of everything she had lost. And more than that, it reminded her that she was still here. She had survived where Bianca had not, and there was a part of her that found that difficult to reconcile.

What made her so lucky? Bianca had so much more to lose, so many more people who relied on her.

"Well, you're just in time," Drew said. "Do you want to take a trip over to the university?"

She wrinkled her nose at him. "Is it the crime scene?"

He shook his head. "No, I'll fill you in on the way there."

She tried to read his expression, but he was closed off as he ushered her from the office.

In the car, she tried to keep quiet, waiting for him to open up to her rather than attempting to drag the truth from him. Finally, impatience won out and she swivelled toward him, the seat belt halting her progress.

"What is it? What aren't you telling me?"

"We think we know who our newest victim is," he said quietly.

"What? How?" Harriet felt her heart sink. "Please don't tell me there's another body so soon."

Drew shook his head but kept his gaze firmly on the road ahead. "No new body. We received a phone call from a guy by the name of Michael Barrows. He saw the appeal on the news and called the station."

"What did he have to say?"

"I'm getting to that part," Drew said as he tossed

her a quick glance. "He thinks his boyfriend is missing."

Harriet slumped back against the seat. "Another man. He doesn't take many of them."

Drew nodded, and Harriet watched as his knuckles whitened over the steering wheel.

She chewed her lip thoughtfully. "So, who is his boyfriend?"

"His name is Gabriel Hopkins."

Harriet felt her heart stutter to a halt in her chest. "Oh, god..."

"Wait, you know him?" Drew looked at her before he whipped his gaze back to the road.

"He's one of my Ph.D students. I've been giving him extra hours because he got a little behind on his thesis."

Drew's expression was implacable as he manoeuvred the car in and out of the lanes of traffic expertly, but she could see the cogs moving in his head.

"I don't like this," he said finally. "Everything leads back to you."

"But doesn't it always, with this killer?"

"Not like this," he said. "It's too much of a coincidence, Harriet. I know he chose you to be his puzzle master, but this is taking it too far. The victims are never usually so closely associated with the puzzle master."

She glanced down at her hands. "He's trying to

punish me for something," she said quietly. "I just wish I knew what it was."

"So do I," Drew said.

"Well, if we don't have a new body, and we know who he's taken, why are we going to the university?"

"Because Michael also mentioned that Gabriel had met someone new in the run up to his abduction."

Harriet felt her heart begin to gallop. "Who?"

"Some guy from the library."

"And you think this might be our guy?"

Drew shrugged and her irritation peaked. "You can't just do that. Don't just shrug. Do you think so or not?"

He twisted his hands over the wheel. "It could be. Until we get there and speak to him, we won't know anything, though."

She flopped back in the seat. He was right, there was no point in jumping to conclusions until they knew for certain.

However, there was no denying the fact that it would fit the pattern she believed the killer followed. Working in the library would have given him the opportunity to observe his victims, giving him the right opportunity to interact with Gabriel the way he had. The more she thought about it, the more plausible it all seemed.

"What are you thinking?" Drew asked as he parked the car near the library.

"I'm thinking there's a good chance that this guy fits the profile."

He cocked an eyebrow at her. "Oh? What gives you that idea?"

"Well, he's in the hub of it all. It fits, doesn't it? Being here gives him the chance to get closer to Gabriel. Even Rachel managed to get on the register for the university so she could get closer to me for her story. Spending time in the library would give him the opportunity to study them all."

"Including you," Drew said thoughtfully. He squared his shoulders. "We can't go in there thinking this is our guy. We need to stay objective."

Harriet nodded, and brushed her hands over her face. "I know. You're right." She stepped out of the car and drew in a deep breath of the crisp air. "Do we know if he's even working right now?"

Drew nodded. "I had Crandell and Maz check out the schedule before I left. There's a Christopher Thomas on the desk."

Harriet picked up her pace in order to keep up with Drew's longer stride. They pushed in through the doors of the library, and Drew pulled up short as he came face to face with the turnstiles in the entrance.

"Since when did books need so much protection?"

"Books are a precious commodity here," she said. "We've got to keep a record of all the comings and goings of the students as they move in and out. Here..." She stepped forward and pressed her key fob against the scanner, allowing Drew to pass through. She repeated it again and slipped through after him.

"Over here," she said, directing him to the front desk.

A young woman with multi-coloured hair sat on the other side, and she glanced up with a disinterested expression as Harriet reached the counter.

"Christopher Thomas. Is he here?" Harriet asked.

The woman glanced over her shoulder and then shrugged. "I think he could be on his break."

"Where does he normally go?"

"He tends to pop home. He doesn't live very far from here. At least, I don't think he does." The woman returned her attention to the book in her lap.

"Do you have an address on file?" Harriet persisted.

"Can't you just wait for him to come back?" the woman said, without glancing up from the book.

"No," Drew interjected flashing his warrant card. "I want to know where Christopher Thomas is. Now."

The woman sighed and pushed to her feet. "Fine, give me a minute."

Drew drummed his fingers against the counter and Harriet fought the urge to place her hand over his to silence him.

"Has the palynologist narrowed the area yet?" she asked.

Drew glanced up. "What?"

"You said earlier this morning, when I rang you, that the palynologist thought she could narrow the geographical area for our killer. Has she managed to do that, yet?"

He shook his head. "I haven't heard anything."

"Well, it might be interesting to cross reference it with Chris' home address."

"He's back," the girl said, pointing to a young man who was, at that moment, sauntering in through the side door. His eyes widened when he spotted Harriet and Drew, and an expression of confusion swept over his features. His steps faltered.

"Chris, this copper wants a word--" The girl's words cut off as Chris doubled back in the direction he'd just come from and took off through the stacks of books.

"Shit," Drew muttered as he took off after him, leaving Harriet to stand there with the girl at the counter.

"Where does that lead to?" Harriet asked.

The girl stared over at her blankly.

"That way. Where does it lead?"

"The back doors. Loading bays and stuff back there. It's where we park our cars."

Harriet nodded. "Is there a quicker way to get there?"

The girl pointed to the front doors. "Go out the way you came in and cut down the alley at the side of the building. It'll take you straight out there, and you won't need a keycard like you do the other way."

Harriet started toward the door, her ballet pumps threatening to slip off as she picked up her pace.

As she made it outside the door, she followed the route the girl on the desk had suggested and slipped down the alley at the side of the library.

She emerged in time to see Chris pushing a large wooden pallet in front of the back door he'd obviously just exited through.

The door rattled from the inside, and as she hurried across the loading area, Harriet could hear Drew's rage fuelled bellows coming from inside.

"I don't know what you want. I haven't done anything wrong," Christopher said, the panic in his voice causing its pitch to rise.

"We just want to talk to you, Chris," Harriet said, softly, as she approached. He spun around to face her, his eyes wild and filled with fear. His gaze travelled past her, and Harriet was suddenly acutely aware of the fact that she was standing between the young man and his planned means of escape.

"Chris, we just want to talk." She raised her hands as she repeated the sentence.

He jumped the railing, landing in front of her, as his gaze darted to the left. "I haven't done anything wrong."

"Nobody thinks you have. Like I said, we just want to talk."

He feinted to the right, but Harriet had seen the telltale flicker in his eyes and knew he really intended to move to the left. She went after him, grabbing him as he tried to slip past her.

"Let me go," he said, jabbing at her with his elbows as she attempted to get a grip on him. Pushing her face in toward his body, she tried to protect her head from the blows he tried to rain down on her.

"Chris, please--"

He pummeled her back, winding her and cutting her off mid-sentence.

His weight disappeared, and Harriet stumbled forward onto the hard tarmac. She glanced up in time to see Drew pushing Chris onto the ground, face first.

"I'm arresting you on suspicion of the murder of Rachel Kennedy and the abduction of Gabriel Hopkins," Drew said, sounding out of breath. "You do not have to say anything..."

He continued on with the rights of the young man he'd cuffed on the ground, and Harriet sucked down mouthfuls of clean air.

Drew finally glanced over at her. "You all right?"

She nodded and straightened up. Her body felt bruised, but it was nothing compared to how she'd felt after Robert Burton had attacked her.

"I'm fine." Harriet turned her attention to the man on the ground, who had now started to sob.

Drew helped him up.

Chris' head hung down as he refused to meet their gazes. "I haven't murdered anyone," he said, his voice high and panicked.

"Then why run?" Drew asked, before he sucked in a deep breath.

The sound of sirens broke the air, and Harriet glanced over at him.

"I called in back up," Drew said. "They'll take Chris to the station." His words were followed by the sound of running feet. A couple of uniformed officers appeared a moment later.

"I swear I haven't hurt anyone," Chris moaned. "You've got this wrong."

"Then why run?" Drew asked again.

Chris shook his head. "If I tell, I'll be in so much trouble."

"Guilty people run," Drew said, as he handed Chris over to the uniforms. "Get him processed."

As they led Chris away, Harriet turned to the row of cars and vans parked behind the library. "One of these is his."

Drew nodded. "We'll get this whole place looked over." He took a step toward her, and Harriet was suddenly aware of the rage he was barely suppressing.

"What?" she asked.

"Why did you do that?"

"Do what?"

He sighed. "Throw yourself at him like that?"

"Well, we had to stop him and--"

"Harriet, he could have had a weapon. We're looking for a deranged killer who cuts chunks off his victims before posting them to police stations. Don't you think your behaviour was a little reckless?"

She glanced down at the ground. He was right, but she hadn't even considered the consequences at the time. With her adrenaline pumping, all thoughts of risk and personal safety had gone out the window. Why was that?

"What were you thinking?" Drew asked.

She shrugged. It wasn't as though she had a good enough answer; at least not one that would make sense to him.

"Tell me."

"I don't know," she said finally. "I *wasn't* thinking. Is that what you want to hear?"

"You don't do anything without thinking about it first."

She sighed. "We should go after them."

"We need to get you checked out first," he said, the authoritarian tone in his voice grating on her nerves.

"I'm fine. We don't have time. If he's the one holding Gabriel, then we need to find out where he has him."

Drew started to protest but Harriet cut him off. "Please. I promise I'll get looked at when this is over and done with. But right now, we need to focus."

He sighed. "Fine. But the next time there's a suspect fleeing on foot, do you think you could let the trained officers do their job?"

Rolling her eyes at him, she stalked away from the loading dock.

———

REACHING the front of the library, Harriet watched as the uniformed officers loaded Chris into the back of one of the cars. There was something about the entire situation that didn't sit right with her, and no matter how she looked at it, she couldn't put her finger on exactly what it was.

His reaction to Drew coming after him. His reaction to her. It just didn't fit with who she thought the Star Killer was.

However, there was no ignoring the very obvious fact that when confronted, Chris had run. Why was that? What was he afraid of?

"Are you ready to go?" Drew asked.

"What about finding out which one is his car?"

He nodded in the direction he'd come from. "We've got his van. They're going to open it up and do a full check on it while we get him down the station."

Harriet nodded.

"Harriet, what is it?"

She shook her head. "I don't know. Something doesn't feel right."

Drew shrugged. "He looks pretty guilty to me. Why else would he run?"

She chewed her lip thoughtfully. "I don't know. But I can't shake the feeling that we're missing something."

"Well, look we'll have a chat with him and see what the SOCOs come up with in the meantime."

He was right. Until they spoke to him, there was no point in her speculating. Christopher Thomas held his own secrets, and the only way they would get to the bottom of them was by talking to him.

"Fine. You're right," she said. "Do you like him for this?"

Drew glanced over at the car and Harriet could tell from the set of his jaw that he was as unsure as she was. "I don't know. But I do know he's hiding something. Whether it's the kind of something we're looking for is another matter altogether."

"Well, let's go and talk to him then. We're not going to get our answers hanging around here."

CHAPTER FORTY

"THE DI WANTS us to look into a Rosemary Cline," Olivia said, as she slipped into the darkened room where Maz sat staring at a set of monitors. Black and white footage of cars on streets dominated the images, and she closed her eyes against the constant motion.

The longer she sat and stared at the screens the more motion sick she began to feel, which was weird because she'd never felt car sick in her life.

"What?" Maz asked, swivelling in the chair to face her.

"Haskell wants us to go over one of the old case files."

"Again?" Maz pulled a face and Olivia found herself agreeing with him. What was wrong with good old-fashioned police work? Why did every-thing have to be dictated to them by the head doctors? It didn't make sense, and felt, to her, like a complete waste of time. If all it took to get inside the head of another person was a few extra years in uni, then any Tom, Dick, or Harry could be a shrink.

"Yeah," she said, with a sigh. "The good doctor thinks the first set of murders warrants a second go 'round."

He sighed and started to climb to his feet. "Where are we supposed to start?"

Olivia shook her head. "Nah, you stay there. I'll look over the file on this Rosemary woman. You keep an eye on the CCTV."

Maz pulled a face at her. "Why do I get the distinct impression you're trying to pull one over on me?"

She batted her lashes at him and did her best to imitate the voice of Dr Perez. "Would you rather 'brainstorm' on the old files with me, Maz? Perhaps you'd be a lamb and go to the coffee shop for me too. I can't stand the taste of this office swill."

"She doesn't sound like that," he said, irritated, as he turned his chair back around. "Why do you have to be such a bitch sometimes?"

Olivia laughed as she turned on the reading lamp and set the files down on the small desk in the corner. "Seems I touched a nerve there."

She could tell he was ignoring her based on his sudden forced interest in the CCTV video, and his silent fuming only made her laugh harder. Maz was definitely too easy to wind up.

His sensitivity reminded her of her younger brother, and Olivia had found herself wanting to take him under her wing. Maybe a little too much judging by the sulk he seemed to be having.

Flipping open the file, she scanned over the notes made by the previous detective. She'd say one thing for Dr Quinn, the woman had an eye for oddities. As she read over the notes, Olivia found herself somewhat agreeing with the good doctor, which felt a little uncomfortable.

Jotting down the name of Rosemary Cline's husband, Olivia carried the file into the squad room. DI Haskell stood in the Monk's office, having what appeared to be some kind of heated debate with DCI Gregson.

Haskell looked pissed off but from the distance between her and the office, not to mention the closed door that lay between them, Olivia couldn't figure out what they were arguing about. Some other aspect of the case which had come to light, no doubt.

She dropped the file onto the desk in front of a free computer and settled in. Her fingers flew over the keys, and in moments, she'd pulled up a home address for George Cline, Rosemary's husband. Luckily for her, he hadn't moved away, as she'd first suspected he might have done.

Grabbing her maroon leather jacket from the

back of the chair, she contemplated letting the DI know where she was headed to, and then changed her mind as he stormed from Gregson's office with a face like a slapped arse. If she went to him now, he'd probably take her head off for interrupting him.

On her feet, she headed back to the darkened CCTV room and poked her head around the door.

"Oi, I'm going to go and check up on something. You all right to hold down the fort here?"

Maz swung around in the chair, his expression one of somebody who was looking for any excuse to get away from the job at hand. "I could come with you."

She shook her head. He definitely reminded her of her brother Robbie, and that was the problem with siblings; there was always something to compete with them about. If Maz thought she was going to share this potentially interesting tidbit she'd dug up, then he had another think coming. No, this lead--if it even was a lead--was all hers.

"Nah, someone needs to stay here and go through the CCTV footage."

Maz stretched. "But I'm the senior detective here. I get first dibs on whatever it is you've got."

She pulled a face at him. "Are you serious? What are we, twelve? No way am I handing over my stuff to you. Do your own homework."

He pushed onto his feet, but she waved him off. "Look, I'm just following up on that information for

Haskell's pet doctor. If I get something, you'll be the first person I come to. In the meantime, I don't think you'd fancy going to speak to some old bloke whose wife died eighteen years ago."

Maz wrinkled his nose. "You're probably right," he said dropping back into the chair. "He's probably senile anyway, so it'll just be a waste of time."

Olivia nodded. "Definitely. You stay all cosy in here and I'll run this down."

Maz rolled his eyes at her and swung back to the monitors. "Try not to have too much fun," he said sarcastically.

Olivia grinned. "I'll try."

She ducked out of the office and made a beeline for the door before anyone else could collar her.

CHAPTER FORTY-ONE

PARKING the car in front of the two-storey farm-house, Olivia killed the engine and sat in silence as it cooled and ticked over. The drive out to Newholm had taken longer than she'd thought, and she glanced down at her watch.

Maz would cover for her if anyone came looking for her. At least she hoped he would. She contemplated calling him to make sure they had their story straight, and then changed her mind.

Better to get this over with. On the drive, she'd thought of all the possibilities she might find here and the most obvious one seemed to be a giant dead end. The doctor was probably just having some kind of mental episode. Olivia had heard the reason she wasn't at the station this morning despite this whole case being about her was because she'd had to go to her mate's funeral. The same mate that had met her

Waterloo at the hands of the sick bastard who'd murdered those kids.

Olivia had been there the day they'd found Dr Quinn dangling at the end of the sicko's rope in his basement, and it hadn't been pretty. Of course, the doctor was one of the lucky ones.

There weren't many people who went toe to toe with a killer and came out the other side of it fine and dandy. There wasn't even a scratch on her, now.

She had taken to wearing high-necked blouses, though, and on more than one occasion, Dr Quinn had caught Olivia staring.

She couldn't help it. It was just one of those morbidly fascinating things.

As she pushed open the car door, the sound of the alarm indicated that she'd left the lights on. Clicking them off, she pulled the keys out. Close call. The last thing she needed was to accidentally leave the lights on and end up with a dead battery.

Locking the car, she glanced around at her surroundings and shuddered. There wasn't a hope in hell you'd catch her living out here. It was far too isolated. And with the winter nights closing in, the place would become an eerie reminder of just how far you were from civilisation.

Crossing the gravel drive, she noted the silver Audi parked by the side of the house and knocked on the door. From somewhere deep within, she heard the sound of a television. Either George had gone out and left the telly on, or the man was going a little deaf. *Please don't be senile.* It would be just her luck that Maz was right.

A couple of seconds ticked by, and she lifted her hand to knock a second time when she heard someone shuffling on the other side.

"Who is it?" The man sounded frail, and Olivia glanced down at the notes she'd brought with her. At sixty-seven, George Cline probably shouldn't have been frail, but then again, it was amazing what grief could do to people. She'd watched her own grandfather wither away after her MayMay had passed. MayMay was the name she'd given to her grandmother when she'd been unable to say the word grandmother when she was young. It had stuck.

"Mr Cline, I'm DC Olivia Crandell with Yorkshire CID. Could I come in and have a quick chat with you?"

He opened the door and it came to a shuddering halt as the chain caught. "Let me see your credentials."

Olivia found herself at the receiving end of a penetrating hazel eyed gaze. She lifted her warrant card into view.

Mr Cline scanned it before his gaze flickered back to her face. He shut the door and she took an involuntary step backwards. Why wouldn't he--

The door opened, wider this time and she realised he'd only shut it to remove the chain.

"What do you want to talk to me about?" he asked. His upper body was stooped forward and Olivia's eyes travelled down to the gnarled wooden stick he used to prop himself upright.

"I'd like to ask you a few questions about your wife Rosemary, if that's all right with you?"

His white eyebrows came together so they more closely resembled a uni-brow that sat furrowed over the top of his angry eyes.

"Why do you want to talk to me about Rosie, now? Why now, when you wouldn't talk to me about her then?"

Olivia shook her head. "I'm sorry, Mr Cline, I wasn't a part of the original investigation into your wife's murder, but--"

"She trusted you lot. Trusted you to do your job and look at where that got her. Dead and buried. Her whole life was tied up in the job, but we had plans, you know? She was going to retire, and we were going to travel around the country in our camper. See a few things. But..." He trailed off and turned his head aside.

Olivia gripped the notes tighter, feeling the paper-thin file crumple beneath the force of her fingers.

"I am terribly sorry for your loss," she said, at last feeling as though she could speak without an abundance of unnecessary emotion in her voice. "I can't begin to imagine how you feel."

"No," he said. "You can't. And if you're lucky, you won't ever have to." George sighed and leaned against the doorframe suddenly, as though all the fight that had been in his body just moments before had slipped away on his breath. "Rosie would have my head if she heard me speaking to a police officer the way I just did."

"I'm sure that, given the circumstances, she'd understand," Olivia said with a slight smile.

He shook his head. "No, you didn't know my Rosie. She never put up with any of my nonsense. What did you want to talk to me about her for?"

Olivia drew in a deep breath. "Would it be possible for us to discuss this inside, maybe?"

He gave a quick bob of his head and shuffled in from the door. Olivia followed him inside.

"Make sure you close and lock that door after you," he said. "I like to keep the chain on, just in case."

She did as he asked, noting the heavy-duty bolt that sat across the middle of the door.

"You've got a lot of security," she said, following him into the living room.

"You have to. My family are worried I'm too isolated out here on my own, but like I told them, I'm more than capable of looking after the place on my own. Besides, this is where I know Rosie is. She never left me, and I couldn't leave her."

Olivia kept her thoughts to herself. It wasn't down to her to comment on the religious beliefs of another person, even if they didn't remotely gel with her own.

"Mr Cline," she began, but he interrupted.

"Call me George, everyone else does." He directed her to a chair opposite the sofa and she sat.

Olivia smiled. "George, before your wife was..." She faltered and glanced down.

"Murdered," he said. "You can say it. Rosie was murdered. By a cowardly piece of scum."

"Before your wife was murdered, was she concerned about anything or anyone in particular?"

He shook his head. "She was the bravest soul I knew," he said. "She had to be, to do her job."

"It says here in the file that she worked as a police officer?"

He nodded. "She did but before her death, she'd taken up a role working with young delinquents who had some issues."

"What kinds of issues?" Olivia asked, making a note on her pad.

"Mental ones," he said bluntly. "Mentally disturbed, the lot of them. Some of them heard voices and everything, but Rosie didn't mind. It was what she'd always wanted to do."

Olivia jotted it all down. "But did she have any concerns regarding the people she was working with?"

He shook his head. "No, the police looked into all of that, and there were no red flags."

"And she wasn't worried about anything?"

He started to shake his head, but then paused. "There was something. We said it to the police at the time, but they dismissed it as not connected to the case."

Olivia sat forward on the chair. "What was it?"

"Before she ever got the first package from him, she had her tyres slashed outside of her work."

"You don't remember how long before she received the first package this happened, do you?"

"A couple of months, I think," he said. "Or maybe a year. I don't know. Over time, everything starts to blur together. If she were here now, she'd tell you. She always did have a sharp memory. Nothing ever got past her."

Olivia nodded and made a couple of notes. "George, do you think your wife ever had any suspicions as to who she thought the Star Killer was?"

He glanced down at his slippers. "She wouldn't want me to say this. Rosie always believed that when your time was done, you'd paid your penance so there was no point in opening up old wounds unless you had good cause."

"So, she had her suspicions?"

He nodded. "She did. She kept telling me she was looking into it."

"And did she tell you who she suspected?"

"She never gave me a name but what she did tell

me was that it was someone she had helped in the past."

Olivia felt her heart flip over in her chest. "She didn't happen to say where or even how she helped this person, did she?"

He screwed up his face. "I never really asked, but I always suspected it had something to do with those parole board hearings she helped out with."

"Parole board hearings?"

He nodded. "Before she started working with the youths, she used to attend parole board hearings for the young people she'd picked up off the streets for selling drugs or what have you. She'd keep up with them, and if she thought she could help them readjust back into society, or they were due for release, she would go and give her tuppence."

Olivia smiled. "Thank you, Mr Cline, this has been very helpful."

He nodded. "Is there any chance you could help me with something?"

She cocked her head to the side.

"Over the years since Rosie's death, people have thought they could frighten me out of here."

"In what way?"

"Oh, you know, the usual. Intimidation tactics. A broken window here, a flat tyre there. Nothing too serious. But last week, someone came around and set fire to the shed."

He stood, and Olivia followed him to the back

window where he pointed to the garden and the
remnants of what had once been a wooden shed.

"Do you have any idea who might be doing this?"

He shrugged. "My son thinks it's just youths, but
I'd like them to stop."

"Have you reported these things to the police?"

He nodded. "Every time. But it's always the same
old, same old. Nobody knows anything, nobody saw
anything. I swear, around here you could get mugged
right in front of them, and they wouldn't see it
happen."

"Well, I can look into it for you."

"That'd be lovely. Thank you."

"Did you have anything of value in the shed?"

He shook his head. "No, I moved all of Rosie's
files out of there a couple of years ago."

"Files?"

He nodded. "She kept notes on every case she
worked on. Or at least all the ones she wanted to
keep track of. It's what made her so useful when it
came time to go back and speak on those parole
boards."

"Do you still have those files?" Olivia couldn't
believe what she was hearing. He was basically
admitting that they had a potential record of the
person she'd suspected of being her murderer. What
if that was why the Star Killer had broken form eighteen years ago and murdered her? What if he'd found

out about her suspicions and, in order to maintain his secret, he'd offed her?

It was certainly possible.

George nodded. "They're in the attic now. I'm not fit enough to go up there and get them myself, but you're welcome to go and have a look, if you'd like."

Olivia glanced down at her watch and made a snap decision. "That would be great, Mr Cline. Thank you."

A COUPLE OF HOURS LATER, with dusty cobwebs in her hair, Olivia drove the four boxes of files back to the office. It had seemed like too small of a haul for a woman with such a varied career as Officer Rosemary Cline, but her husband George had assured Olivia that the contents of those four boxes were what mattered to his wife most.

As she crept closer to the station, Olivia thought of the look on Maz's face when she informed him that she alone had cracked the case wide open. She pressed her foot down a little harder on the accelerator in an attempt to get back to the station just a little faster.

CHAPTER FORTY-TWO

"SO WHY DID YOU RUN, CHRIS?" Drew asked, sitting across from the frightened-looking man.

"You don't need to answer that question, Chris," the duty solicitor said, before he addressed Drew. "My client has instructed me to read you a statement he has prepared."

Drew sat back in the chair and placed his hands behind his head. Chris kept his gaze trained on the floor; the white coveralls they'd given him only served to wash him out in the harsh fluorescent lighting from overhead.

He looked much younger than his thirty six years suggested. Clearly, he was doing something right all this time.

"My client wishes to begin by stating categorically that he was not involved in, nor has he any

320

knowledge of the whereabouts or the abduction of one Gabriel Hopkins.

"While he had, in the short amount of time he has known Mr Hopkins, struck up what he believed to be a mutual friendship, my client would like to stress at this time that that is all it was.

"He has never had any interactions with Mr Hopkins outside of the University Campus. He would also like to state that on Wednesday, the 18th of October, he did offer to take Mr Hopkins in his van for a 'takeaway coffee' at the drive-thru MacDonald's but Mr Hopkins declined. This was the last he saw of Mr Hopkins.

"Furthermore, my client would like to state that he has never knowingly had any interactions with Ms Rachel Kennedy."

"Is your client going to tell me why he ran away, when all we wanted to do was have a friendly chat with him?" Drew asked, leaning his elbows on the table. He ignored the solicitor, keeping his gaze trained on Chris, who with each passing moment looked more and more like he wanted to disappear into himself completely.

Harriet was right to think there was something not quite right about the entire situation. As far as Drew was concerned, even though Chris had run when they'd tried to speak to him, he just didn't fit the idea he had in his mind of what their killer was like.

Everything about the Star Killer suggested somebody with a lot of confidence and swagger, which Chris simply didn't seem to possess.

"My client has nothing further to add at this time," the solicitor said, a little too smugly.

"Chris, you know we've got a warrant for your house. If you're lying to us about anything we're going to find out."

Chris shrank backwards, and Drew sighed. "Interview terminated at 16:37."

Pushing up from his chair, he clicked the button on the recorder and started for the door.

"DI Haskell, I would like to know just how long you think you can keep this charade up for?" the solicitor asked.

Drew cast a glance over his shoulder.

"We both know my client is an innocent man," the solicitor continued. "And when it breaks in the news that you've been hauling in innocent people, the public are going to discover that the police force tasked with protecting them from the Star Killer is none the wiser as to his identity than they are."

Ignoring the obvious barb, Drew pulled the door open and stepped out into the hall. He met Harriet as she was leaving the observation room. Dr Perez was hot on her heels, and from the expression she wore, he could tell she wasn't best pleased.

"The solicitor is correct," she said. "You may as well cut him loose now."

Drew shook his head. "It doesn't work like that. He ran when we tried to question him. He's hiding something."

Harriet gave him a sympathetic smile. "Hiding something, he may well be, but I'm going to agree with Katerina and say it's not murder or abduction."

Drew nodded, and scrubbed his hands up and over his face. "I know that. Christ what a mess."

From the corner of his eye, he caught sight of Harriet checking her watch. "I know," he said softly.

"What?"

"That Gabriel is running out of time."

She nodded. "He doesn't like to keep them beyond a maximum of seventy-two hours and Gabriel has already been gone since last night. The longer we go on like this, the more likely it is that we're going to end up with a body on our hands."

"I'm aware."

She looked chagrined and Dr Perez sighed frustratedly. "I'm going to get a coffee," she said impatiently.

Once they were alone in the hall Harriet turned to him. "Any luck with the hunch I had about Rosemary Cline."

It was Drew's turn to look chagrined and he glanced down at the floor. "To be honest, I passed it off to Maz and Olivia this morning and I haven't heard anything from them."

He could tell from the strangled expression on

her face that she was trying not to look irritated. "Oh." Was all she managed to say. "Well, I suppose you had other things on your mind."

Drew nodded. "Look, I'll go now and--"

Harriet shook her head. "It's fine. I can check in with them myself. It was my hunch after all."

She spun on her heel and sauntered down the hall, leaving him frustrated. Shit, why couldn't anything around here run smoothly, for once?

CHAPTER FORTY-THREE

HARRIET SLIPPED into the CCTV booth and paused silently behind DS Arya. The sound of his gentle snores did nothing to appease her irritation. Here they were waiting for a serial killer to drop his next body, and those working the case either couldn't be bothered to follow up on things or were sleeping on the job. Literally, in the case of Maz.

Deliberately leaning in over his shoulder, Harriet scanned the notes Maz had doodled on the pad in front of the monitors, before she straightened up and cleared her throat loudly.

He started in the chair and very nearly wound up on the floor.

"Christ," he said, clearly flustered, as he smoothed a hand down over his hair and glanced sheepishly up at Harriet.

"Sorry," he said. "I didn't hear you come in."

"Evidently," she said. "Any luck with the CCTV?"

He shook his head. "On Wednesday night, I've managed to track Gabriel on the route he takes to get home, but once he short cuts into the park, he disappears."

"You mean he doesn't come out the other side?"

"That's what disappears means, yeah."

Harriet shot him a sharp look, but his gaze was fixed on the screens.

"What about cars or vans in and around the area at the same time?"

He shrugged. "Take your pick. The road that runs alongside the park is pretty busy. There's always something coming and going on it."

"Right, but this vehicle would be accelerating off a slip road near the park. Can't you crosscheck it with the vehicles seen in the area at the time of Rachel's abduction?"

Maz glanced down at the paper in front of him. "But there aren't any cameras in the parking complex."

"But there are traffic lights going in both directions that our killer would have had to pass through in order to drive off," Drew said.

Harriet dug her nails into the palms of her hands to keep from yelping. She'd been so intent on studying the screen that she hadn't heard him enter the room.

Maz sat up a little straighter. "I hadn't thought of that," he said. "Now that you say it, there was a van in the area that seemed to pass up and down a little too much. I dismissed it because it looked like it might be making deliveries or something."

"When was this?"

"On the Tuesday," he said. "Actually, Rachel went to the same sandwich place every Tuesday, from what I can tell."

"How do you know?" Harriet asked.

"We got her schedule from her online calendar," Maz said. "I was able to cross reference it with the rough outline of her whereabouts that her boyfriend gave us, and the sandwich shop was a regular haunt for the last three months."

"How far back has the van being doing that round on a Tuesday lunchtime during the time Rachel would have been there?"

Maz shrugged. "I'd say nearly every Tuesday." He typed on the keyboard in front of him and a grainy black and white image came up of a white van trundling slowly through an intersection.

A couple of keystrokes later and an image of a car passing through the same intersection flashed onto the screen. "That's Rachel's car," he said. "In nearly every instance that I've seen, the van passes through the intersection around twenty to thirty minutes prior to Rachel's arrival."

"And when she leaves?"

"The van can be seen moving in the opposite direction usually five to ten minutes after she leaves the sandwich shop with her lunch."

Harriet chewed her lip. "Can I take a look at Rachel's schedule?"

Maz nodded. "Sure, I'll print you out a copy. How far back would you like it to go?"

Harriet contemplated her answer. "I guess give me the last year."

He whistled through his teeth. "That's a lot of info, Doc. You sure you want to go back that far?"

Harriet nodded. "Yeah, I'm sure."

Maz shrugged and pushed up from his chair.

"What are you thinking?" Drew asked as Harriet started toward the door.

"What I'm thinking," she said. "Is that whoever our guy is he's the one who told Rachel about the sandwich shop."

Drew gave her a funny look. "That's a bit of a leap, isn't it?"

She shook her head. "I don't think so. Look at it this way; Alyssa, Rachel's friend, told me she started speaking to a Nathan somebody or other. She couldn't remember his last name over the last few months about the story she was working on."

Drew nodded. "Right. I don't see the connection."

"The story she was working on was the story concerning Freya. This Nathan claimed he could..." Harriet trailed off.

"What is it?" Drew asked, his brow corrugated with concern.

"How would you go about getting information on medical negligence?" Harriet asked aloud.

"Well, for one, the physician in charge would have access to the pertinent information," Drew said. "I don't see how this connects to Rachel or this mystery Nathan."

"Nathan told Rachel he could get her some information for her case." Harriet closed her eyes. "I need to make a phone call."

"Who to?"

"Alyssa, Rachel's friend. We have her information on file now, right?"

Drew nodded. "Yeah, the uniforms will have followed up on that by now."

She darted for the door and he caught her arm before she could slide past him. Harriet glanced up into his face, half hidden in the shadows.

"Are you all right?" he asked. "You know, after everything with your friend's service and then with Christopher Thomas?"

There was no mistaking the concern reflected in his eyes as he looked down at her, and it warmed Harriet from her toes up to know that, despite everything, despite her lying to him when they'd first met, he could still look at her like this. But now was not the time to get caught up in personal emotions. She needed her head clear so she could focus. There were so many thoughts crowding her brain all at once, that she wondered if she was actually losing her mind completely.

"I'm fine," she said honestly. "Or at least I will be fine when we catch this guy."

Drew nodded and took a step backwards. "I know what you mean."

"You don't look as though you've been sleeping," she said.

He shook his head. "I haven't been home yet."

Harriet opened her mouth to say something, but he said, "I'm fine. I caught a couple of hours in one of the side rooms last night."

"You should go home and get some sleep," she said. "And something proper to eat. You can't live on whatever it is you've been getting from that vending machine."

He grinned at her. "Monster Munch, Hot and Spicy. They're my favourite."

Harriet pulled a face at him and moved for the door. "One of these days, you'll turn into a preservative if you're not careful."

"At least I won't fade away," he said. "Preservatives just mean I'll live longer."

Laughing, she pulled open the door. "I'm going to ring Alyssa and ask her just what this Nathan had promised her friend Rachel."

"You really think it's important, don't you?"

Harriet nodded. "Yeah, I do. Like I said, I think

he's been following and stalking them for months. Inserting himself into their lives in any way he can."

Drew nodded. "Well, while you do that. I'll run down this lead with the guy Michael saw in the coffee shop."

"Want me to come with you?" Harriet asked.

Drew shook his head. "After last time, no chance. I'll take Maz with me."

Harriet smiled. "I thought I handled it quite well."

Seeing his expression darken, she backed out of the office into the squad room, leaving him to stew in his own anger. He clearly still wasn't at a point where making jokes about the situation was suitable.

CHAPTER FORTY-FOUR

DREW PARKED the car next to the university and hopped out. Daniel Sykes was one of the people hired by the university for cleaning and some minor repairs.

Crossing the car park, he stepped into the maintenance office that sat at the outer edge of the campus. There was a woman behind the desk who seemed to be finishing up for the day, judging by the way she'd tugged on her coat and flung her bag over her shoulder.

"I'm sorry," he said. "I'm DI Haskell, I was wondering if you could tell me the whereabouts of one of the men who works for you. Daniel Sykes?"

Flustered, she huffed out a short breath and pulled a book from beneath the desk. "Danny is currently over in the psychology building," she said.

"He's replacing the bulbs that were on the blink in the main staircase."

Drew smiled and started back out the door.

"Why, what's this about?" she asked.

Shaking his head, he said, "I just wanted to ask him a few questions about an incident."

"Is this about that young man who thought he was going through his locker at the gym? Because Danny has a perfectly reasonable explanation for that."

Drew paused and quirked an eyebrow at her. "Go on."

She sucked in a deep breath. "The man bumped into Danny when he was cleaning in the psychology building on Monday. Danny said he noticed the man had dropped his driver's license, so he picked it up. When he saw him on Wednesday evening, going into the gym, Danny thought he'd do the guy a good turn and return the licence. That's all there is to it."

Drew had heard flimsier true stories. "This guy whose licence he found, he didn't happen to be a Gabriel Hopkins, did he?"

She shrugged. "I don't know. Danny didn't say."

Drew nodded. "Thanks."

"Wait. You're talking about the student who was taken on Wednesday night?"

Drew nodded. "That's the one."

"Well, I don't know if it was the same man. You'd

have to ask Danny. It was just awful, what happened though. None of us can believe it."

Drew smiled sympathetically and attempted to leave for a third time.

"You're not thinking Danny has anything to do with it, are you?"

"I can't discuss an ongoing case," Drew said swiftly as he backed out through the door.

"Well, for what it's worth, Danny has an alibi for Wednesday night."

Drew paused. "Yeah?"

She nodded and glanced down at the desk. "We've kind of being seeing each other for, going on four months, now... That's how I knew about the guy and the licence," she added quickly. "Danny's a good guy."

"You said he had an alibi?"

She flushed and nodded, several bottle blonde strands working their way loose from her high pony-tail. "He took me out Wednesday night. We went to the French department's special showing of some foreign thing I can't even pronounce the name of, never mind actually remember. But we were in the main theatre hall from around quarter to nine until midnight. And then, he drove me home."

Drew nodded. "And for the rest of the night?"

If he thought it should have been impossible for somebody to blush even more, he was mistaken. The rosy hue on her cheeks deepened until she was a vibrant red. "He stayed over."

Drew pushed open the door. "Thanks for your time, Ms?"

"Chantelle Smith."

"Thank you Ms Smith. If I need any further information can I reach you here?"

"Mondays to Fridays," she said cheerfully.

Drew stepped back out into the evening air and sighed. So much for a potential lead. He was still going to speak to Mr Sykes. It was always better to dot your i's and cross your t's, in case something down the line came back to bite you on the arse. But he could see the whole trip as being nothing more than a complete waste of time.

He glanced down at his watch and sighed. Harriet had been right; time was definitely running out for Gabriel Hopkins. And as far as Drew was concerned, they didn't seem to be any closer to finding the so-called Star Killer.

CHAPTER FORTY-FIVE

HARRIET PUT the phone down and twirled the pen between her fingers. Alyssa hadn't shed much light on the subject of the mysterious Nathan. But something she'd said had definitely caught Harriet's attention.

Nathan had promised Rachel an exclusive story about a young man who'd been mistreated, or misdiagnosed--Alyssa had been a little hazy on the facts-- by a prominent psychiatrist.

As far as Harriet was concerned, it seemed a little odd that Rachel had started to pursue a case involving Dr Connor shortly after this revelation from the mysterious Nathan. The same Dr Connor who had very kindly pushed the blame her direction as soon as it had become a little uncomfortable for him.

DEATH IN PIECES

Was it possible that this Nathan was the young man in question?

"I've got us the motherlode!" DC Crandell declared as she appeared in the doorway of the squad room, her face hidden behind a stack of boxes.

"What are they?" Harriet asked, getting to her feet before she hefted down one of the boxes and set it on the desk next to her.

"You're not going to often hear me say this," Crandell said as she dropped the pile down onto another free desk. "I think you were right Dr Quinn."

"I was?" Harriet tried to keep the surprise from her voice as she peered into the box closest to her.

"The DI asked me to look into Rosemary Cline, as you suggested."

Harriet paused her perusal and turned her full attention to the DC. Maz joined them and, from the corner of her eye, Harriet spotted Dr Perez as she wandered out of the conference room.

"Well, Rosemary's husband George told me his wife had her suspicions about who was behind the murders."

Harriet felt her heart stall in her chest, and she gripped the edge of the desk in order to stay on her feet.

"Please tell me he gave you a name," Maz said, sounding as excited as Harriet felt.

Crandell shook her head. "No name, but he gave me these instead." She gestured to the boxes.

337

"But what are they?" Maz asked, as he popped the lid off one and began to rummage around in it. "They look like old files and notebooks."

"George said his wife used to do some work when she could, on parole board hearings. Mostly for young offenders, after she'd arrested them, and they'd served their time. She liked to help reacquaint them with society, so to speak." Crandell sighed. "Well, according to George, Rosemary thought the killer was somebody she'd helped."

Something clicked in Harriet's brain. "Oh, my god," she whispered more to herself than the others, but they heard her, nonetheless.

"What is it?" Katerina asked, drawing level with her.

"I knew the name was familiar to me, but I couldn't remember where it was from."

The others stared at her as though she had completely lost her mind. "Rosemary Cline. I remember the name from an article I read in Dr Connor's office, once. He has it framed in there. Something about the excellent work he and others like him were doing with rehabilitating violent youngsters who'd been placed in juvenile detention centres."

"And how does Rosemary play into all of this?" Katerina asked, perching on the desk next to Maz who stared up at her in awe.

"Rosemary's name was listed in the article as one

of the police officers who was giving up her free time to help these youngsters rejoin society after prolonged stays in detention centres."

"What has this got to do with Crandell getting us yet more paperwork to sift through?" Maz asked.

"Don't you see? Rosemary thought that one of the youngsters she'd helped was the one behind the murders. She figured it out and he murdered her because of it."

Maz eyed her speculatively. "I don't know..."

"I think Dr Quinn may be on the right path here," Katerina said.

"Rachel's friend mentioned a man named Nathan who had contacted her in the months leading up to her death. He was said to have told her he had information pertaining to a misdiagnosis or mistreatment of a young man by a prominent psychiatrist."

"What's this now?" Drew's voice cut in, and Harriet swung around to see him sliding out of his coat.

"DC Crandell has just cracked the case wide open, Guv," Maz said, as he swung around on his chair. "The only problem is that she thinks the answer is in one of these boxes."

Drew glanced down over at Harriet. "What was that I heard you say about Rachel and a young man who'd been misdiagnosed by somebody?"

"Alyssa told me that Nathan had promised

Rachel a story about such a young man, and I realised where I'd heard Rosemary's name before."

He cocked a questioning eyebrow at her.

"Dr Connor," she said. "He's the common denominator in all of these things. Somebody he treated, that Rosemary helped to rehabilitate, is the Star Killer."

Drew pursed his lips, his unhappiness palpable. "I'm not sure," he said.

"Think about it, Drew," Harriet said. "It makes sense. Why kill the first puzzle master unless she'd figured out who he was?"

Despite the look of scepticism he wore, Drew nodded reluctantly. "And you think Rosemary Cline has written down our killer's name in one of these boxes?"

Crandell lifted a stack of photos from the box. "I think she's done more than given us a name, Guv; I think she has the photos to go with them."

"Then we'd better get to work," Drew said.

Harriet turned to the box in front of her and pulled the lid off. Staring down at the notebooks, and despite the daunting level of work ahead of them, she felt the first stirrings of hope since the case had started.

They were going to catch him.

Now they just needed a name.

CHAPTER FORTY-SIX

"I THINK I'VE GOT SOMETHING," Maz said, pushing a notebook across the desk. "This guy here, Nolan Matthews, was a patient of Dr Connor during his time in juvenile detention. Rosemary was the arresting officer when, at age twelve, Nolan attempted to murder his brother by dosing him with rat poison."

He held the notebook out towards Harriet, who took it.

"Dr Connor believed the boy was simply looking for attention and that his intention was not to kill his brother," Maz continued. "According to the records, Rosemary sat in on the parole board hearing and spoke on Nolan's behalf when he was up for early release at age seventeen. It was the parole board's opinion and that of Dr Connor that he showed sufficient remorse for his crimes and had learned coping mechanisms with which to live by."

Harriet glanced over at Maz. "How long ago does it say this happened?"

He flipped through the file. "Nolan was released in 1999."

"And the first murder was committed in 2001," Crandell said. "That fits with your timeline, Doc."

Harriet nodded but her attention was riveted to the notebook in her hands. "According to this, his brother only survived because upon tasting the poisoned packet of crisps, he immediately threw up and was rushed to hospital by their parents when he began suffering from convulsions."

"That doesn't sound to me like the actions of someone who did not truly have the intent to kill his brother," Dr Perez piped up. "It sounds like this Dr Connor misread the situation completely."

Harriet scanned the page and felt her stomach turn over.

"His brother's name was Nathan."

Drew met her eyes across the table. "What did you say Rachel's informant's name was?"

"Nathan..."

Crandell pulled a stack of pictures out. "I'm sure I've seen a Nolan Matthews in here somewhere."

"I want to speak to the Detective in charge!"

The unfamiliar voice rose above the general din

in the squad room, drawing everyone's attention. "I want to know what they're doing about Gabriel."

"Who is that?" Harriet asked, as Drew got to his feet and crossed the room to where the commotion was taking place. A drunken man, shirt askew and hair disheveled, wheeled around as soon as Drew approached him.

"What are you doing about Gabe?" His words were slurred, and he gripped the wall in an attempt to stay upright.

"You weren't here earlier when DI Haskell spoke to Michael Barrows about the missing man Gabriel," Katerina said, sounding almost bored. "He wasn't very helpful then, so I'm not sure why he's come back now. And in this state." She rolled her eyes. "Some people enjoy nothing more than to be overly theatrical."

"Who is he?"

Katerina glanced over at the grouping near the door. "Gabriel's boyfriend. Well, his ex-boyfriend. He cheated and they had a fight... It's all here in the statement." She passed the folder to Harriet who scooped it up and skimmed the contents, one line in particular stood out to her and the hairs on the back of her neck stood to attention.

"What is it?" Katerina asked, eyeing her as though she had just sprouted a second head.

"Michael says here in his written statement that

on the night in question, when he cheated on Gabriel, his friend Taff *Cline* was out with them."

Katerina nodded and Harriet knew she hadn't seen the connection. "Michael continues, and says that Taff was the one who sent the offending images to Gabriel's phone. Why would he do that?"

Katerina shrugged. "I have no idea. Revenge? Jealousy? Hatred?"

Harriet pushed onto her feet as Crandell pulled a photo from the pile triumphantly. "Got it."

"Can I borrow it?" Harriet said.

Crandell handed it over and Harriet made her way towards the doors to the squad room. She found Drew and Michael in the hall. The other man was sobbing, and Drew shot her a panicked look as he struggled to console the heartbroken ex.

"Hi, Michael. My name is Dr Quinn. You can call me Harriet if you'd like."

Michael lifted his head and glanced over at her before he wiped his eyes with the sleeve of his jumper. "When are you going to get him back?"

Harriet gave him her best sympathetic smile. "Michael, there are a couple of questions I'd like to ask you, if that's all right."

He nodded and wobbled unsteadily on his feet. "I feel so useless. I just want to help. I don't care what it is, I just want him home."

Harriet inclined her head toward the seats in the hall. "Maybe we should take a seat."

He followed her to the benches, and Harriet could feel Drew as he hovered behind her. "Michael, you said in your statement that when you were out on Monday night you--"

"Oh, not this again. I didn't mean to do it. I love him."

"I know that," Harriet said softly. "You said in your statement that it was a friend of yours, Taff Cline, who sent the images and videos to Gabriel. Is that correct?"

He nodded miserably.

"Why would Taff do that, do you think?"

Michael shrugged. "I don't know. He's always been the jealous type. We were only friends with him because Gabe took pity on him."

"How did you meet Taff?"

Michael sat back in the seat and let his head drop back against the wall. "He was a mature student, like Gabe. Taff is older though, he started at the university, he's getting a degree in philosophy or some such bullshit." He rolled his eyes. "I mean, what is he going to do with a degree in philosophy?"

Harriet nodded. "What else can you tell me about Taff?"

Michael shrugged. "Nothing much. He lives at his mother's house. She died a year ago and he moved back from London. He said he was down there for work."

"Did he tell you what he did in London?"

Michael shook his head. "No, we were never that close."

"But you were close enough to go out with him on Monday night?" Drew cut in.

"And look where that got me. He blabbed to Gabe and now--"

"Michael, is there anything else you can tell us about Taff? Anything at all?"

He turned toward her. "You think he's got something to do with this, don't you?"

"We're just exploring all avenues, and it's important that we get as rounded a picture as is possible from you, and everyone else who knew Gabriel."

He swallowed hard. "Taff is harmless."

"What makes you say that?"

"He's a total nerd. His idea of fun is spending the day with his head stuck in a paper, doing a crossword, or sudoku."

"What about jigsaws?" Drew asked, and Harriet could feel the quiet tension that radiated from him.

"Yeah, he's obsessed with them. How did you know? He's got this huge collection he keeps in his shed."

"Michael, have you got a current address for Taff?"

The other man nodded and pulled his phone from his pocket. "I can call him now if you'd like. Tell him to come in and--"

"No," Harriet said, shaking her head gently.

"'That's not necessary. It's getting late. We'll just nip over there and have a quick word with him."

Michael nodded. "Yeah, I suppose..." He started to cry again, and Harriet pulled a tissue from the packet she kept in her pocket. When he started to quieten, Harriet tried again.

"Do you think we could have Taff's address?"

Michael blew his nose loudly. "If it's him, I'll never forgive myself."

Harriet shook her head. "You can't think like that. You've done all you could for Gabriel and giving us the address is helping him further."

He glanced down at his hands. "He lives in his mother's house over in Newholm. I can't remember the exact address."

Harriet shot Drew a quick look and he headed back into the squad room leaving her with Michael. Placing her hand on the man's arm, Harriet smiled. "You've been a big help, Michael."

He leaned forward and buried his face in his hands. "How will he ever forgive me?"

A COUPLE OF MINUTES LATER, Harriet joined the others back in the squad room. DCI Gregson had been briefed and was handing out the last of the assignments.

"You'll meet armed response at Nolan Matthew's

residence. I want this done by the book, people. No screw ups. And just pray to God that when we get in there, Gabriel Hopkins is still alive."

Drew nodded and paused next to Harriet as the others bustled around. "You should stay here."

She shook her head. "I'm not getting left behind."

He opened his mouth to argue, but she cut him off. "Look, I'm not saying I want to be a part of the raid, just that I won't be left here twiddling my thumbs while you all go off and confront him. He chose me as his puzzle master. Let me see this thing through."

She could feel his gaze on her face before he finally inclined his head. "Fine. But you're staying in the car the whole time, with the doors locked."

She grinned up at him. "No problem. We both know I'm more of a thinker than a fighter."

"I thought it was more of a lover than a fighter?" He quirked an eyebrow at her and Harriet found herself beginning to laugh.

This was how it was supposed to be between them. The constant back and forth arguing and the silent grudges had done nothing but wear her down. Not that she could blame him.

"Let's go." DCI Gregson's voice cut through the disarray in the squad room.

"You coming?" Drew asked as he grabbed his coat from the back of the chair.

Harriet nodded, and slipped her arms into her

own coat. Nolan Matthews had chosen her. He'd believed he could outsmart her, and he'd been wrong. However, she couldn't shake the unease that coiled in the pit of her stomach. What if, when they got there, they were too late and he'd already murdered Gabriel?

It was an unsettling thought and no matter how hard she tried, she couldn't rid herself of it as she followed Drew to the car.

CHAPTER FORTY-SEVEN

THE JOY DREW had felt over finally getting a name for the bastard who had caused so much heartache and pain down through the years had faded; leaving only nervous tension in its wake.

What if they were too late? What if he got away? What if he wasn't the man they were after?

The last question was just his brain's way of trying to throw him off. Despite knowing that, he couldn't shake it off.

What if they were wrong? What if they'd got everything wrong up to now? It wouldn't have been the first time where this guy was concerned. Other officers in the past had thought they were getting close to him only to have the whole sorry mess blow up in their faces.

They parked down the road from Nolan's

Matthew's house. Drew turned to Harriet who had taken up her usual position in the front passenger seat next to him.

"You're going to have to wait with the other personnel who aren't going in at the house."

She nodded and smiled over at him. "That's fine."

Pushing open his door, he stepped out and was surprised to find the wind had picked up. That, at least, would help them and give them more of an element of surprise.

Hurrying along the dark road, he got to the armed response van and found the guys already preparing for the breach.

Standing there, listening to them speak, Drew felt suddenly out of his depth. Armed response would be making all the calls on this one and all he was supposed to do was sit back and twiddle his thumbs, only following them inside once they'd cleared the area of threats.

Somebody passed him a vest and he shrugged out of his jacket and slipped it on. He didn't mind the discomfort of wearing it.

"Is everybody clear on their jobs?" DCI Gregson asked, his gaze scanning the crowd until it came to rest on Drew. "I want absolutely no heroics here. Just in and out as cleanly as possible."

Despite it being so dark, Drew couldn't help but feel as though his boss was speaking directly to him.

Maz moved up next to him. The DS practically buzzed with energy and he bounced on the balls of his feet.

"Do you really think this is him?" Maz asked as they followed the others down the short cut that took them to the top of Nolan's driveway.

"I hope so," Drew said softly.

"Sshh." The voice came from somewhere just ahead of them and Drew fell instantly silent.

THE SECONDS TICKED by as he waited for the signal that the first group had breached the house. With each moment that passed, he felt his heart rate rise. Sweat trickled down his spine, turning icy in the cold wind that buffeted them.

There was a flurry of excited activity ahead of them, and suddenly they were moving.

Drew's legs pumped, carrying him forward of their own volition as they crossed the dark drive.

They entered the house through the front door, the darkness closing in around them.

Somebody flicked on the lights as the call went up that the place was clear.

"Have they got him?" he asked one of the armed response guys who'd led them inside.

"Not yet, mate."

Drew felt his heart rate speed up. "But the house is clear, yeah?"

The bloke nodded and picked up his radio as it crackled to life. "House is all clear. No sign of the suspect."

Drew's heart sank. "There have to be outbuildings or something around here," he said. "This can't be it."

The guy ahead of him started to shrug when there was another burst of static from the radio. They fell silent and Drew found himself holding his breath as he waited for the message to come through.

"We've got an injured male here, in the shed at the back of the house. Weak pulse, blood loss. We need paramedics."

"Is it Gabriel?"

The guy ahead of him shrugged. "No idea, mate. You heard the same message I did."

Drew nodded and started to move through the house with his heart hammering in his chest.

Moving through the kitchen, he barely registered the mess and the boxes piled high on every surface. Papers and cut-out images were strewn across each counter.

Picking his way to the open back door, he stepped out onto a small path that led down to a shed near the back fence.

A light in the garden lit the place up, making it look like a football ground.

Gregson intercepted him halfway down the garden. "It's not him," he said. "It's not Nolan."

"And Gabriel?"

Gregson glanced toward the ground. "He's unconscious. He's in a bad way. We can't do a visual ID on him."

Drew's stomach flipped over as Gregson's words sank in. "What do you mean, we can't do a visual ID on him? It's either him, or it's not."

"It's impossible to tell, and we don't know who the third victim was supposed to be," Gregson said. "For all we know, the bastard already dumped Gabriel and we just haven't found his body yet. This could be the third victim."

Drew pushed past the other man and headed for the shed.

"Drew!" Gregson called after him.

Drew ignored him. He made it as far as the door to the shed before the paramedics rushed in, jostling him out of the way. But not before he got a glimpse at the inside of the shed.

The victim in question was still seated in the middle of the room but Gregson had been right to say there would be no visual identification. The man in the chair jerked and a bloody bubble appeared at the end of where he thought his nose should be. It took Drew a moment to realise what he was looking at and when it dawned on him, he felt his stomach churn.

Drew flung himself backwards and away from the shed as bile raced up the back of his throat. He made it as far as the perimeter fence before the acrid vomit filled his mouth.

Dropping to the ground, he ignored the damp grass as it soaked his trousers. He retched until his stomach was empty, and still he felt the need to purge himself of what he'd just witnessed.

How had the victim survived that? It seemed impossible, and yet there was no doubt in his mind that whoever it was, the poor bloke was still alive beneath the suffering that had been inflicted upon him.

"You all right, guv?" Maz's voice filtered through the rushing in his ears and Drew turned his face to see the young DS standing next to him.

Wiping the back of his hand across his mouth, he nodded. "I'm fine." Slowly, he climbed to his feet, in time to see the paramedics wheel the covered victim from the shed.

"Do you think he'll make it?" Maz asked, his face twisted up in consternation.

"I don't know," Drew said hoarsely as the memory flashed in his head. He would have nightmares about that image for a long time to come.

"Armed response has gone over the whole property. They said Nolan's nowhere to be found."

Drew sighed and shoved a hand back through his hair. "We need to know where he's gone to. He can't be allowed to get away with this."

Something tugged at the edge of his vision and he glanced up to see Harriet picking her way over the grass to where he stood.

"They didn't get him." She sounded as disappointed as he felt.

He shook his head. "No. His van isn't here either."

She sighed and glanced back up at the house. "There's so much in there."

Drew jerked his head in the direction of the shed. "I'm going to go out on a limb and say that's where all the pertinent evidence will be found."

Harriet followed his line of sight and he noted the way her body stiffened. "They don't know if the person they removed from the shed was Gabriel or not. I mean, he fits his build but..." She trailed off and glanced up at him. "You saw him, didn't you?"

Drew turned his head away, not wanting to meet her penetrating gaze. If he saw pity reflected in her eyes, he knew it would be his undoing. He didn't need pity, or sympathy. What he needed now was to do his job. He needed to focus; to concentrate on catching the bastard who had started all of this.

"We're going to get him," she said, as though she could read his thoughts.

He nodded. "We have to."

"Agreed," she said. "He's done enough damage. It's time for all of this to come to an end."

Drew glanced back at her and was surprised to find her expression wasn't one of sympathy or pity but, instead, held a look of determination. He gave her a tight smile.

"We've got work to do then."

CHAPTER FORTY-EIGHT

DRESSED IN A TYVEK SUIT, Harriet stepped into the shed. The SOCOs were far from finished but they'd agreed to give her a few minutes' worth of access, considering the situation regarding Nolan Matthews. The metal platforms set up around the room allowed her to move above the floor without stepping in anything that might be evidence.

She paused next to the desk in the corner and scanned the surface. Once they were done going through his things, forensics had promised to bag everything they didn't need and send it over to the station. At the earliest, she would get to see the items tomorrow but until then, Nolan's scribbled writings would have to remain a mystery to her.

"Do you see anything useful?" Drew asked, pausing behind her.

She shook her head, the sound of the suit crinkled around her blocking out the other sounds. "There's nothing here to tell me where he's going. At least nothing I can see just by glancing at it. I mean, there might be something in these piles of writings but..." She trailed off. "We really need to get a proper look at these, Drew. Is there any way they can speed up the process?"

He shook his head. "The fact they've let us in here at all is a miracle."

Disappointed, she returned her attention to the items scattered about the desk's surface. "He'd started making another puzzle," she said, pointing to a partially covered jigsaw piece.

"For all we know, that's part of one of the old ones."

Harriet shook her head. "I don't think so. I'm sure it was Gabriel they removed from here. I don't think he's taken his third victim yet."

"He could have them right now," Drew said, his voice muffled by the mask he wore.

Harriet's stomach clenched painfully as her gaze fell on the shelves, half shrouded in darkness at the back of the room. "Is that what I think it is?"

"Trophies," Drew said.

"Success stories," she added. "Remember, each victim he took, each piece he cut off them and kept, was proof that he was smarter than anyone else."

Following the steps around the room, she crossed to the other side and halted next to the small camp bed. "He didn't sleep in the house while he was working," she said.

"It doesn't look like he did, no." Drew stood next to the desk, his eyes dark and unfathomable in the room.

"He didn't," she said. "He wanted to be close to them. Like a vampire he fed off their misery and pain. In order to satisfy himself completely, he needed to be with them all the time. Otherwise how else could he get everything he needed?"

"There are pictures of Rachel here," Drew said, as he turned and stared down at the desk. "These must have been taken after..."

Harriet nodded and inclined her head toward the video camera positioned in the corner of the room, offering the widest possible angle of the scene. "I'm guessing the video and photographs were just another opportunity for him to relive his crimes. It's what gave him the ability to fall dormant for a time."

"Like a snake that's gorged itself," Drew said, the disgust evident in his voice.

Harriet nodded but her mind was whirling with unspoken thoughts. There was something about the entire set-up that felt off to her.

"What is it?" Drew asked.

"Hmm?" Harriet lifted her face and met his gaze.

"You've got the look in your eyes again. The one that says you've thought of something."

"It was just something I was thinking about. Somebody with a compulsion this strong wouldn't have been able to just go completely dormant for years at a time."

Drew cocked his head to the side as Harriet crossed toward him and ushered him outside.

Once out in the crisp night air, Harriet pulled the mask from her face and pushed the hood back off her head. "He didn't just stop, Drew. He couldn't. Everything he did to them--every cut he inflicted, every wound, every bruise--it's part of his compulsion. He needs this; needs it like you and I need air to breathe."

Drew slipped the mask onto the top of his head. "What are you saying?"

"I'm saying what he's been doing here with us, I think it was just the tip of the iceberg. I'm willing to bet, if we could trace him back to the places he's been every time he went dormant, we would find other crimes with a similar signature to the ones here."

"Wouldn't we have seen it before now?"

She shook her head. "We've been looking for the Star Killer all this time. We believed he needed a specific set of circumstances to do what he does, but I think we were wrong. His MO can change--and I think it has--but the signature, the thing that makes it uniquely him, will be the same for those other murders."

"How do we find them?"

Closing her eyes, Harriet tried to imagine Nolan. London would be relatively easy to disappear in but that didn't mean it would be easy to murder with impunity.

"High risk victims," she said finally. "He'll have targeted prostitutes, the homeless, people he thinks society has ignored, much like he believes it's ignored him. In them, he'll have seen something kindred. But the other part of him, the aspect that craves destruction, will view them as expendable. He knows they won't be missed."

Harriet drew in a deep breath. "Let's be honest; as much as I hate it, how much attention is given to a prostitute who disappears? And when it comes to the homeless, unless they self-police and report it, then who is going to even notice?"

She could tell from the expression on his face that she'd struck a nerve.

"Fine. Say you're right. How are we going to track down these murders?"

Folding her arms over her chest she turned and glanced back at the shed. "Leave it with me and I'll compile a potential report for other police forces to look out for where past crimes are concerned. Once you can see the signature, everything else is relatively straightforward."

Drew shuddered. "I swear, sometimes the way you talk about this stuff..."

Surprised, she took a step back. "What do you mean?"

"You're so relaxed around all this..." He gestured with his hands as though searching for the right word. "All this *horror*. It's like you're at home with it. It's a little hard for me to wrap my head around, sometimes."

Harriet let her gaze drop back to the ground. It wasn't the first time she'd had that accusation levelled at her. People mistook her ability to empathise with the killer, as well as his victim, as a sign that she somehow condoned the behaviour, when really nothing could have been further from the truth.

"If I don't do this, then who will?"

"I'm sorry," he said. "I didn't mean it to sound like that."

She shook her head, her dark hair sliding noisily over the collar of the suit. "You did mean it and I get it, within reason. But make no mistake, Drew. I don't gladly go looking for the darkness. It finds me everywhere I am. I can't escape it, any more than you can. And I think that I can do what frightens you."

He stared at her, his eyes like two chips of hardened ice before he turned on his heel and strode away. She let him go. The case was beginning to get to them all by now and going after him would do no good. He needed time with his own thoughts to get them affixed in his own mind if he was going to carry on doing his job.

Drawing in a deep breath, Harriet began to strip out of the Tyvek suit. There was nothing more she could do here. And until forensics gave them the go ahead to begin going through the items they'd discovered, she was as good as useless.

Shoving her coverall into an evidence bag, she followed the path out of the garden. Bumping into Maz, she schooled her features into a smile.

"Could you give me a lift back to my house?" she asked.

He seemed surprised by her request. "Sure, but I thought Drew would have done that."

Harriet shrugged. "I don't think he's in the mood for that now."

Maz looked her over. "Did you two have a fight?"

"No, I think I hit a nerve with him is all."

Maz's expression shifted. "I don't think he's feeling himself. He saw the poor guy before the paramedics got in there and I found him vomiting in the bushes."

Harriet tried to conceal her surprise but failed as Maz grinned at her. "You didn't know that, did you?"

She shook her head. "No, he never mentioned it."

Pulling his keys from his pocket, Maz gave her a brief smile. "That's pretty typical of the DI. Around here, you have to be capable of reading between the lines."

His canny observation made Harriet laugh and he shot her a surprised look. "What did I say?"

"Nothing," she said. "Just don't ever change."

Looking a little pleased with himself Maz led her back to the car. "I'll try not to."

CHAPTER FORTY-NINE

"HASKELL!" the Monk's voice roused Drew from the fitful sleep he'd fallen into and he jerked awake. Glaring up at the older man above him, Drew tried to shrug him off and turned over on the couch in the corner room.

"Have you been here all night?" Gregson's voice continued to bore through his skull.

"I didn't want to leave in case there were any developments overnight," he said, his voice muffled by the cushion he'd sank his face into.

"For God's sake, man, get up and go home. You're no good to me in this state."

Drew shook his head. "Sir, I'm fine. I just need a quick kip and I'll be right as rain in the morning."

"Haskell, go home, get some sleep, shower, and come back when you're halfway human again. I don't

366

want to see you in this office until you do all of that. Got it?"

Groaning, Drew rolled off the couch and onto his feet. He pulled his keys from his pocket, but Gregson snatched them out of his hand.

"I'll have a uniform drive you home."

"Sir, I'm more than capable of driving myself home." Drew wasn't able to keep the irritation from his voice. It had been a long time since he'd been a teenager in need of looking after and even back then, he'd been capable of taking care of himself. He definitely didn't need Gregson trying to fill the role of father figure in his life. The one he'd had was more than enough.

Gregson shook his head. "You can barely see straight, Haskell. I'm not a fool. I know a man teetering on the edge when I see him."

"Bullshit," Drew said, his anger spilling over into his voice.

Gregson raised an eyebrow. "Go home."

Drew held his hand out for the keys, but Gregson shook his head. "No. Get a uniform to drive you."

"I'll walk," Drew said, hating the sullen note in his voice as he headed for the door. In the doorway, he paused. "Any word on the victim they brought to hospital?"

Gregson sighed. "He's hanging in there."

"Have they identified him yet?"

"It's Gabriel Hopkins," Gregson said. "Michael

Barrows confirmed it based on a tattoo Gabriel has in a particularly intimate place."

Drew sucked a breath in through his teeth. "They didn't let him see Gabriel like that, did they?"

Gregson shook his head. "Of course not. They asked him about identifying marks and he described the tattoo perfectly." Gregson dropped onto the couch and scrubbed his hand over his balding head. "If the poor bloke pulls through this, he's never going to be the same again."

Drew shook his head. "No."

"You saw him, didn't you?"

Drew's shoulder's stiffened and he struggled to let some of the tension go from his body and failed. "I did. I think if I was in his shoes, I'd prefer not to survive."

Drew didn't turn around to see Gregson's expression, he could practically imagine it.

"People are resilient, Drew. Don't underestimate the desire to survive."

"With all due respect, sir, the bloke had no face. Nolan skinned him alive. If he survives, and that's a pretty big 'if' considering the seriousness of his injuries, how is he going to cope with everything he's been through?"

Drew finally glanced back at the other man, who spread his palms in a helpless gesture. "I don't know what to say to you."

"Neither do I," Drew said finally.

"Go home, get some sleep, shower, and come back so we can finish this," the Monk said. "It's important to us all that we get this over with once and for all."

Drew gave a jerky nod as a sign of his assent.

Slamming out of the office, he made it into the squad room. There were only a handful of officers lingering and they looked at him hopefully. Clearly, he wasn't the only one waiting for some kind of break in the case. With a sigh, he left. Outside in the cold early morning air, he cast his mind back over the raid. How had they missed Nolan?

It seemed impossible that he could have hidden from them, so he must have known they were coming.

"Shit." As he crossed the road in front of his house, he pulled his phone free of his pocket and dialled Maz's number. There was no answer, and he hung up in frustration. Squaring his shoulders, he dialled Harriet's number as he fished the keys to his apartment from his jacket pocket.

"Dr Quinn," she said. To him, she sounded as though she'd been sleeping, and he suddenly wished that he was doing the same thing.

"Harriet, it's Drew."

"Have you caught him?" Her voice was immediately alert.

"No. Nothing yet. But there's something bugging

me. When we got there, Nolan should have been there."

There was silence on the other end of the line, and he paused, but when she said nothing, he decided to continue. "Everything he did to Gabriel. You said yourself that he would have wanted to be there, to witness it. To soak it in."

"Yeah, it's part of his compulsion. He needs to be a part of the suffering. He craves the control. And he enjoys taking from his victims everything they hold dear. He took Rachel's tongue as an ironic commentary on her job as a journalist. Figuratively speaking he was removing her ability to tell her stories."

"But you said he did this because of jealousy?"

Harriet sighed. "Envy is not an easy emotion to pin down. He envied Rachel for what she represented and so he sought to destroy it."

"And Gabriel?"

"He was handsome," Harriet said. "Popular. Loved by those who knew him. It's possible that on some level, he felt a particular attachment to Michael and wanted to destroy the relationship he and Gabriel had. Because he's not capable of getting that close to another human without ultimately destroying them."

"Do you think it's possible somebody tipped Nolan off that we were coming?"

"You think Michael called him, after all?"

Drew pressed his head against the wooden door

frame. "Maybe. I'm not sure. But after everything you said, something spooked him. He skinned Gabriel. Wouldn't he want to hang around for that?"

"He flayed him alive?" Harriet asked. The horror in her voice was palpable and Drew felt suddenly guilty for everything he'd said to her earlier. Deep down, he knew why she did the things she did. She was good at her job because of her empathy but he'd seen the cost it exacted on her soul.

To suggest anything other than that had been unnecessarily cruel on his behalf. She deserved better than that.

"He did," he said.

She sucked in a sharp breath. "Then, yes, I would have thought he would have wanted to stay for that. Wounds like that would have eventually proved fatal, the fact that he is still alive now is nothing short of a miracle."

Drew said nothing.

"I think you're right and that Michael called him. He wouldn't have left and willingly walked away from such an achievement."

"That's what I thought," he said. "Right I'm going to call Olivia and ask her to bring Michael Barrows in for another chat. If he has a way of contacting Nolan, we need to exploit that."

"Where are you now?" Harriet asked.

"On my way in through my front door; the Monk

371

sent me home. I'll be in later in the morning though, so we can regroup then."

"I'll see you, then," Harriet said.

The words he longed to speak stuck on the tip of his tongue.

"I'm sorry about earlier..."

"Don't," she said. "Let's not go over old ground."

"But..."

"It's fine, Drew. I get it, I really do. I'll see you in the morning."

The line clicked, and he was left to stare at the phone. The battery light blinked up at him and he swore under his breath as he shoved the keys into the lock. The door swung inwards and he hurried inside.

He would call Olivia as soon as he got the phone onto charge. Coffee was next on the list. Screw Gregson and his demands for sleep. A quick shower and a shot of caffeine would be all he needed to...

His thoughts cut off as his foot scuffed against the edge of something plastic. In the early morning sunlight that was slowly beginning to creep through the windows he spotted the sheet of plastic that lay across the living room floor. His gaze snagged on the kitchen chair right in the middle of it, but it was too late.

Something heavy and hard struck the back of his head and he dropped to his knees. The phone skittered across the plastic and out of his reach.

Something warm dripped down the front of his

head and into his eyes. He raised his hands and his fingers came away smeared with blood.

His heartbeat began to pound in his head, and he tried to turn but something heavy caught him on the side of his chin and the world was plunged into darkness.

CHAPTER FIFTY

EARLY THE NEXT MORNING, Harriet sat in Dr Connor's office and stared at the certificates that lined the walls. It was the last place she wanted to be, but the appointment had been made, and she wanted answers. At least she would be able to kill two birds with one stone.

Rearranging herself in the chair, she glanced surreptitiously down at her phone and, satisfied that the little red light was still blinking, settled back.

Lifting her gaze again to the pictures on the wall, she paused at the image of the magazine article Jonathan had framed.

The very one where Rosemary Cline had been mentioned and the pieces of the puzzle had finally begun to slot together. The headline of the piece read '*Star Patient Receives New Lease of Life After Wonder Intervention of Psychiatrist.*'

It was the word 'Star' that stuck out to Harriet. Nolan had spent his life cutting stars out of the bodies of his victims, each one his attempt at proving to Dr Connor that he was special.

"I'm sorry to have kept you waiting." Jonathan breezed into the office and closed the door softly behind him.

His smile was wide and beguiling as he moved around to the other side of the desk and took up his position.

"You wanted to discuss your mother, is that correct?"

"Why is she being denied visitors at the moment?"

"Straight to the point," he said. "I always liked that about you, Harriet."

"Why is my mother being denied visitors?"

He shrugged, hands splayed out in front of him. "She requested for her visitation privileges to be suspended. And considering her behaviour, I didn't think it was a bad idea."

"What behaviour?"

"Well, there's the attack on the assistant."

"That was weeks ago."

Jonathan shook his head. "You know how these things are, Harriet. I can't go risking a visitor's safety by allowing them inside a volatile patient's room."

"You had no problem the last time."

"That was before we reassessed the situation." He

sighed and folded his hands on the desk before him. "I know you've got strong feelings about all of this; after all, this is your mother we're talking about. But you, of all people, should understand the necessary precautions we've had to take."

"Are you telling me she's injured another member of staff?"

"You're just going to have to trust me on this, Harriet. I'm doing it for your own good."

She leaned back in the seat. "Tell me, do you remember Rosemary Cline?"

For a moment his expression was blank and then he recovered. "I don't think I do. Was she a patient here?"

"What about Rachel Kennedy?"

Jonathan's expression shifted and he glanced down at the desk. "This is not the best time to discuss this," he said. "It seems petty to speak ill of the dead."

"So, you do remember her?"

"What does it matter? The woman is dead."

"What about Nolan Matthews?"

He stared blankly at her. "What is this?"

"Do you remember him?"

"I've never heard of him. Now tell me what this is all about?"

Harriet inclined her head in the direction of the wall behind him. He glanced up at the framed pictures and then returned his attention to her face. "I fail to see what this has to do with--"

"Look again, Jonathan. Look closely."

He opened his mouth to protest. "Look at it, Jonathan."

Sighing heavily, he pushed onto his feet and stared at the images. "What am I supposed to be looking at?"

"How about the write up in that prominent magazine about the wonderful work you did with those youths back when you were starting out?"

He glanced over his shoulder and swallowed hard. "What about it?"

"So, you do remember Nolan Matthews?"

"Why do you want to know?"

"You said he was your greatest success. You built your career on the back of his recovery, didn't you?"

"There were a lot of different factors surrounding that case," Jonathan said as he turned and sat back down.

"Have you known all this time what he's been doing?"

There was a flicker of discomfort that flitted momentarily across his face. "He's in London now, isn't he?"

She shook her head. "No, he's been back in York-shire for the past year. You're telling me you didn't try to keep track of your star pupil?"

"What are you getting at, Harriet? You know I've never enjoyed stupid games like this."

"Why did you say he was cured?"

He sighed and leaned back in his chair. "Is that what this is about? You think you can dig a little dirt up from my past and use it to blackmail me?" He grinned at her triumphantly. "It is, isn't it?" Jonathan pushed onto his feet and moved around the desk.

He stopped in front of it and sat down on the edge, crossing his legs at the ankle he deliberately brushed against her.

Harriet fought the urge to shift away from him.

"What can I say? There's nothing you can do. I've got the proof of your little fuck up and there's nothing you can do about it."

Harriet ducked her head in an attempt to hide her smile. "You didn't answer my question, Jonathan. Why say the boy was cured when you had to know he wasn't?"

Dr Connor snorted, the sound vulgar and inelegant in the confined space of his office. "There was nothing wrong with him. He was nothing more than an attention-seeking little shit who thought he was smarter than he was."

"So, you thought he was faking?"

"I told him he was. He would cry and tell me he had all these urges but one look at him and I knew he was bluffing. He just wanted people to think he was special. His parents, in his mind anyway, showed more affection and attention to his brother. In a fit of jealousy, he tried to kill the competition."

"And he used rat poison," Harriet said. "Did you

not think that showed a kind of forward planning, a level of premeditation and cruelty?"

Jonathan shook his head. "Premeditation, have you listened to yourself? He was a pathetic idiot who liked to make puzzles. He still does, you know."

Harriet stared up at the man she'd once idolised and felt a hollow ache open in the centre of her chest. Nolan had needed help. He'd been vulnerable and confused, and his doctor had dismissed his fears because he thought he knew better.

"What do you mean he still does? How do you know?"

"Over the years he's sent me bits and pieces of jigsaws he's made. They don't make any sense. They're just pieces."

Harriet's heartbeat accelerated in her chest.

"Do you have the pieces?"

Jonathan nodded. "I got the latest one this morning."

He crossed behind her and Harriet turned in the chair and watched him open a filing cabinet. He pulled several envelopes free and tossed them to her. "There."

"Do you have gloves?"

He stared at her incredulously. "What for?"

"Do you have some gloves I could use, Jonathan, or not?"

Rolling his eyes, he left the office. Harriet's fingers itched to dig into the envelopes, but she resisted. He returned a moment later and set a box of single use gloves down in front of her.

"I don't know why you're going to such effort. They're just puzzles."

She slipped on the gloves and quickly went through the packets. Checking the postage marks on them, she found the most recently dated envelope and pulled it open. There were three packets inside, still wrapped in their sandwich wrappers.

Harriet opened them up and went through the pieces. He was right, the pieces would have meant nothing to him. There was no context to any of them and without knowing what the puzzle was supposed to be, they would be impossible to figure out. But Harriet had seen the other half of the puzzles and she knew what each one represented.

The first packet, when completed, would undoubtedly be Rachel Kennedy, and the second had to be Gabriel Hopkins.

Harriet pulled the third packet open and spilled the pieces out onto the envelope.

"I told you, they mean nothing..."

Harriet's gaze roamed over the pieces, but he was right. The puzzle didn't mean anything to her. They were just pieces that didn't fit together. Frustrated, she climbed to her feet and swept all the puzzle pieces back into their envelopes.

"Where are you going?" he asked, moving to block her path.

"The police station," Harriet said.

"You can't prove I did anything wrong," he said. "You have--"

"Get out of my way, you buffoon," Harriet snapped. "Despite what you might think, not everything in this world is about you."

He stared at her, shock etched into every aspect of his face.

"You can't speak to me like that. I..."

"Do you know what your great treatment did for Nolan Matthews? Do you have any idea what you did to him? He tried to confide in you, tried to tell you the truth and you turned him away."

"He was faking."

"Faking so much that he grew up to be the Star Killer," Harriet said harshly. "He trusted you to help him and instead you spun a fairytale that fitted your career."

Jonathan backed up until he hit the edge of his desk and then dropped down onto it. "You're wrong, he's not..."

"The puzzles he sent you," Harriet said as she held the envelopes up to the light. "Each one of these is part of a larger puzzle that was sent to a police officer. An impossible puzzle to solve because they never had all the pieces you did. Each puzzle is a portrait of a victim he murdered because of your carelessness and negligence.

"And if you think I'm just going to sit back and let

you mistreat my mother in here, then you've got another thing coming, Jonathan."

Harriet was gratified to see him blanch beneath the strength of her tirade. With one last look of disgust, she strode from the office, leaving him sitting on the edge of his desk.

BACK IN THE CAR, Harriet tried calling Drew's number but to no avail. Each time she called she found herself instantly redirected to his voicemail, which was full.

Slamming her hands against the steering wheel, she started the engine.

"Where are you, Drew?"

CHAPTER FIFTY-ONE

DREW WOKE to find himself tied to the kitchen chair in the middle of the room. His brains felt scrambled and he stirred restlessly as his head began to throb. Struggling against the bonds that held him down, he tried to remember how he'd got there but his mind refused to put the pieces together.

"Finally."

Drew jerked his head upright and found a sinewy man standing in the doorway. His dark hair flopped over a serious and somewhat owlish face dominated by a pair of large glasses.

Drew recognised him from the picture they had of him. He was older than the one Rosemary Cline had kept in her files but then it was over eighteen years ago since the picture had been taken.

Nolan pushed upright, straightening his gangly

frame as he padded across the sheet of plastic on the floor to where Drew sat.

"You were out for quite a while. I thought maybe I'd done some permanent damage..." Nolan circled him slowly before he reached out and trailed a hand down over Drew's arm. "You're a big guy. Gabriel was big too but not like you... But then you know what they say, the bigger they are, the harder they fall."

Nolan giggled, managing to sound like a school-girl as he paused in front of Drew. He crouched down and peered up into his face, his large brown eyes solemn.

"Did you think you'd slip away from me?"

"What do you mean?"

"You're my third... I needed someone close to Dr Quinn and, well, there's nobody closer than the man she wants in her bed."

Drew shook his head. "I don't know what you're talking about. We just work together."

Nolan pouted, his bottom lip jutting out as he looked Drew over. "We both know that's a lie."

"It's the truth. We're colleagues, nothing more."

Nolan grinned up at him. "I know how to make you tell me the truth." He pulled a Stanley knife from his back pocket and Drew felt his stomach clench as Nolan slid the blade out. "Do you know what this will do to her when she eventually finds you? It's going to break her heart."

"You don't have to do this," Drew said, careful to keep his voice measured.

Nolan smiled. "No I don't. But I want to."

CHAPTER FIFTY-TWO

HARRIET CARRIED the jigsaw puzzle pieces into the squad room. "Did we get any of the pieces from Nolan's house yet? Any bits of the third puzzle?" She was breathless, her words garbled together.

Crandell glanced up at her. "Woah, doc, slow down. What was that?"

"The third puzzle," Harriet said. "Did they find it?"

Crandell indicated the box of items on the conference room desk. "Everything forensics have sent over so far is in there."

Harriet nodded and started toward the conference room. Rummaging through the items, she pulled a packet of puzzle pieces from the bottom of the box and her heart flipped in her chest as she carefully spilled them out.

"What are you doing?" Crandell asked, joining her.

"I've got the rest of the puzzle," she said. "We can..." Her voice trailed off as a photograph wrapped in plastic at the bottom of the box caught her attention. Her hands shook as she reached in and pulled it free.

"What is it?" Crandell asked, but her voice seemed to come from very far away.

"Harriet?"

"It's Drew..."

"What?"

"Drew," Harriet said, her heart skidding into overdrive. How could she have been so stupid? How could she not have seen it? Of course it would be Drew.

"Where's Drew?" she asked, turning her attention to Crandell. "Did he come in? Did you speak to him? He said he was going to call you and--"

"Slow down!" Crandell snapped. "What about Drew?"

Harriet sucked in a deep breath, but she couldn't slow the panic that spread through her. "Drew. Nolan's third victim, the one close to the puzzle master. It's Drew. He's the next victim."

Crandell shook her head. "That can't be. I mean, Drew is..."

"I'm telling you," Harriet said, as she held the

image up for Crandell to see. "He's going after Drew next."

"Shit!" Crandell's eyes widened as they focused on the picture.

"If he's not here then he has to be at home."

Crandell nodded. "Try and get him on the phone and I'll get armed response over there."

Harriet put the picture down on the desk as Crandell took off at a run. Without wasting a moment, Harriet scooped her phone from her bag and dialled Drew's number, hurrying from the office. The call went to voice mail as she took the stairs two at a time.

"Please be all right, please be all right." She muttered the words beneath her breath like some kind of mantra as she pushed out of the station and headed for her car.

He would be all right. He had to be. He just had to be.

CHAPTER FIFTY-THREE

GRITTING HIS TEETH, Drew tried to ignore the searing pain as Nolan raked the Stanley blade over the skin of his stomach. Each time, he allowed the blade to bite a little bit deeper, and Drew's boxers were already soaked in crimson blood.

"You're allowed to scream if you want to," Nolan said, watching him with a look of consternation on his face. "I won't mind."

"If it's all the same with you, I'd rather not."

"Why fight it?" Nolan asked, sitting back on his feet.

Drew found it hard to concentrate on the other man's blood-spattered face. The situation didn't feel real, and the longer it went, on the more dreamlike it became.

"Fight what?"

"The truth? I know what you are to Dr Quinn. I know you want her. I've seen it in your eyes."

Drew shook his head, more in an attempt to clear his mind than as a denial. His head continued to throb painfully, and the blood loss was slowly creeping up on him.

Nolan cut into him again, and Drew let out a low hiss of pain as the blade bit into his body. The steel pressed deeper and the pain turned to a numb burning as it severed the nerve endings.

"Whoops, too deep."

"You know, you're going to rot in jail," Drew said. Sweat beaded on his forehead as Nolan trailed the blade down across the inside of his thigh.

"They'll have to catch me first. Now, hold still. This is going to hurt."

Drew screwed his eyes shut as Nolan used the blade again. The pain was intense, and as hard as he tried to bite back the scream that bubbled in the back of his throat, he felt his resolve weakening.

Nolan dug the blade into him, and Drew finally stopped fighting.

CHAPTER FIFTY-FOUR

PARKING THE CAR HAPHAZARDLY, Harriet abandoned it with the keys still in the ignition. She raced up the path to Drew's door and hammered on it.

The curtains were drawn, and she tried to peer through the gap at the edges, but she couldn't see anything beyond her own face reflected back at her. Returning to the door, she pushed open the letter box. The sound of a pained scream poured out to greet her.

Her heart clenched in her chest as she recognised the owner of the voice.

"Drew!" She balled her hand into a fist and hammered on the door but there was no answer.

Pressing her face against the letter box, she sucked in a deep breath.

"Nolan, it's Dr Quinn, I know you're in there."

The silence continued to mock her, and Harriet's fear crawled into her throat like an animal desperate for escape. It was too quiet. What if Drew was dead? What if she'd heard his final cry, and Nolan had murdered him while she was standing out here on the doorstep?

"Nolan, I know you can hear me. Let me in, so we can talk."

The door clicked and Harriet fell forward onto the front mat. She straightened up and pushed open the door, it wasn't until she was across the threshold that she suddenly wished she'd thought to bring a weapon with her.

Not that there was time to worry about it now.

"Close the door after you." The stranger's voice drifted from the living room but instead of being utterly unfamiliar, as she'd expected, there was something about it that triggered a memory in the back of her mind.

She did as he asked, and then slowly stepped into the living room. Plastic rustled underfoot as she came to a halt. She tried to keep her expression neutral as she caught sight of Drew, slumped in a chair. Harriet hoped he was just unconscious and not as dead as he looked.

The voice in the back of her mind almost became a scream but she held it back. Now was not the time to wonder how much blood he had lost; not when the man next to him held a utility knife against his throat.

"I know you," Harriet said softly, directing her attention to the man next to Drew.

Nolan shuffled as though suddenly uncomfortable beneath Harriet's gaze. "Oh, yeah, and how is that?"

"You were at my lecture," she said. "The one on Nature versus Nurture. You asked me whether killers were born or created."

Nolan shrugged. "So what?"

"So, I remember you. You stood out to me."

"That's a lie. You didn't see me. Nobody ever does."

"Some people see you though, don't they?"

Drew moaned and stirred. He lifted his head and Harriet's breath caught in the back of her throat.

"Harriet, why are you here?" he said weakly.

"Don't worry about that now."

Nolan shifted suddenly and moved behind Drew, repositioning the blade so it was pressed more firmly against his throat.

"Have you ever seen arterial spray?" Nolan asked. "It's truly beautiful, I've watched it arc up and when it hits the floor it makes this wonderful sound..."

"If you're trying to disturb me, Nolan, I'm going to tell you now that it won't work."

Nolan cocked his head to the side like a predatory animal watching its prey. "And why's that?"

Drew looked at her with panicked eyes. "Harriet, get out of here now."

Ignoring him, she kept her gaze trained on Nolan. "Because I get it. I know what it feels like to be driven by darker impulses."

He shook his head and pressed the tip of the blade into Drew's throat, drawing a tiny ruby droplet that balanced on the blade before sliding down Drew's neck.

"You're lying."

Harriet shook her head. "I'm not lying. Look me in the face, Nolan. I'm not lying."

He glanced up at her. "What do you know about dark impulses?"

"More than you think. I know what it's like to crave pain."

"Harriet, go!"

"Drew, shut up, please."

"Yeah, Drew, shut up." Nolan mocked her with a smile, but she could see behind the smile there was a wavering in his emotions that gave her hope.

"I know how it feels to want to hurt," she said.

"Now you're just fucking with me because you want to save his life."

Harriet's gaze flickered to Drew's face. His eyes were wide and unfocused.

"I do want to save his life," she said. "I solved your puzzle, so you owe me."

Nolan scoffed, the sound painfully loud in the quiet of the room. "You're just like *him*."

"Dr Connor?"

Nolan stiffened and fixed her with his gaze. "He's an idiot."

Harriet nodded and she flexed her numb fingers. Where the hell were the armed response unit?

"I'm not going to argue with you there."

"So, tell me what you know about pain? Better yet, show me..."

Harriet stiffened. "Show you?"

Nolan nodded, his gaze a little too eager. "You can practice on the handsome DI here."

Harriet shook her head. "That's not what I meant, Nolan. When I was younger, a teenager actually, I used to cut myself."

"That's crap," he said. "That's not a darker impulse."

She forced a smile. "I liked the pain. It helped ease this hollowness inside of me. Every time things got too much, I took my razor blade out and cut myself. I'm guessing you tried the same thing."

He searched her face. "Show me."

Harriet hesitated, and Nolan pressed the blade against Drew's throat and a second trickle of blood appeared.

With trembling fingers, Harriet unbuttoned her blouse until she had enough room to slip one arm out. "Here," she said, trailing her fingers over the pale and ridged skin.

"Come closer," Nolan said.

"Don't," Drew ordered.

Harriet took a step closer. "Can you see them?"

Nolan nodded, staring down at her arm with a greedy expression in his eyes.

"Let him go, Nolan. I solved your puzzle. The rules of the game say I get to win this round."

He glanced up at her face and moved the blade from Drew's throat.

"Harriet," Drew said, drawing her attention away from the other man's face for just a split second. But it was that lapse in her attention that Nolan was waiting for. He shifted, moving around Drew as he grabbed her arm.

The blade hovered above her arm. The kiss of cool steel against her skin brought back a flood of memories she'd thought long since buried.

"Do you still like it?" Nolan asked, searching her face. "The pain?"

Harriet looked up at him. "There's a part of me that will always crave it, like an addict searching for their next fix. But I learned to manage it, Nolan. You can too."

"What if I don't want to learn?"

"Then why go to all this trouble? You're better than this, better than this petty vengeance against Dr Connor. I can help you."

"How?"

"I can teach you to control the darkness."

He searched her face to see if she was telling the truth or not. "I already know how to do that."

She shook her head. "Let me help you, Nolan."

"Tell me, Dr Quinn, do you know if killers are made or born yet?"

She opened her mouth as he lifted the blade to his own throat and sank it into his flesh. She felt the spray of his warm blood against her face before he hit the ground.

"Police! Get on the floor!" The sound of splintering wood and the pounding of boots on the floor filled the air.

Harriet went after Nolan, pressing her hand over the wound in his neck as he struggled to pull the blade out. She held on.

"I'm not going to let you die," she said through gritted teeth. "I'm not going to give you the satisfaction..."

Nolan kept his gaze on hers until finally, his eyes rolled back in his head and his hand slipped from the knife.

"I'm not going to let you die," she repeated. "I can't let you die."

She stayed like that until somebody came along and moved her, their strong, sure hands covering hers as they took over and worked on Nolan. She shuffled aside and watched them work, all the while acutely aware of Drew's eyes on her.

And as much as she wanted to, she couldn't bring herself to meet his gaze.

He'd seen too much of her, too much of the darkness that resided in her, and sitting there on the floor, she couldn't bring herself to see what she knew would be reflected in his eyes.

CHAPTER FIFTY-FIVE

HARRIET SET the grapes down on the small hospital table and crept towards the doorway of the hospital room.

"You know, I'd have much preferred if that were a bottle of whiskey," Drew said, stopping her.

"I'm pretty sure alcohol doesn't mix with whatever they've got you on," she said, turning to study him from the doorway.

There were large dark circles beneath his eyes, but it was his expression that caused her mouth to go dry and her palms to sweat.

"Why did you try to save him?" Drew asked.

"It was the right thing to do."

Drew shrugged and then winced. He tried to sit up in the bed and finally, dropped back against the pillows.

"How long are they keeping you in here?"

"A few more days at least. I lost a lot of blood and the crazy bastard actually managed to fracture my skull." He smiled at her. "I always thought it was too hard for that, but apparently I was wrong."

Harriet dropped her gaze to the floor. It had been a close call and yet here he was cracking jokes.

"I hear he survived then," he said.

"Yeah, the blade missed the jugular."

He sighed. "Pity..."

Harriet's attention snapped up to meet his. "You don't really mean that."

It was Drew's turn to look away. "No, I don't. He deserves to rot in jail for the rest of his life. Taking the easy way out like that, well it wouldn't have been right."

Harriet nodded. "No, it wouldn't."

"Gregson told me they think Gabriel will pull through, they're looking at skin grafts or something?"

Harriet chewed her lip and gave a quick nod. "Yeah, apparently. I don't really know the ins and outs, but I had heard he was responding to treatment."

Drew smiled and there was a moment of tense silence that seemed to stretch out into infinity between them.

"I suppose I should let you rest," she said finally.

"Harriet, about what you said to Nolan."

"Drew, I'm sorry you had to see that but—"

"I'm not sorry," he said quietly. "I mean I'm sorry about a lot of things but not about that."

She tilted her chin up. "You didn't feel that way at Nolan's house."

Drew shook his head. "I can be an idiot sometimes."

She cracked a smile. "Can't we all?"

He sucked in a breath. "Look, I can't begin to understand how it is you do what you do. There's one thing I do know."

"And what's that?"

"You saved my life."

She shook her head. "I think armed response would have got there on time."

"And he'd probably have killed me before killing himself or getting shot. Without you, I'm almost certain I wouldn't be sitting here getting to eat Muller Rice pots."

"Oh, is that what they're giving you in here?"

He nodded. "Strawberry's my favourite."

Harriet couldn't help herself; she started to laugh.

Drew gave her a lopsided smile and held his hand out to her. "Friends?"

Nodding, she crossed the room and took his hand in hers. "Definitely."

"Good, now that we've got that out of the way, there's something I've been meaning to say."

"What's that?"

"The next time you go running blindly into a situation where there's a lunatic with a utility knife, do you think you could do us both a favour and not do it?"

Harriet quirked an eyebrow at him. "I suppose for the sake of our friendship I could try not to save your life the next time."

"The next time?" He tried to sit up again. "There won't be a bloody next time."

Harriet smiled at him. "Well, we'll just have to hope that's true."

Splinter the Bone - DI Drew Haskell & Profiler
Harriet Quinn Detective Series Book 3

GET THE NEXT BOOK!

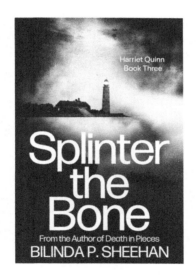

Harriet and DI Haskell return in the next book in the series.
Splinter the Bone

WANT A FREE NOVELLA?

Sign-up to the mailing list to receive Harriet's prequel novella absolutely free when it launches in December

Mailing List

Or Join me on Facebook
https://www.facebook.com/BilindaPSheehan/
Facebook: The Armchair Whodunnit's Book Club

Alternatively send me an email.
bilindasheehan@gmail.com

My website is bilindasheehan.com

ALSO BY BILINDA P. SHEEHAN

Watch out for the next book coming soon from Bilinda P. Sheehan by joining her mailing list.

A Wicked Mercy - DI Drew Haskell & Profiler Harriet Quinn Detective Series Book 1

Death in Pieces - DI Drew Haskell & Profiler Harriet Quinn Detective Series Book 2

Splinter the Bone - DI Drew Haskell & Profiler Harriet Quinn Detective Series Book 3

Hunting the Silence - DI Drew Haskell & Profiler Harriet Quinn Detective Series Book 4

All the Lost Girls-A Gripping Psychological Thriller

Wednesday's Child - A Gripping Psychological Thriller

ALSO AVAILABLE AT AMAZON

At any given time, there are at least three active serial killers in Britain.

A new team has been created to find them...

To get your copy, click HERE

Made in the USA
Las Vegas, NV
21 August 2023